RAINING MEN AND CORPSES

A RAINA SUN MYSTERY

ANNE R. TAN

Author's Note: This is a work of fiction. Names, characters, places, and
incidents are a product of the author's imagination. Locales and public
names are sometimes used for atmospheric purposes. Any
resemblance to actual people, living or dead, or to businesses,
companies, events, institutions, or locales is completely coincidental.

To Emma,
for reminding me that dreams can fly,
but only if I give them wings.

1

PANTS ON FIRE

Raina Sun studied her flushed face in the mirror of the restroom, hoping for an attack of diarrhea or food poisoning. Anything to delay the upcoming confrontation with her graduate advisor. She pulled her shirt away from her body and sniffed. No B.O. Just the industrial strength Pine-Sol and cloying lemon cleanser the janitor had used to clean the place.

She splashed water on her face and toweled it off. The trek from the bus stop to the history building in this August heat had turned her curly black hair into a fuzz ball. A Chinese girl with an Afro. Not exactly the image of a ballbuster.

While Raina would eventually recover from being a fool in love, she wasn't willing to lose two thousand dollars to learn this lesson. Not when she had lawyer's fees gobbling up her savings and bald tires giving her heart palpitations every time she got behind the wheel.

For the first time, Raina wished she was more physically commanding. With her petite frame, she wasn't a real threat to anything larger than a pygmy goat. But it was time to up the ante and to pester Holden Merritt like a fly on a fresh pile of crap. She wasn't walking out of this meeting empty-handed.

Taking a deep breath to calm her fluttering stomach, Raina banged open the restroom door in a show of bravado that echoed through the hall. A paunchy student glanced in her direction but returned to his study of the bulletin boards. Raina stalked into her graduate advisor's office, preparing to do battle. She was all woman. She was a lioness. She was courageous. The cheesy affirmations became a prayer for strength.

Holden continued scribbling on his yellow legal pad and gestured for her to have a seat. "Let me finish this thought." He chewed on his pencil and wrote a couple more sentences.

Raina dropped onto the chair in front of his desk and folded her arms across her chest. So much for ruffling his feathers. The scratching of the pencil and the ticking clock tightened the knot in her stomach. She shifted in the chair, wondering how she should bring up the loan. Her upbringing had made discussing money taboo, and even as an adult, she had trouble talking about it.

Just ask for the money back, said a small voice in her head.

Her skin itched at the neatness in his office. On the shelves lining one wall, books were alphabetized by subject and authors' last names. No crammed volumes in the space above the shelved books like in her apartment. On the opposite wall, framed covers of his published books hung in neat lines, forming a perfect grid. As in previous visits, she resisted the urge to nudge a frame by a small degree just to see how long it would take for him to notice.

A place for everything and everything in its place, just like the blond man with the crisp collared shirt sitting in front of her. The pale light filtering in from the dusty windows behind Holden gave him a tarnished halo. He was a tall man with strong shoulders and a confident aura. She had once found his heavy-lidded brown eyes mesmerizing. Now he just looked tired, but he was still spit-and-polished within an inch of his life.

Holden placed the pencil on the center of the pad and folded his hands on the desk. "Have you decided which countries you want to focus on?"

Raina unclenched the fists resting on her lap. So he was going to pretend they were nothing more than a professor and grad student. "China and Japan look to be a good option."

"Good choice. Unfortunately, you'll need to take beginning language classes with the undergrads. It's too bad classes from your undergrad engineering degree don't apply towards your graduate degree." He turned to open the low filing cabinet underneath the window and pulled out several sheets of paper. "We need to declare your area of focus before the end of the semester."

Raina scowled at his back. If he wanted to pretend nothing had happened between them over the summer, she could do the same...after she got her money back. She smoothed her face and tugged at her earlobe. "My car is having problems. When can you pay me back?" Great. She sounded like a pansy.

Holden flashed a commercial-worthy smile. "Sorry, I don't get paid until the end of next week." He scribbled on the margin of the top page of the pile and pushed the stack toward her. "Here's the information for this semester."

Raina took a deep breath. She couldn't believe this. He made it sound like she was asking him for a favor. "That's what you said last time. Why don't you post-date a check for me? I'll deposit it next week."

"Sorry, I don't have my checkbook with me."

Her forced smile became brittle. "Why don't you log in online and post-date a bank check? I can wait."

He tapped his pencil on the desk. "Look, I don't have time—"

Raina sagged against the chair. "I need the money. I'm late—" The knot in her chest tightened until it strangled her voice. He wouldn't care about her late bills. This angle wouldn't appeal to a selfish person.

Holden licked his lips. He gave her a wobbly and hopeful smile. "I...I don't know what to say. Are you sure?"

Raina nodded, not trusting her voice. There was something in his voice. Was he listening to her for the first time? She cleared her throat and opened her mouth. To do what? Threaten to expose their affair? She closed her mouth, waiting for his next move.

They stared at each other, and the clock leisurely swallowed the minutes and filled the silence between them.

"The money?" Raina finally whispered.

Heels clicked on the hallway floor, and someone knocked on the open door.

Holden jerked up like a tangled puppet, and his chair scuffed against the floor. He grabbed the pile of papers in front of him and knocked over the mahogany pencil caddy Raina had given him for his birthday.

Raina glanced behind her.

Gail, the history department's secretary, stood at the door. Her thick brows were a tight line across her forehead. "Sorry to interrupt. Holden, you're late for the meeting with the Dean. He's in the conference room."

Holden squeezed Raina's shoulder as he stepped around his desk. "Let's talk later," he whispered.

The fluttering returned to Raina's stomach. She resisted the urge to brush the feel of his hand from her shoulder.

"Are you okay, hon?" Gail asked.

"Yes. I..." Raina nodded. "Yes, thank you."

"Just let me know if I can help." Gail left the room and the sound of her clicking heels faded in the hall.

Raina took a couple of deep breaths, staring at the tiny window in front of her. Holden's reaction was strange. What was up with that strange smile? He looked as if Raina had given him a gift...

Her eyes widened. Wait! Did he think she was late late? Did he think she was pregnant? Her gut twisted at the thought. Why should she feel guilty about wanting her money back? It wasn't her fault he jumped to the wrong conclusion.

Her eyes flicked to the knocked-over pencils and the small framed photograph next to them. She turned the frame around, and her eyes widened in surprise at the blonde. New girlfriend already? He sure got over her fast enough. She replaced the picture frame face down on the desk. Yes, it was petty, but she'd never claimed to be gracious.

Raina left the office and trudged toward the computer labs for her shift. She didn't expect Holden to pay up with a smile, but now things were even more complicated. Tomorrow's fundraiser committee meeting would be awkward with a fake pregnancy hanging between them. Awkwardness she could power through, but her lawyer wasn't going to work for an IOU.

THE SKY WAS TURNING pink when she drove home through the downtown area. Most of the mom-and-pop shops were closed, but there were still people frolicking in Hook Park, enjoying the delta breeze after another hot, record-breaking day. The strands of lights in the outdoor seating areas and the few bicycles rolling next to parked cars were part of the charm that made Raina seek refuge in the small town of Gold Springs. Far enough away from her family in San Francisco, where the two-hour drive was a convenient excuse to skip out on birthday parties and last minute family gatherings.

At the corner of Second and B Street, Raina slowed and squinted at the bank's parking lot. Was that Holden? Two heavyset men in dark suits with bored expressions held Holden by the elbows between them. Holden's wide eyes had the trapped appearance of an animal in a cage. The three of them got into a shiny black SUV with chrome spinners.

The car behind her honked, and Raina drove through the intersection. By the time she circled the block, the black car was gone. The two well-dressed men had to be thugs, and apparently they worked for someone who cared about appearances.

Should she call the police? But what would she tell them? Her ex-boyfriend got into a car with two big men? She shook her head. This was none of her business. She needed to focus on getting her money back and clearing the air with Holden. It had crossed her mind to let him continue to believe she was pregnant, but this was plain stupid. She didn't want to come off as a vindictive girl using a pregnancy lie to get back at a man.

Raina drove home on autopilot. She lived in a small complex on the edge of the downtown area, which consisted of two strips of four units facing each other like the little green houses on a Monopoly game. She threw her purse on the narrow side table and turned on the lamp next to her olive-colored sofa. The soft glow filled the living room and cast shadows into the breakfast nook. She glanced around the space with pride. Her apartment might be small, but it was bigger than the attic bedroom in San Francisco. And it was all hers.

Above the TV, the clock with gilded koi fishes swimming around the dial said it was past dinnertime. And because Raina was no longer on someone else's dinner schedule—her mother insisted on dinner at five thirty— she didn't have to eat until she felt like it. Even after a year of being on her own for the first time, it still felt great.

Raina flopped down on the new-to-me sofa, shifting on the thick cushions, and picked up the book on the floor. She was immersed in the world of Middle Earth when there was a sharp knock on her front door. Cocking her head, she waited, in case it was the dressed-up church people trying to convince her to give up her Sunday mornings. The knock came again. She glanced at the gap between the curtains of the closed window above her sofa. No church person, but she wasn't sure an inquisitive reporter was much of an improvement.

Eden Small, her friend and neighbor, hunched and squinted at the peephole like she thought Raina was watching her. She worked for the *Gold Springs Weekly*, the town's newspaper and sometimes entertainment rag. Eden wasn't the type to let a closed door stop her. With one hand holding a pizza box, she whipped out her cell phone and tapped on it.

When the phone in the kitchen rang, Raina laughed. Her friend wasn't someone who took no for an answer. Raina tossed the book on the sofa and opened the front door to look up, up, and up.

Even without her three-inch heels, Eden towered over Raina by a good seven inches. Her deep brown skin shone with health and vitality. Before Raina could utter a greeting, Eden shoved the pizza box into Raina's hands. "I forgot my soda."

Her graceful friend turned, and her silky brown weave fanned out like a shampoo commercial, glittering in the dim light. The scent of lavender lingered in the air even after she hustled across the courtyard toward her apartment.

Raina left the door open and dropped the pizza box on the square Goodwill dining room table. She filled a glass of water for herself and grabbed some napkins.

Eden returned with a can of soda and locked the front door. "Did you get your money back?"

Raina told her friend everything that had happened

on campus and the strange incident at the bank. "I haven't seen Holden in two months, but he seemed diminished today. A little less larger than life."

"It's called taking off the rose-colored glasses," Eden said. "I can't believe he jumped straight to the pregnancy idea. I'm surprised he didn't shove a check into your hands to get rid of you."

"I'm not quite sure what to make of it. It almost sounded like Holden wanted to be a father."

"He's playing mind games with you."

Raina grimaced. Her friend was probably right. "Back in June, you should have snatched those glasses from me and smacked my nose with them."

Eden rolled her eyes. "As if you would have listened."

Raina ignored the comment. Her friend was probably right about this one too. "So when is Phil supposed to pick his EIC trainee?"

"Assistant Editor-in-Chief. Not trainee. Unofficially, the position is supposed to be his replacement when he retires. I need a story that'll make me stand out. I'm thinking about resurrecting an old gossip"—Eden gave her a sideways glance—"about Holden and Olivia."

Raina played with the cheese on her pizza. Did she want to get involved in this? A smart woman would probably change the subject. "I'll bite. What is the rumor?"

"This has nothing to do with you. It's perfect timing with the upcoming annual Christmas fundraiser."

"Got it! It's not about me. What's the rumor?"

"The history department got a huge grant. It was supposed to be divided among the other professors, but Holden got fifty percent." Eden wiggled her eyebrows.

"He spent far too much time in the boss's office to be strictly professional."

"Olivia Kline is old enough to be his mother!"

"I'm just repeating what the wagging tongues said."

Raina flushed, and she shifted her gaze to the pizza on her plate. So Holden cheated on her while they were together?

"This was before you came on the scene," Eden added quickly. "But that's not the interesting part." She paused. "Another twenty percent of the grant money grew legs."

"What makes you think Holden has anything to do with the missing money?"

Eden shrugged. "But wouldn't it be juicy if he did?"

Raina didn't reply. This sounded more like gossip mongering than news, but wasn't there a grain of truth in every story?

After Eden left, Raina sorted her mail. On top of the pile of junk mail was a cream-colored envelope from her lawyer. Apparently, another cousin had decided to join the suit contesting the inheritance from her grandfather. At the rate things were going, the lawyer fees would swallow the entire three million dollars. Her grandfather didn't do Raina any favor by asking her to forward the money to his secret second family in China. Once again, being the good girl had backfired on her.

She took a deep breath. One thing at a time. First, Holden. Then, her family.

2

FLY CAUGHT IN A WEB

Raina trudged into the history building. Bright lights streamed into the reception area through the skylights on the vaulted ceilings. The large windows along one wall pulsated with trapped heat. The open space was too large to cool or heat efficiently, so everyone either shivered or sweltered. Whoever approved the design for the building preferred style over function.

"Psst. Raina," her frenemy Gail called out. The sliding glass partition above the front counter was open. She was in the middle of stuffing paper into folders, but her bright eyes and slightly parted lips suggested she had exciting department gossip to share. No one got this hot and heavy from filing.

Raina walked over and leaned her elbows on the wooden front counter, resting her chin on her hands. "I'm all ears. Is Olivia giving the grad students more paid hours this semester?" She quickly calculated that if she got five extra hours a week, she could pay for a new set of tires by the end of the month. Maybe she could charge it now and pay off the bill later.

"It's about the fundraiser," Gail fake whispered with one hand next to her mouth.

A knot settled in Raina's stomach. Forget new tires. She might have to eat ramen for the rest of the semester.

"The Dean axed Olivia's idea of having the grad students work on the fundraiser. So the grad students would truly be 'volunteering' their time." Gail's fingers curled into air quotes.

The secretary gave Raina a closed-lip smile that was meant to be sympathetic, but her eyes twinkled. Raina returned with a half-smile of her own and continued to the conference room after thanking Gail for the heads-up. She didn't want to give the receptionist more fuel for her gossip.

Raina peeked in the conference room. The newly decorated space had light maple furniture and sleek mesh office chairs. The remodel was one of Olivia Kline's pet projects when she became the department chair. Unfortunately, she didn't upgrade the HVAC system, so the musty paper odor from the other parts of the building seeped into here.

Sol Cardenas, a fellow graduate student, was inside, staring at his coffee cup. He wore his signature stained T-shirt and a greasy ponytail. The college had assigned Sol to show her around campus when Raina first arrived a year ago. Since that one fateful meeting, he badgered her for a date at every encounter.

Raina glanced at the wall clock. Ten minutes of small talk? No way. She ducked back out.

"Raina!" Sol called out.

Not fast enough.

Raina turned around and mumbled a good morning. She sat across from Sol and pulled out her cell phone, hoping he would take the hint.

Sol tapped the coffee sleeve on his cup. "I stopped by yesterday, but you weren't home. What are you doing Sunday afternoon?"

"I'm busy."

Sol scratched his paunchy stomach. "Is it because I'm fat?"

"I'm just not interested. Sorry."

Sol took a large gulp of his coffee. "Uh-huh." A thin dribble slid around his chin and plopped on his chest. His T-shirt now sported a small brown dot in the middle of the existing pale green stain.

Raina glanced at the clock and tapped her pen on the table. If she kept this up for the next three minutes, would he stop talking?

"I can't believe you went out with Holden." Sol's hazel eyes darkened, and he sneered. "Like everyone else, you fell for his charm. You think he's so smart—writing his groundbreaking new book. Ha! He can't even name his sources." He threw the coffee sleeve at the table. It slid and hit her hand.

"None of your business." Raina flicked the sleeve back at him. How many others knew about her secret relationship?

Sol reddened, and his shoulders slumped. His flash of aggression popped like a bubble. Talk about being socially awkward. If Raina gave him even the smallest smile, he would take it as an encouragement, so she stared at her hands.

The wall clock ticked uncomfortably until Cora Campos rushed in with a tray of coffee cups. Raina exchanged pleasantries with the blonde undergraduate student assistant.

Olivia Kline and Andrew Rollinger came in half a minute later. The department chair and professor were making small talk about the upcoming school year. Olivia was about sixty years old and clinging onto her youth with bottles of fake tan, hair dyes, anti-aging makeup, and anti-gravity underwear. The only things genuine on her were probably the icy blue eyes. By contrast, Andrew was in his mid-thirties with green eyes and a flat monotone voice. His red hair was a tad too long and his pants a tad too short, but he didn't seem to notice. They each grabbed a coffee cup without glancing at Cora.

Holden strolled in, wearing a wrinkled shirt and gray trousers. Raina knew the exact moment he saw her. His step paused discernibly. He sat on Raina's other side and reached across to grab a coffee. The scent of his spicy aftershave lingered in her nose. At his mumbled thanks, Cora lowered her brown eyes and blushed.

Olivia frowned at the exchange. The thick mascara lashes twitched like spider legs wrapping an insect for lunch. She watched his face and tapped her watch. "About time."

Cora pushed her thick glasses up her face and hunched her bony shoulders as if she could blend in with the furniture by hunkering down.

Holden shrugged and took a sip of the coffee. Raina wondered if there was any truth to the rumor that Holden and Olivia were ex-lovers. The man had nerves of steel. If her boss spoke to her in that accusatory tone, she wouldn't be drinking coffee like she had all the time in the world.

Olivia droned on about what an honor it was to be the chairperson of the committee again. Raina wanted to poke her eyes out. The others in the room threw out half-hearted suggestions, but it soon became clear that Olivia was looking for automatons to do her bidding.

After a few more minutes of Olivia's soliloquy, Raina cleared her throat. "I heard the grad students wouldn't get paid for their time."

Olivia flipped her fake, youthful, chestnut hair over a shoulder. "Yes, the Dean announced his decision this morning. But it's still a good networking opportunity."

"I can't afford to volunteer my time."

"Of course, you can." Olivia's smile faded, and her eyes narrowed. She leaned in and lowered her voice. "Think about how many classes you'll have with one of us. This will be a great networking opportunity."

Raina pressed her lips into a tight line. If she stopped showing up, Olivia Spider Lashes would make her entire grad school experience miserable. For a moment, nausea assaulted her. She didn't want to be in a power play with the department chair.

Everyone avoided eye contact—either watching the clock, doodling on their notepads, or picking at their nails. She had no idea why the department chair wanted her on the fundraiser committee, but she didn't believe for a minute it was for her computer skills. She sighed and nodded.

Olivia beamed and returned to her monologue.

Raina massaged the sides of her head. She should have... done something. A twitching fly caught in a web had more fight than what she'd just given. There was always the dead grandma excuse. She didn't want to sink to that level, but Olivia had left her with no choice.

Holden squeezed her knee under the table.

Raina stiffened. What the—?

He slid a note into her lap.

She glanced at Olivia and then at the note.

WE NEED TO TALK

She balled up the paper and slipped it in the pocket of her shorts. She wasn't talking until he showed her the money.

After an hour, Raina raised her hand. "Where are the snacks?"

Olivia's face darkened at the interruption, but she glanced at the clock.

Andrew's face got even redder. "Sorry, Lori will be here with the snacks as soon as she is done with the photo shoot of our backyard for the Garden Club's newsletter."

Olivia announced a short break and Raina rushed out along with the others. They scattered like roaches at the end of a flashlight beam.

Raina pulled out her work schedule from her purse. It didn't look like Olivia would wrap up the meeting any time soon. She would have to skip lunch to make it to her shift at the computer lab. With each step toward the vending machines by the stairwell, her annoyance increased. Not so much for the volunteer hours, but the indirect blackmail into volunteering.

A few minutes later, Raina leaned against the vending

machine and stuffed mixed nuts into her mouth. She closed her eyes at the guilty pleasure. Chocolate and salt for lunch. Yum. Her mother would be horrified.

The hair on the back of her neck stiffened. Raina's eyes flew open. Holden stood in front of her, blocking the exit. She jerked and banged her elbow on the trashcan. Stifling a yelp, she clutched the bag of nuts to her chest. The silence stretched until the low rumble from her stomach snapped Raina from her deer-in-headlights position.

"Do you have my money?" Raina popped a nut into her mouth, trying to appear nonchalant. The nut irritated her dry mouth and stuck in her throat. She coughed, hoping to dislodge it without hacking.

"I never intended for things to end the way they did. You surprised me yesterday." Holden leaned against the wall. "In a good way."

Raina held up a hand. "I don't need a song and a dance." It would be just her luck for Holden to want a baby.

"Let me finish. I've spent the whole night thinking about the baby. I think we could be great together—"

"If you have feelings for me, how come you haven't paid me back? I've been asking for weeks." Since when did he want to be a father? Did he think she would want to share a child with him?

Holden paled and held onto his stomach. Sweat popped up on his upper lip. "It's complicated."

Raina took a step back. If he was sick, she didn't want to catch whatever he had. "Right. It's always complicated."

"I'm so ashamed. I wished—"

The sounds of clattering footsteps increased in volume as several people walked down the staircase. Holden glanced behind him and froze. Olivia strolled by, pointing at her watch.

Raina's breath came out in a small whoosh. As she rushed past Holden, his hand snaked out and clamped onto her arm.

"We have unfinished business. Stop by my office this evening," he whispered. "Please."

Raina shook off his hand and trotted back to the conference room. This evening? No way. She was going home after her shift. Holden had his chance; it was not her fault he got interrupted by Olivia. He could play any games he wanted, but she wasn't engaging.

When Raina slipped into her seat, Olivia glanced at the clock. Big deal. So Raina was a few minutes late. It was not as if she missed anything important. Holden didn't even bother coming back.

"As I was saying, Raina could organize the donor's list. You'll also need to ask them to give us something for the silent auction." Olivia slid a pile of papers across the table. "Mention that it's a tax deduction. It usually works."

Raina blinked. "But I'm an introvert."

Olivia nodded and wrote something on her planner. "I'm sure you'll do fine. Lori can help you."

"Lori isn't even here." Raina glanced apologetically at Andrew. "I'm sure your wife wouldn't want to get stuck talking to all the donors." She eyed Olivia. "I thought you wanted me on the committee to help with the computer stuff."

Olivia winked, twitching her black spider lashes.

"The donors' list is on a spreadsheet. You'll need to update it and print out thank you cards later."

Raina pressed her lips together to prevent a snarky comment from escaping. Olivia wanted computer skills for a spreadsheet? She apologized silently to her ancestors, but she would send out an email using the dead grandma excuse tomorrow morning. Besides, she didn't want to spend any more time with Holden. If he wanted a baby, what was she supposed to say? The truth wouldn't get her money back. And technically, she didn't lie to him. Why couldn't he be like a normal man and hand over money to get rid of his problem?

3

CAT IN A TREE

As Raina climbed the main stairs to the history department building, she squinted against the glare of the sunlight glinting off the windows. It was quitting time, but the sun wouldn't set for another three and a half hours during the summer. She hadn't planned on meeting Holden after her shift, but his text messages were too enticing. She knew all about curiosity and the cat, but there was something to be said for satisfaction.

Leaning against the handrail, Raina pulled out her cell phone to bring up Holden's last message again.

I HAVE THE CASH. WAITING FOR YOU

She couldn't figure out why he didn't demand proof or deny his responsibility. His behavior was odd, and it made her curious. Maybe she would learn why he broke things off without an explanation. Some women might think closure was overrated in a brief relationship, but

Raina liked relationships to be tidy. Closure was important.

Distant sirens broke the tranquility of the lazy August day. She looked behind her and didn't see anything unusual. The campus employees hurried to the parking lots, probably eager to get home. A handful of students tossed a Frisbee on the lawn. The sirens got louder, but she shrugged. The evening news would undoubtedly report on the sirens. Even a cat stuck in a tree got at least thirty seconds in Gold Springs.

Raina stuffed the phone back into her purse. She marched up the rest of the stairs and into the lobby. Once the money was firmly locked in her bank account, she would have a photo-burning ceremony with her friends Ben and Jerry to cleanse Holden Merritt from her life.

Her sneakers squeaked in the empty corridor. The front desk stood in silent sentry to her passage. Gail had probably gone home for the day. She turned the corner, and the open door of Holden's office beckoned at the end of the hall. Her steps slowed, and a knot settled in her stomach. What if he refused to give her back the money? Should she threaten him? Was this how good people turn bad?

A muffled buzz snapped Raina from her spiraling thoughts. She pulled the cell phone from her purse, wondering if Holden decided to cancel their meeting. Before she could tap on the screen, a whoosh of air threw Raina's hair into her face. The scent of lemon cleanser and vomit hit her. She grimaced and brushed the hair off her face. Her gaze caught sight of movement on her right. She turned toward the open doorway and froze.

A large person charged out of the men's restroom and

slammed into Raina. They fell into a tangled heap on the tiled floor. The air flew out of Raina's lungs, and her cell phone clattered to the ground. As she pushed the person off, she encountered the softness of a woman's body. When she glanced up, a unibrow on an ashen face loomed over her. Gail?

Gail grabbed Raina's forearms, digging talon-like nails into her skin. Her flared nostrils made tiny squeaks with each labored breath. "My...my phone!"

Raina winced at the pain and batted at Gail's hands. She shivered at the bulging eyes on Gail's face. "Are you okay? Do you need me to call someone?"

"I need to stay on the line!"

Raina crawled over to her phone, grabbed the shattered screen, and popped the battery back in. "Mine is toasted. Where's your phone?"

Gail pointed a trembling hand at the men's restroom. "In there." A small moan slipped from her pale lips. "Holden's dead."

Raina shook her head. Had Gail been drinking? She didn't smell alcohol on the secretary. "He texted me an hour ago." Her voice came out squeakier than she intended.

Gail closed her eyes. "He's dead. He's dead."

Raina shook her head again. Dead? She opened her mouth, but no sound came out. There had to be some other explanation. She got up on wobbly legs and tiptoed the short distance to the restroom doorway. With shaking hands, she pushed it open. A body lay on the floor, the head cocked at an odd angle. She jerked at the loud bang behind her and dropped her hand. She backed away, glad she didn't have time to see more.

The clamor of footsteps grew louder. Three uniformed men and a woman filled the hallway. The entire police force was on duty. Gail covered her mouth with her hands, but the moans continued to escape. As if from a great height, Raina watched a couple of the officers enter the restroom. Another officer ducked into the doors along the hall. Cold seeped into her body, and Raina shivered. She felt disconnected from the activity before her. The noise should have been deafening, but there was only roaring in her ears, and her heart thumped rapidly.

A gentle touch on Raina's arm snapped her back into her body. She blinked, feeling lightheaded. Someone had thrown a blanket around her shoulders. She clutched it against her body as if it were a life preserver.

A policewoman gripped Gail under her elbow and half supported her toward the lobby. "Please follow me."

Raina stumbled after the two women, touching the walls occasionally to keep from floating away. Holden just died. She tripped and fell on the tiled floor. The sharp pain from her knees was an improvement compared to the numbness in her body.

The policewoman asked if she was okay, and Raina nodded mechanically. At the lobby, the policewoman opened the office door and helped Gail into a chair. She huddled underneath a blanket, moaning as tears continued to run down her face.

Raina leaned against the front counter in the lobby. She closed her eyes and took deep breaths. Someone pushed a warm mug into her cold hands. Her nose twitched at the burnt day-old coffee scent. She inhaled it greedily. This was something she understood.

She opened her eyes to thank the person, expecting the policewoman. A jolt went up her spine, and Raina stiffened. A tall Asian man in a knit polo with an embroidered badge stood in front of her. Their eyes locked and a low buzzing sounded in her ears. Little spots of light danced before her eyes as her brain registered who she was seeing.

Elliot Matthew Louie?

He gave her a curt nod. "Rainy."

The coffee mug slipped from her hands and clattered on the floor. Her eyes followed its descent. She stared in horror as the dark liquid spilled across the floor, splattering droplets onto Matthew's dress shoes and khaki pants. Her mind had to be playing tricks on her, digging up her past at this stressful moment. She glanced at her hands. No hives yet.

Raina stared at the golden flecks in the familiar warm brown eyes. His expression was no longer as carefree as she remembered. A dead body had a way of doing that. His lips were pressed into a thin line, and the furrow between his eyebrows reminded her of the years they had been apart. He was her childhood friend, first boyfriend, and ex-husband.

"Matthew?" She crossed her arms to stop her hands from shaking. The police officers milling around the hall were unaware that her world had stopped spinning. A shudder overtook her, and gooseflesh popped up on her arms and shoulders.

He grabbed the blanket and tucked it more firmly around her. "Did you find the body?"

Raina shook her head.

Matthew wrapped her hands around the ends of the

blanket. His warm hands sent another jolt down her spine. He was real.

"Please don't leave before an officer gets a statement from you." He walked away without a backward glance.

A police officer greeted Matthew. They conferred and disappeared around the corner. To everyone else, he might look normal, but Raina noted his ramrod straight back and stiff walk. He was just as disconcerted at seeing her again.

Raina picked up the pieces of the mug and placed it on the front counter. The sour scent of vomit made her swallow the bitter tang in the back of her throat. She peered into the interior of the office. Gail hunched over a wastebasket and dry heaved. Raina backed away and fought for control of her stomach. She shifted her weight from foot to foot. What if Matthew came back to take her statement? What if he left without talking to her? Her heart skipped a beat at the thought.

"Raina!" Eden stood on tiptoes, trying to get around a pug-faced policeman blocking the entrance to the lobby.

"No reporters. This is a crime scene," said the policeman.

Eden grabbed her lanyard press pass and stuffed it in her pocket. "I'm here to take my friend home. She called to say she needed a ride."

"You can wait here. She'll come over when she is allowed to leave."

Eden pushed against the policeman's extended arm. "Look at her. She needs me."

"Stop. Or I'm going to have to arrest you for obstruction."

Eden dropped her arms and stalked over to the

benches next to the wall. "Raina, I'll wait for you here." She pulled out her cell phone and ignored the chaos in the hall but aimed her phone at the two medical examiners arriving at the scene.

At any other time, Raina would have laughed at her friend's antics. The floating sensation left her body. This was normal. This she understood. The more Eden pretended to be absorbed in her phone, the more the police should worry. She was probably using the video camera feature to record the police activities and any conversation within earshot. Raina walked back to the front counter and peered inside the office.

The policewoman tucked her notepad and digital recorder under her arm. "Give us a call if you remember anything else. Do you need to call someone for a ride home?"

Gail brushed a strand of hair back with a shaky hand. "My husband is out of town. I'm okay to drive."

The policewoman shook her head. "You're not in any condition to drive."

"I'll drive you home," Raina called out.

The policewoman squinted at her. "I don't think you should be driving either. I'll find an officer to take both of you home after I get your statement."

Raina gestured behind her. "My friend is in the lobby. She can take both of us home."

The policewoman stood up and looked over the counter. She frowned as she watched Eden working her cell phone and whispered into her walkie-talkie. She gestured for Raina to come inside the office.

Raina gave her contact information and described what happened after she set foot inside the building.

"What were you doing here this late in the day?" the policewoman asked.

"He sent me a text asking to meet with me. I thought he forgot to give me something. We met about my classes the day before." Raina hadn't technically lied.

"I see." The policewoman studied her.

Raina clamped her mouth shut to prevent talking to fill the silence. She crossed her arms so she wouldn't fidget.

After asking the same few questions again in more creative ways over the next half hour, the policewoman said, "We'll be in touch if we have further questions."

Raina grabbed Gail's elbow and guided her into the lobby. The woman was still trembling. Eden glared at the pug-faced policeman still standing sentry in the hall. Her phone was M.I.A.

Eden wrapped her arms around Raina. "Ready to go home?" she asked, her eyes softening with concern.

Raina nodded. "Where's your phone?"

Eden jerked her thumb at the policeman. "Mr. Pug took it."

Raina looked behind her. Matthew kept his eyes on the three of them as he talked to the policewoman. They both had on professionally blank expressions. When she met his dark eyes, she shivered. What was Matthew doing in Gold Springs? And with the police no less.

4

NO NEWS IS BAD NEWS

R aina jerked up, heart racing and fists clutching the tangled sheets. She turned on the lamp and looked around her bedroom. As her gazed moved around the room, her heart rate slowed, and her chest stopped heaving. The digital alarm clock next to the lamp read 3:30 A.M.

She flopped back onto the queen-sized mattress and stared at the whirling ceiling fan, trying to keep her thoughts away from what had happened a few hours ago. Her sweat-drenched body eventually cooled. She padded to the kitchen to get a drink of water. Leaning against the counter, she kept seeing the still body.

How could Holden be dead? He'd spoken to her just yesterday morning. They'd sat next to each other. He'd touched her. A tear leaked out the corner of an eye. "Darn allergies," she mumbled.

With shaking hands, she set the glass on the table, grabbed a tissue, and blew her nose. Okay, maybe it wasn't allergies. Holden didn't have any family left, just a few distant cousins. Would anyone plan a memorial service for him?

Raina placed the cool glass on her forehead and closed her eyes. Her life had morphed into a soap opera in the last forty-eight hours. When Holden had cornered her by the vending machines, she should have told him the truth. Then she would have gone home after her shift, and Matthew wouldn't have reappeared in her life again.

She dragged her tired body back into the bedroom and drifted off into an uneasy sleep until a chirping noise woke her. She peeled her gummy eyes open and lifted her heavy head to glance at the cell phone display. Wincing, she turned off the volume. Her grandma would only add to her stress.

Raina studied her hands and found two pink bumps on her right pinkie finger and one bump on her right ring finger. Surprise, surprise. The hives were here. A sure sign she'd reached her stress threshold. Why did she let Holden believe she was pregnant? It was a stupid, stupid mistake.

She swung her legs off the bed. Crumpled tissues littered the bed and carpet. She trudged to the kitchen to start the coffee maker and slathered a thick anti-itch cream on her hands. It would suffice until she could stop by the Student Health Center to refill her prescription.

Raina watched the coffee squirt out of the coffee maker like a predator watched its prey. There was no way she would be able to focus today without the brew. Rapid-fire knocks on her front door competed with the coffee for her attention. Her grainy eyes and heavy heart didn't want company, so she ignored it and reached for a mug. The taps came again. She shuffled to the living room to peer through the closed drapes above her sofa.

As Eden took a long gulp from her large traveler mug, she bounced on her toes. Yellow paint on the mug brazenly declared "No news is not good news."

Raina sighed and opened the door. It was bad news to be Eden's friend today. And her friend wasn't one to take a closed door for an answer.

"I'm on my way to Gail's house. Want to come with?" asked Eden.

"No."

Raina trudged back to the kitchen to finish fixing up her coffee and carried it to the sofa. She sat and curled her legs up. When the first sip of the hazelnut-flavored coffee hit her taste buds, she closed her eyes in bliss. If she didn't open her eyes, she could almost pretend she was alone. The birds outside her window chirped like they did every morning. Normal. Everything was normal.

When the plush cushion on the sofa shifted beneath her, Raina's perfect moment was ruined. She tightened the grip on the mug to stop the coffee from pouring onto her lap. Eden could not sit on a sofa like a normal person. She had to throw herself on it like she was playing whack-a-mole with her butt.

"Don't you want to know how Gail is doing?" Eden asked.

"My guess—poorly. There's no need to traipse over to Gail's house to verify it, especially with a reporter in tow."

"I'm not going there as a reporter. I am going there as a concerned friend."

"No."

"I'm not doing this for me. Look at you." Eden waved

in Raina's direction. "You're a mess. You need to talk to someone who was there. This visit is not for me. This visit is for you. I've already sent in my article last night." She smiled. "Healthy professor drops dead in his prime. Isn't that a wonderful headline?"

Raina took a sip of coffee to hide her frown. She hadn't thought about how Holden had died. She figured he had a health problem. "Cut the bull. What are you trying to find out?"

Eden leaned forward, wiping the faux concern off her face. "All right. Maybe Gail knows how Holden died. The police are having a hard time finding the next of kin, so they wouldn't release any info."

Raina lowered her gaze. "I have a lot of stuff to do today. I need to buy my textbooks, get a new cell phone, and get new tires. Sorry. I don't have time to go with you."

By the end of the day, her credit card would be bloated, but she needed retail therapy. She didn't want to stop and think. Her thoughts fluttered between Holden and Matthew, swirling in a confused windstorm that she didn't want to analyze now. But spending money she didn't have? This she understood.

"We should strike while it's hot. It'll take the police another day to announce foul play. I need this exclusive, Rainy. I need the promotion."

Raina stared at the gleam in Eden's eyes. So sensitivity was not one of Eden's strengths. But foul play? Was this hopeful thinking on her friend's part or did she know something Raina didn't?

"I'm going with or without you. I probably would inflict less damage if you're with me," Eden said.

Raina stared at the mug in her hand. There were no

answers in the coffee. It would be wrong to let Eden barge in on a friend at a time like this, even though her friendship with Gail was questionable. The only way to rein in the intrusive questions was to go with Eden.

"You are just as curious as I am to find out how Holden died," said Eden.

"No, I'm not. I want to forget the whole thing." *Pants on fire,* said a small voice in Raina's mind. With Matthew in the picture, she had to stay off the police radar.

"There's no shame in a little curiosity. It's not like we're ambulance chasers."

Raina pinched the bridge of her nose and squeezed her eyes shut. Did that just come out of Eden's mouth? Couldn't she pretend to feel something for Raina's sake? The lingering emotions from last night must have made her more sensitive than usual. This aspect of Eden's personality had never bothered her before.

Eden touched her knee. "You okay?"

Raina opened her eyes. "I need to take a shower first."

Thirty minutes later, Raina pulled her thirteen-year-old faded red Honda Accord out of the driveway. She had inherited the car in high school after her dad passed away from prostate cancer. It still had the dent in the rear bumper where her teenage self had backed into a pole. Her dad's reaction to that particular incident had been a raised eyebrow and a new bus pass. From that moment on, each time she got behind the wheel, she felt his comforting presence.

"He's not worth getting upset over," said Eden.

Raina shrugged, pretending a nonchalance she didn't feel. "A man I know is dead. I may not have liked him at the time of his death, but I liked him enough at one point to loan him money and let him see me naked." She clamped her mouth shut as her voice trailed off. Eden wouldn't understand the confusion she felt.

"You should think about that yummy detective instead. I saw the way he looked at you last night." Eden wiggled her eyebrows and smacked her lips.

"Eden! Get your mind out of the gutter."

"You should join me. You'll have more fun this way. You need to stop moping after a man who didn't give a sh —" Eden splashed coffee on her shirt. "Ouch!" She pulled her shirt away from her body and glanced at the brown spot. "I need to get you a wide cup holder for your birthday."

"You mean you need to get a cup holder for your extra-large traveler mug." Her friend was trying to help, but thoughts of Matthew only made Raina want to scratch her hands. "When was Matthew watching me?"

"Like that, huh?"

"What?"

"Matthew." Eden rolled the name off her tongue, and her grin widened. "When did Detective Louie become Matthew?"

When Raina punched him for stealing her sister Cassie's lollipop at eight, when she saw him naked at sixteen, or maybe when he got their marriage annulled in Las Vegas. She and Matthew went way back and not all the memories were as good as ice cream with sprinkles.

She parked in front of a ranch-style house with bright blue curtains. The quiet street had a handful of minivans parked on the driveways. A young mother with an infant on her hip and a large diaper bag on one arm locked her front door, while a strawberry blonde preschooler jumped on the raked pile of leaves on their lawn. Normal. Everything was so normal for the rest of the world.

Raina patted her unkempt ponytail, tucking a ringlet back into place. "You didn't answer my question."

"Neither did you." Eden leaped out of the car and jogged up the driveway.

Raina trudged after her friend, scratching her pinkie. Right now the last person she wanted to think about was Matthew. Eden bounced on her toes by the front door, waiting for Raina. She took a deep breath and raised her hand to ring the doorbell.

RAINA MIGHT HAVE LOOKED as if she had spent the night dragged through an alley by a stray cat, but the bruises below Gail's eyes and the sagging jawline were prime examples that age didn't like loveless nights with Mr. Sandman.

The brick-red accent wall of the kitchen and festive dinnerware behind the frosted glass cabinet doors made Raina feel even worse to be sitting across from the distressed woman. This room was made for parties, not for the fake small talk. While Eden asked a few "concerned" questions, Raina made tea for everyone. After everyone took a sip, Eden went in for the kill.

"What made you decide to go into the men's restroom?" asked Eden.

"If you'd rather not talk about it, that's okay," said Raina, earning a dirty look from her friend.

Gail's finger traced the rim of her mug. Around and around it went. "The women's restroom ran out of toilet paper. I found a dead body because of toilet paper." She gave a mirthless laugh that dissolved into a cackle, which thankfully ended when she jammed the mug to her mouth.

Raina shifted in her seat as the hair on the back of her neck stiffened. Did she want to hear the rest of the interview?

As Gail placed the mug on the table, her hands trembled, sloshing the black tea onto the tabletop.

Raina resisted the urge to hug the secretary. She was here under the guise of friendship, but she wasn't a friend.

Eden waited while Gail took several more calming sips of tea. "What was the first thing you saw?"

"I'm not supposed to talk about this," said Gail, glancing down at her lap. She peeked at Eden from under lowered lashes.

"Don't worry. I could say you're an anonymous witness. I protect my sources."

"Anonymous sounds good. I don't want to lose my job," Gail said, nodding eagerly.

Raina opened her mouth but promptly shut it when she caught Eden's eye. There were only two eyewitnesses at the scene. It wouldn't be hard for anyone to guess who talked to the press. Even if she flashed a red stop sign, she doubted Gail would have stopped. She probably needed to tell someone the story. And besides, Raina was curious as to how Holden died.

Eden leaned forward in her seat. Her brown eyes focused on Gail. If a naked fraternity guy fell on her lap at this moment, Eden would have shoved him aside for blocking her view of the witness. "What did you see?"

Gail stared at the sliding glass patio door. The silence stretched until Raina cleared her throat, which earned another dirty look from Eden.

"Something was behind the door," Gail finally said. "I had to push to open it. That should've been my first clue that something was wrong. I should've stopped pushing. I should've left."

Raina nodded in agreement. "I should've gone home after my shift." She shared a look with Gail, a moment of regret for making the wrong choice.

"So you pushed open the door..." prompted Eden.

"The first thing I noticed was the smell. Pine-Sol, vomit, and feces. Holden was on the floor." Gail shuddered and closed her eyes. "I didn't want to touch him, but I had to check. The skin was clammy and still warm." She opened her eyes and grimaced. "Then I called the police and went outside to wait for them."

Eden shifted her gaze to Raina. "Did you see the body?"

Raina recoiled. "Only for a second before the police arrived."

"How did he die?" asked Eden, shifting her attention back to the secretary.

"I don't know. Don't people die from accidents in the shower all the time?" Gail asked.

"You think he slipped and fell?" asked Raina. Holden wasn't much of a gym rat, but he certainly had more natural grace than she did. Even if the floor was wet and she had on high heels and the sink was positioned right next to her head, she couldn't imagine slipping to her death in a public restroom.

"Did Holden seem odd that day?" Eden asked.

ANNE R. TAN

"No, but he had asked if I had something for an upset stomach after lunch. I gave him Pepto-Bismol tablets," Gail said.

"Why did he ask you?" Eden asked.

"Probably because he didn't want to walk across campus in the heat," Raina said.

"I was asking Gail," Eden said, giving Raina a pointed look.

Raina slumped in her chair. She was only trying to speed this up.

Gail shook her head. "I don't know."

"Did anything unusual happen recently?" asked Eden.

"No..."

"Do you know if Holden had any enemies?"

"I don't know." Gail averted her gaze. "I don't pay attention to office gossip. I've been busy. Classes start in two weeks."

Raina choked mid-swallow on her tea. She coughed again to dislodge the drop of liquid in her throat. "The tea went down the wrong pipe." She waved for them to continue.

Eden asked a few more questions that Gail answered halfheartedly, but Raina had stopped paying attention. When did Gail ignore office gossip? In a world where squirrels stop hoarding for the winter? Raina was willing to bet the secret stash of chocolates in her nightstand drawer that Gail knew more than she let on about Holden's private life.

5

5

PEEING ON THE HYDRANT

Raina dropped Eden off at the newspaper's office and drove to campus. After parking at the faculty lot with her homemade parking pass, she moseyed over to the bookstore—only to find it closed. It was still on summer hours. She strolled over to a shaded bench and perched on it, flapping the collar of her shirt.

The hardest thing to get used to about Gold Springs was the heat. It was barely ten o' clock and already seventy-eight degrees. It would be another triple-digit day. She sniffed at her armpits and jerked back. She had forgotten to put on deodorant in her mad rush out of the apartment with Eden. Great. Her day was getting better by the minute.

She pulled a pocket notebook from her purse and stared at the blank page. Holden had broken up with her a month ago without even a simple good-bye. His current desire to work things out over a supposed pregnancy was

39

bizarre. If his death wasn't from natural causes, she might be the last person he had contacted. Would this make her a potential murder suspect?

She pushed the thought aside. Time for panic later. As she re-created his day, her hands flew across the page.

10 AM H AT FUNDRAISER MEETING

12 PM FUNDRAISER MEETING ENDED. LUNCH?

2 PM H ASKED G FOR PEPTO

3 PM H TEXTED R TO MEET

4 PM H TEXTED R TO MEET

5:05 PM G FOUND BODY

5:15 PM R AT SCENE

What happened in five hours to cause a healthy thirty-six-year-old man to drop dead in a public restroom? What did he eat for lunch? Eden had asked about enemies. Did her friend have a reason to suspect murder or was that hope for a big story?

Raina shivered at the morbid thoughts. Her life should be filled with cream puffs and coffee, not thoughts of murder and mayhem. Her imagination was running away from her.

The doors clicked open. Raina scurried inside the bookstore, nodding thanks to the employee who held the door open for her. She bypassed an assortment of gifts, campus gear, and study guides and clattered down the metal staircase in the middle of the store to the basement where all the textbooks were stored. As she browsed the shelves, she could hear the low hum of quiet conversation, the ding of the cash register, and squeaking shoes. It was so ordinary that she felt silly for her earlier thoughts of foul play.

She picked up two used textbooks and made her way

upstairs to purchase the rest of her school supplies. As she turned a corner, she spotted the policewoman from the night before at the end of the aisle. What was her name? Hippo? Hook? The policewoman closed her notebook and strolled away.

Raina picked up her pace. At the end of the aisle, Cora Campos, the blonde student assistant, stood next to a rack of study guides. Her face looked ashen like she was feeling sick. By the time Raina swept her gaze around the store, the policewoman was no longer in sight.

"Why is the policewoman talking to you?" Raina asked.

Cora dabbed behind her glasses at her red-rimmed eyes and blew her nose. "I'm in big trouble. I know they are going to blame me."

A hormonal teenager was no laughing matter, but Raina couldn't resist. If nothing else, it would lighten the mood. She mocked a gasp. "So it was you."

"Of course not. I thought about it, but I have nothing to do with it."

Raina wiped the smile off her face. Okay, this was no longer funny. "I'm sure whatever it is, it's a misunderstanding."

"Not when you're dead." Cora's eyes widened, and she backed away. "I have to pick up my nephew." She turned and fled through a side door.

Raina pounded after her on instinct, even as her mind tried to process what had just happened. Was Cora talking about Holden's death? As Raina flew out the door, an alarm went off. Her steps slowed as she looked around in confusion. Cora disappeared around the building.

She saw movement out of the corner of her eye. A

strong hand clamped onto her arm, and she turned to find herself looking at a pair of amused gold-flecked eyes. The textbooks slipped from her hands. Matthew!

He retrieved the books and held them out to her.

Raina grabbed the books and hugged them to her chest. "What are you doing here?"

Matthew hooked his thumbs on his jeans pockets. "Police business, but arresting a shoplifter is just as good."

Heat raced up her neck and onto her cheeks. "This isn't what it seems."

"Did you pay for the books?"

She shook her head. "I was trying to catch someone."

"Was someone else trying to steal these books?" Matthew waited for a beat. "There is no other culprit. You went through the doors with the books. Seems like a clear-cut case to me."

"You know I'm not a thief."

"I haven't seen you in a few years. I say you're a stranger."

Raina straightened and lifted her chin. Stranger, huh? That sounded good to her. "Have the police released information about Holden's death yet?"

"Are you the next of kin?"

"No, but Holden doesn't have any family."

"When did Professor Merritt become Holden? Are things that informal on campus?"

She narrowed her eyes. Her relationship with Holden was none of Matthew's business. "I'm wondering if someone will plan a memorial service for him."

His jaw tightened. "Why are you in such a rush to get rid of the body?"

Raina blinked. Why would she want to get rid of the body?

Matthew peered into her face. Whatever he saw must have satisfied him. "He had a sister. We'll be releasing the body to her soon."

A chill ran through her, and she stiffened. Holden had said he was an only child. Could this be a mistake? She glanced at the police logo on Matthew's polo shirt. No. The police couldn't be that incompetent. Why had Holden lied about his family?

"How well did you know Holden Merritt?" Matthew asked.

"Apparently, I don't know him at all. I didn't even know he had a sister."

"Then why do you care about a memorial service?"

Raina scratched her pinkie. This whole situation was a mess. If Matthew found out about the supposed pregnancy... She never uttered the words. She couldn't help if someone made the wrong assumptions. It was not her fault.

Matthew held out his hands. "Let me see."

"What?"

He grabbed her textbooks and tucked them under one arm. His warm hands enveloped hers, sending a tingle from her fingertips up to her toes. He inspected her hands. Leaning back slightly, Raina held her breath, afraid of the scent from his skin, how it would affect her. She counted the few white hairs among the black on his head.

He gave her a soft smile. "Rough night, huh?"

Raina nodded, not trusting her voice. Beads of sweat popped out on her forehead.

Someone cleared her throat. "Detective Louie."

Raina snatched her hands back. She was saved by the bell. Matthew turned to the speaker behind him. His broad shoulders blocked her view momentarily, and she leaned forward, trying to catch bits of the mumbled conversation. Were they going to charge her for shoplifting? By the time he stepped aside, the butterflies in Raina's stomach had knotted into a slick clump.

Matthew gestured at Raina. "Officer Hopper, you remember Miss Raina Sun?"

Officer Hopper nodded. Her flinty gray eyes ran up and down the length of her.

Raina stiffened under the inspection, fully aware that her unruly black hair and wrinkled shirt, while appropriate on campus, made her look like a slob everywhere else. She lifted her chin slightly, uncertain as to the cause of the sudden chill from the once nice policewoman. Her gaze slid over to the brown-skinned man standing next to Officer Hopper.

"Tony Fuentes. Campus Security." The Hispanic man stepped forward. "Thank you, officers. I'll take it from here."

Raina wiped a trickle of sweat running down the side of her face. She had gotten to know Tony last year when she tutored his daughter in calculus. He would probably let her off with a stern warning. Her nose twitched at the musky scent oozing from her armpits. If she stood in this sun much longer, the stench would become a mushroom cloud over everyone.

Matthew stiffened at the dismissal.

Officer Hopper scowled. "And what can you do about

a misdemeanor? Take away her access to the campus gym?" She turned to Matthew. "I'm going to run her through the system. Maybe there might be an outstanding warrant."

Raina's eyes widened. "I swear I was going to pay for the textbooks. I was running after someone. I forgot I had the textbooks in my hands. Let me pay for them now." She snapped her mouth shut to stop the babbling. She was overexplaining the situation. The tension in the air was thick enough to strangle her.

"I'm sure you were." Officer Hopper jogged over to the police cruiser parked across the street.

Matthew handed the books to Tony. "We'll take care of this."

Tony ignored the books. "The police don't have jurisdiction over student affairs on campus."

Raina grabbed the books and hugged them to her chest. Several students stopped and stared at the commotion. She picked out Sol's greasy ponytail glinting in the sunshine. "Could we go someplace more private to continue this conversation?" she whispered.

Both men ignored her.

"Campus Security doesn't have jurisdiction over a misdemeanor. She could be looking at six months of jail time." Matthew shifted until he stood between Raina and Tony.

Raina curled her itching hands into fists. She wanted to laugh at the two men facing each other with spread feet. Neither man would have pressed charges on her if they were alone. But together, one of them might end up arresting her under the misguided attempt to protect her from the other person. Men could be such convoluted creatures.

She glanced at the tight jaws and narrowed eyes, and another bead of sweat rolled down her back. Maybe this wasn't funny after all. What if she ended up in jail?

Officer Hopper returned, glowering at Raina. "No warrants."

Raina blinked at the tears filling her eyes. How did a simple errand to pick up her textbooks degrade into a public pissing match between Campus Security and the police? Wasn't it enough she found a dead body a few hours ago? She covered her face with her hands and burst into sobs. The textbooks landed with a thud.

"I'm so sorry." She opened her purse, rooting for a tissue. "It won't happen again. I don't know what came over me."

The men broke their staring contest.

Officer Hopper snorted in disgust and stalked back to the police cruiser.

A red-faced Tony grabbed the textbooks. "I'm sure it's a misunderstanding. No harm done. I'll bring these back to the bookstore." He trotted away with a look of relief on his face.

Matthew sighed. "You're so much trouble."

Raina dabbed at her gummy eyes. Red nose, puffy eyes, grungy hair, and BO. She didn't want to be alone with Matthew looking like this. "Can I go now?"

"For now, but I'm coming over for dinner tonight. I'm in the mood for something hot." He gave her a roguish wink and trotted toward the police cruiser.

Did he think she would cook for him after this...this

fiasco? She cupped her hands around her mouth. "No, you're not!"

Matthew waved in acknowledgment but didn't turn around. Officer Hopper, who was smiling at Matthew's approach, raised an eyebrow.

Raina had the feeling she made an enemy today.

6

THE GREAT GUACAMOLE COVER-UP

Raina stomped to the Eatery, the cafeteria-style dining hall in the middle of campus. The nerve of the man to assume she would slave over a hot stove for him. She was no longer a love-stricken teenager. She didn't have to impress him. Her stomach growled, reminding her she hadn't eaten anything all morning. A fat overstuffed steak burrito layered with gooey cheese and creamy guacamole would hit the spot nicely.

The Eatery had yellow pastel walls and gleaming wood counters. It was busy as usual. Student-friendly pricing also attracted the local townspeople. All the food stations had lines, except for the Mexican food counter. The lights were off. No steak burrito today.

With some reluctance, Raina paid for her iced coffee and Cobb salad from Java Java. For the same price, the Mucho Steak Burrito could be both lunch and dinner. Today was turning out to be a bad day. The floor-to-ceiling tinted windows facing the grassy quad area pulsated with trapped heat. She cringed at the thought of sitting anywhere near those windows.

"Raina! Over here!" Eden waved at Raina from a table near the other entrance.

As Raina weaved her way through the café-style tables and chairs, Eden spoke to a freckle-faced undergraduate student with a stained apron next to her. She slipped something into his hands. He winked at her and resumed picking up discarded trays by the trash bins.

Raina placed her tray on the table and sat opposite her friend. "Have the police released any more information?" She glanced at Eden's roast beef sandwich and regretted buying the salad.

Eden glanced at her watch. "I've got two hours to kill before they release a statement. They haven't found the next of kin yet, so I don't think it will be anything important. But I'll be there just the same."

"Are they looking for Holden's sister? Know her name?" Raina pretended nonchalance as she pushed a straw through the lid of her iced coffee.

"Natalie Merritt." Eden shot Raina a furtive look. "Know anything about her that might interest me?"

"I didn't even know she existed until an hour ago."

"Then who told you about her?"

"Matthew."

Eden straightened. "What else did he tell you?"

Raina hesitated. She didn't want to mention her dysfunctional relationship with Matthew. "Nothing."

"How about a ride to the cell phone store? I used my twenty dollars for the week already. I need to get one of those pay-as-you-go phones."

"You need to up your weekly gas budget. Twenty dollars barely gets you to Sacramento."

Eden munched on a fry. "I like food on my table better. How about that ride?"

"What happened to your phone?"

"The police are keeping it. Something about preserving evidence." Eden winked. "It'll give me an excuse to stop by the station to harass them whenever I feel like it."

Raina chuckled, but her mind was whirling. Had Eden found out anything else about Holden's death? Would her friend be offended if she agreed to the ride in exchange for information? "I have an appointment to get new tires after lunch. The cell phone store is a block away. We can walk there while we wait for them to work on my car."

"I thought you didn't have money to replace them?"

"I needed some retail therapy after last night. They are going on the credit card."

Eden snorted. "Most people hit the mall for retail therapy."

"But that's not an excuse to buy things I don't need." Raina tilted her head toward the freckle-faced teen picking up trays at the other end of the cafeteria. "Was that guy hitting on you? I thought you prefer guys that are...older."

"He cleaned up Holden Merritt's vomit yesterday."

Raina frowned. Holden didn't look well when he cornered her by the vending machine. At the time, she thought he was nervous about their discussion. "Food poisoning?"

"Here's the thing. Holden came with a skinny blonde

girl in a red T-shirt and glasses to pick up the lunch orders for the department. He threw up while he was picking up the lunches."

A knot settled in Raina's stomach. Did this have anything to do with the trouble Cora alluded to at the bookstore? "Did they pick up Mexican food?"

"Yep." Eden wrinkled her nose. "I can't believe you eat that stuff voluntarily. I only have salads in front of dates."

"I wanted a Mucho Steak Burrito." Raina pulled a slice of roast beef dangling off the side of Eden's sandwich. "What about that bump on the head?"

Eden swatted her hand. "Get your own sandwich. You'd have to be mighty lucky, or unlucky in this case, to die from a bump on the head."

"I wonder if anyone else got sick from eating the Mexican food."

"The food poisoning is a cover-up. I talked to someone from the hospital and at the Student Health Center. No one else showed up complaining about a stomachache, just Holden. So you were wrong. He did make the trek across campus to the Student Health Center."

"What time was this?"

"After he asked Gail for Pepto. They told him it was indigestion and gave him something for it."

Raina took a sip of her iced coffee. Whatever they gave him must have helped if he felt well enough to meet with her later. If it wasn't a bump on the head or food poisoning, then how did Holden die? "Why did you say cover-up?"

Eden shrugged. "A man died on campus. The police wouldn't release any information. Parents are already phoning in for answers. Something fishy is going on here. It's much easier to point fingers at bad guacamole."

Raina laughed, but it sounded hollow even to her ears. If there was something fishy about Holden's death, would she become a person of interest for being the last person he'd contacted? What if Matthew found out about the assumed pregnancy? He wouldn't understand. He would blame her...at least when it came to this subject.

Eden waved a fry in front of Raina's face. "I need a sidekick. Your practical side and my instinct could blow this story wide open. The promotion will be mine if I get an exclusive on this."

"I'm nobody's sidekick."

"Well, someone has to be the sidekick. I can't be the sidekick. Look at me." Eden flipped her hair over her shoulders and straightened in her chair. "You're physically smaller. The sidekicks are always peanuts."

"That's because they are usually younger, Obi-Wan."

"What?"

"Never mind. I don't want to get involved."

"But you're already involved. The bitter break-up, the fake pregnancy, the money, and the text messages." Eden ticked the points off on her fingers. "They always suspect the ex-lover. It's only a matter of time before you become a suspect."

A piece of lettuce stuck to Raina's throat. She gulped some coffee, but her voice still came out in a squeak. "That's crazy talk. No one would be interested in me."

Eden raised an eyebrow. "Do I need to go through the list again?"

Raina slumped in her chair. How did she get herself into this mess? She was a good person; she loaned money to friends. And now she was a murder suspect. "You really think someone killed Holden?"

"It's only a matter of time before the police start knocking on your door."

Raina sighed. Her friend had confirmed her worst fear. Her skinny butt would be in a holding cell rattling a metal cup on the bars before the week was out.

"You're part of the inner circle for the history department, and it looks like you have an in with the police. Just keep your eyes and ears open. I'll even share my byline with you if you help me solve the murder before the police."

Raina shuddered. Murder. Who could hate Holden that much? "That's generous, but no thanks. I want my name to stay out of the newspaper. And I want us to share information. Either we're a team, or we're not."

Eden nodded. "What do you know about Olivia Kline?"

Raina shook her head. "Not much. She's willing to spend mega bucks to look forty when she's already on the other side of sixty." Should she tell Eden about the bookstore incident? No. It wouldn't be ethical to sic Eden on Cora without any real proof of her involvement with Holden's death. It would be less traumatic if Raina spoke to the girl before Eden did.

Maybe Raina could ply Matthew with wine over dinner and get him to squeal. He always did have a soft spot for her even if he always left her crying later. She stabbed at a piece of lettuce, twisting it into bits with her fork. Was she ready to walk down this familiar path again with Matthew?

Raina was having second thoughts about plying Matthew with wine and cheesecake when she bumped into the potbellied man with the greasy ponytail at the grocery store. Eden had disappeared into the smoothie shop next door, preferring to play with her new phone rather than watch Raina shop.

"I've been hoping to catch you. I'm sorry about my behavior during the fundraiser meeting." Sol Cardenas rested his basket on top of her shopping cart, trapping her to the spot. "I've been under a lot of stress lately with the fellowship and my sister's wedding."

"Don't worry about it." Raina looked around for an escape. Another shopper's cart blocked the end of the aisle behind her. Unless she wanted to ram her cart into Sol's stomach, she was stuck.

"What are you doing this Sunday? My sister is having her wedding reception at the casino's banquet hall. Want to come as my date?"

"No, thanks." She pressed her lips into a thin line. Seriously? Again?

"Why won't you go out with me? I'm a nice guy. I could show you a good time." He wiggled his eyebrows suggestively and scratched his armpit.

"I'm just not interested." She stared pointedly at the mustard stain on his once white T-shirt. While she was inclined to give the guy points for persistence, the way he always went about asking made her want to cringe. His sister should give him pointers on how to talk to women. A person could be socially awkward and still come across as sweet, but in Sol's case, he reeked of desperation.

"I clean up real good. My mama always said I'd be a catch for the right woman. Trust me; you don't want to let this ship pass you by."

She averted her gaze until the desire to laugh passed. "I'm sure you are, but I'm not the woman for you."

He glared at her and took a step toward her. "Is it because I don't have money? Do you have something against poor people?"

Raina straightened. Enough of this. She was already having a bad day as it was. "No. It's not because you're broke. It's because you're moody, and you come off as creepy. You go around with a chip on your shoulder. I don't want to be around that negativity."

He jerked around, and his shoulders slumped, but not before she saw his shaking chin.

She bit her lip to stop the automatic apology from escaping. When did she become so mean? She scratched at her hives, and the inflamed pinkie throbbed with her guilt.

He swung around, squaring his shoulders. His face twisted into a sneer. "I didn't want to do this, but you forced me. You're going to my sister's wedding as my girl-friend." He narrowed his eyes. "Or I'm going to the police. Pregnant ex-girlfriend killed boyfriend over another woman. Wouldn't the police be interested in that?"

She recoiled with a gasp. "What are you talking about?" How did he know? "I'm not pregnant."

"Oh, even better! Bitter ex-girlfriend lied about a pregnancy, then killed cheating boyfriend over another woman."

Blood rushed to Raina's head, leaving her breathless

and dizzy. "What?" Her grip tightened on the shopping cart. Was he blackmailing her... for a date?

Sol rocked back on his heels and folded his hands on his protruding stomach. "I know all about the fake pregnancy. You didn't close the door. I was in the hallway when you told Holden you were late." He tapped on his cell phone and played her conversation with Holden.

Raina licked her stiff lips. Was a recording even admissible in court? "Why would the police care? It's just a prank."

"Uh-huh. I'll pick you up Sunday. 10:00 A.M. Make sure to bring a gift."

There was no way she was going to be a trapped passenger in his car. "I'll meet you there." Oh, no. Did she just admit to something she shouldn't? "Who is this other woman?"

Sol peered into her face, and his grin widened. "You've no idea." He shook his head at her naiveté. "Olivia Kline."

Raina shook her head. No way. "The relationship was over before I came into the picture."

"They were still in a relationship the last I heard, and I hear things." He looked pointedly at her. "People always forget to close doors."

"Are you blackmailing me?"

"Let's call it a mutual cooperation." He picked up his basket and strolled away with a swagger.

Her breath came out in a whoosh. The police wouldn't care. Women had lied about a fake pregnancy throughout history. What she did was harmless. Harmless.

Except Matthew wouldn't understand. His mother

had lied about a pregnancy to force his father into marrying her. Their brief marriage had been filled with the clamor of raised voices, slammed doors, and smacked fists on skin. He'd disappeared with another woman when Matthew was in the first grade.

Her hands shook. The skin on her fingers was tight and pink. The scratching had spread the hives to a middle finger. Her mind focused on the burning sensation on her hands. If Holden had died from foul play, she needed to find the killer before Matthew realized what she did.

Raina paid for her groceries and loaded the bags into the trunk of her car on autopilot. Wait a minute! She straightened and banged her head on the lid of her trunk. Ouch! With tears in her eyes, Raina straightened a second time, albeit more carefully, and leaned against the bumper, rubbing her head.

How did Sol come to the same conclusion as Eden that Holden was murdered? Raina swayed and braced her hand against the bumper. What if he tells Matthew about the fake pregnancy? Her hands balled into fists, and she thumped her bumper with frustration. No way. She'd sit through ten weddings if necessary to shut Sol up.

Eden waved her smoothie cup in front of Raina's face. "What are you staring at?"

Raina jumped at her friend's sudden appearance. "You should have stayed with me. You missed a great show." She described her encounter with Sol inside the grocery store.

Eden's eyes widened and then narrowed in anger. "The nerve of that guy. Gosh, you sure know how to pick 'em."

"Why do all the crazy ones pick me?" Raina slammed the trunk closed and got into the car. "It's one thing if I know he only needs a date for the wedding. But what happens if he pulls this stunt again later?"

"Then you need to dig up some dirt on Sol. That's the only way to shut him up."

Raina glanced furtively at Eden playing with her phone in the passenger seat. At least she could trust her friend to keep her relationship with Holden a secret. Eden was right. And Sol had given her the perfect opportunity for some digging at the wedding.

7

A RED SUITCASE OF TROUBLE

Raina stuffed the Oreo cheesecake in the freezer and slammed the door shut. She snatched the dinner plate, scraped the untouched food into the trash, and flung the plate into the dishwasher. She poured another glass of wine and settled down to eat her cold dinner. Alone. It was nine fifteen. Matthew hadn't even bothered to call and cancel their evening plan.

"Fool," she muttered to herself. Matthew wouldn't have divulged police information over dessert. It was only an excuse to hide her eagerness to see the man again. She shredded the steak into lumpy pieces and hid the meat under mashed potatoes and congealing gravy. She stared at her dinner for another half-second before clearing the table. There was no point in making a show at eating when no one was watching.

Raina opened the freezer again, grabbed a pint of Cherry Garcia, and stomped to her sofa with the bottle of wine tucked under her arm. The only thing she wanted was the escape promised by her friends, Ben and Jerry.

She poured a little wine into the carton, tipped the carton, and slurped the wine and ice cream mixture. Her back relaxed into the plush cushions. To heck with it. She wasn't going anywhere later. Raina poured the rest of the wine into the carton. Things were looking better already.

The fan whirled above her, moving the warm stale air. Raina drank some more of the ice cream wine. When Matthew left the first time, he left with her grandfather's money and her heart. When he left her the second time, she wanted to break his knees. And here he was, once again, sending out smoke signals.

She hiccupped and slid down the cushions until she was stretched out on the sofa. Why did all the men in her life walk off into the sunset without her? Of course, Holden couldn't very well explain himself at the moment. Her eyes grew heavy, and her last conscious thought was about Holden's sister.

Bam! Bam!

The pounding on her front door echoed the pounding in her head.

Raina cracked open one gummy eye, glanced at the goldfish clock on the wall above the TV, and promptly closed them. Four thirty. Too early for good news, in which case, it could wait. Her mouth felt like sandpaper, and her breath could make Ben and Jerry rethink their relationship. Definitely not fit for company.

"Open up, Rainy." The familiar voice on the other side of the door cracked with exhaustion.

Matthew! Raina's eyelids flew open, and she jerked up. Not a good idea. She groaned and clutched her head between both hands. She stumbled to the front door and fumbled with the locks.

Raina leaned against the opened door. "Will you shut up!" She cringed. That came out louder than she wanted.

Matthew's bloodshot red eyes held her gaze. He ran his hand through his already tousled black hair. "Have you been drinking? You always get so cranky after two drinks."

"What do you want, Sherlock?"

He stepped closer and enveloped her in a bear hug, resting his chin on her head. He sighed deeply like he just came home after a trek in the wild.

Her traitorous body melted, and her nose greedily breathed in his clean water and sage scent. She raised her hands to push him away, but her hands gave him a quick squeeze instead. She must be drunker than she thought.

He took several deep breaths. His heartbeat was steady under his solid chest.

She pressed her cheek against his wrinkled polo shirt and closed her eyes. Just for a minute. She shivered in the cool air, and he tightened his hold.

Life could be pretty strange sometimes. How did they both end up in Gold Springs? Maybe her ancestors were playing a joke on her. Payback for lying to Holden? She stiffened. He made a false assumption. She didn't lie to him.

Matthew lifted his chin and gently pulled away from her. He stared into her eyes and brushed a ringlet off her face. "I'm glad you're back in my life."

"If you're looking for dinner, it's in the trash."

"Sorry. A five-car pileup. I should have called, but I thought I could make it. And then I got caught up in dealing with the scene. There was a baby"—he swallowed and whispered—"in a ditch."

Her heart twisted. "But the baby is fine, right?"

He squeezed his eyes shut like he was in pain. "I just need a hug right now."

Raina didn't ask more questions about the accident. She had a feeling she wouldn't like the answers. She pulled him closer and blinked at the tears in her eyes.

He took a deep breath, and the tension left his body.

A light clicked on in another apartment unit. Something rustled in the undergrowth.

"I need to go. I'm not done with my paperwork yet," he said.

While Raina was still trying to process his words, Matthew turned and trudged into the dim morning light.

THERE WAS no point in sleeping after Matthew left. After swallowing two Motrin, Raina went for her daily morning run. The sun rose in a blaze of rusted fire, matching her anticipation for the day. When she passed a pair of ducks floating in the pond at Hook Park, she grinned. Everything would work out. It just had to.

As Raina ran up the walkway to her apartment, Eden chatted with a white-haired Chinese woman sitting on her red suitcase next to Raina's front door. Her grandma waved at Raina's approach. A surprise visit could only mean trouble at home.

"Po Po? What are you doing here?" Raina unlocked the front door. "I mean, it's good to see you."

Po Po squeezed past Raina into the apartment. "When you missed my birthday banquet, I knew something was wrong."

Raina bent to grab the handle of the luggage. "Nothing is wrong."

"How did it go last night with Matthew?" Eden grinned cheekily. "Did you get any information out of him?"

Po Po stared with avid interest. Raina cocked her head toward the front door. Eden stepped out, and Raina followed and closed the door. Immediately, her grandma pressed her face against the window to watch the two of them. Raina didn't think her grandma could lip read, but she turned away from the window just in case.

"He didn't show up until early this morning, but he didn't say anything other than he was sorry for not calling," Raina said.

Eden raised an eyebrow.

"I swear, that was it."

"You need to learn to work it." Eden placed a hand on her cocked hip. "Next time, grab the man by the ears and give him a big wet one. I've seen the way he looks at you. You can make him squeal."

Raina laughed. "All right. I'll be sure to bring it next time."

"I'm going to harass the police about my phone again. Maybe someone at the station will be in a gossipy mood. What are you planning to do later?"

"Head to campus to find Cora. I have a feeling the kid might know something."

Raina waved good-bye to Eden and went inside her apartment. Ignoring the questions in Po Po's eyes, she dragged the suitcase into the bedroom, grunting from the effort. How long was her grandma planning to stay?

Either she had clothes for several weeks, or she packed rocks. "Which cousin drove you here?"

Po Po patted her hair. "The family doesn't know I'm here yet. I took the morning train. I looked up the schedule on the Internet."

Raina's jaw dropped. Oh, no. Her mom would descend on this place like a wet alley cat. She swallowed, but her voice still came out in a croak. "Are you going to make the call?"

Po Po peered into her face and chuckled. "I'll call and explain everything."

Was this another blowout between Po Po and her dictatorial Uncle Anthony? Raina hated being the shield between the two Titans. As if she weren't on the poop list with her family already over her supposed inheritance.

Her grandma's relationship with her eldest son was complicated. Her Uncle Anthony spewed directives like some old patriarch in China, which Po Po promptly ignored even though she had been the traditional, obedient Chinese wife when her husband was alive.

"Where did you learn to use the Internet?" Raina asked.

"The Association had a computer class for the seniors. You can find all kinds of nifty stuff on the web these days," Po Po said.

The oldest Chinese families in San Francisco belonged to Associations, which started as a club to help immigrants back in the Gold Rush days. The maternal side of Raina's family, the Wongs, belonged to several Associations. However, the Sun family didn't belong to any, which only confirmed her grandfather's belief that Raina's mom married beneath her.

"What does Mom have to say about your new interest?" Raina asked. Her grandma with unlimited access to information wasn't a comforting thought.

"I don't think she knows. She has problems using her smarty pants phone, so she probably thinks I'm just as clueless with technology." Po Po chuckled. "So what's for breakfast? I'm starving."

Raina opened her refrigerator. Half a bag of spinach and two eggs. She regretted tossing out last night's dinner in an unusual fit of anger.

Po Po made a face when Raina told her the options. "Let's go to that waffle house. My treat."

Raina grabbed her purse. "Did you know Matthew lives here?"

When Raina was a child, Po Po and Matthew's grandma had been neighbors and best friends in San Francisco.

Her grandma nodded.

"How come you didn't tell me about this when I applied for grad school?" Raina asked.

"You shouldn't let a man influence your decisions," Po Po said.

"But you encouraged me to move here. You emphasized the personal attention I would get at a small college compared to U.C. Davis."

"And wasn't I right?"

"Yes," Raina muttered, but it didn't mean her grandma wasn't playing matchmaker.

"Honey, I'm starving. Can we talk about this over breakfast?"

"Fine. Let's roll."

"I need you to drop me off at the senior center after breakfast. I'm meeting Maggie for mahjong."

Raina suppressed a groan. So Matthew's grandma was in town too? This meant the grandmas were in cahoots playing matchmaker again.

If it hadn't been for her grandma, she would be living in Davis and would not be a potential murder suspect. No, she wouldn't think along this line. Holden could have died from natural causes. And if her grandma got a whiff of the death, she would want to play Miss Marple on the rescue train.

8

TWITCHING SPIDER LEGS

R aina dropped Po Po off at the senior center and drove to campus. The history building was a ghost town. There wasn't the sound of footsteps anywhere in the building. As Raina marched through the halls, a sense of unease settled between her shoulders. The fine hairs on the back of her neck stood at attention.

The east wing was a motley collection of glass display cases, bulletin boards, open doorways to classrooms and offices, and a dozen other hiding places. Raina stopped in front of a display case, squinting past her reflection on the glass. No movement.

She deliberately straightened her shoulders, but the sensation of being watched only increased. Her quick steps echoed around her. She flipped her hair over a shoulder and peeked behind her. No one. She struggled to catch any odd sound. Nope. Just the hum of the HVAC.

Raina hustled down the hall until she stood outside

the partially closed door of Olivia's office. All this talk of someone killing Holden had her jumping at shadows. She raised her hand to knock but stopped at a loud bang. Did Olivia drop something?

"I want my money back! I'm telling the police how you helped your brother," Olivia said. Another bang.

Raina lowered her hand. Who was inside the office with Olivia? Should she knock? It was the polite thing to do. But her pinkie finger was covered with hives, and she was a murder suspect. She didn't have the luxury of being polite anymore.

She leaned forward, pressing against the doorframe, and stumbled over her feet. Her shoes squeaked against the floor. She grabbed the doorknob to keep from falling into the office. So much for being a smooth operator.

Taking a deep breath, Raina knocked and pushed open the door. Olivia's office had the same layout as Holden's office, except for the "Save Lake Tahoe" framed poster on the wall. There was only one person in the room.

Olivia glanced expectantly at the door with a slight curl to her lips. She was perched behind her desk with a hand on the receiver of her landline phone. The wrinkles settled into deep grooves around her eyes. Her black spider lashes blended with the purple eye bags. At Raina's finger wave, Olivia's smile slipped. Apparently, Raina wasn't worth the effort of a pleasant greeting.

"Yes?" Olivia said, replacing the receiver on the hook.

"Are you okay? I heard loud bangs," Raina said, making a point to glance around the office.

"The phone fell out of my hands. Are you looking for something?"

Raina glanced at the chipped receiver. Uh-huh. She put on her bimbo smile. "Do you know where I can find Cora Campos? I forgot to ask for her phone number."

"I sent her on an errand yesterday. She came back in tears and quit."

"I lent her my headphones, and I need them back. Do you know where she lives?"

Olivia stared at her, tapping her fingers on the desk. "No. Anything else?"

Raina giggled. Pretending to be brainless was hard work. "I misplaced the donor's list. Do you have another copy?"

Olivia sighed and jerked open the filing cabinet beneath her window. She rifled through the folders, muttering under her breath.

"I'm surprised you're working. The rest of the building feels like a ghost town."

"Why wouldn't I be here? This place would fall apart without me."

Raina rubbed her sweaty palms on her shorts. "I had the impression you and Holden were close. I thought you would be too upset to come in."

Olivia spun around and stared at Raina with a blank expression. "What are you implying?"

Raina coughed, and fear rose to clog her throat. *Keep up the bimbo act.* She wrinkled her brow and hoped she sounded mystified. "Holden often spoke highly of you. I thought maybe you were his mentor."

Olivia stared at Raina for another heartbeat. "No. I wasn't his mentor." She slammed the cabinet shut and turned to her computer. Several clicks later, the printer whirred to life and spat out several sheets of paper.

"If I were you, I would tread carefully." Olivia looked pointedly at Raina and held out the stack from the printer. "You know what they say about curiosity and the cat."

Raina stuffed the sheets of paper into her purse and mumbled a thanks. Was the last comment a threat? As she made her way to the main hall, a knot formed in her stomach. Was Olivia hiding something?

Her steps faltered. Sol had said ex-girlfriend killed boyfriend over other woman. What if Olivia thought Raina was the other woman? And wasn't poison the weapon of choice for scorned women? She shivered at the thought. No, Holden had died from natural causes. She refused to jump at shadows because of Eden's bogus theory for a front-page story.

Raina waved to the two students chatting in front of Gail's empty desk. Snatches of their conversation included "bathroom" and "police." They gestured for Raina to join them, but she shook her head.

She trudged toward the west wing, arguing with herself the entire time to turn around. As she rounded the corner, the crime scene tape blocked access to the men's restroom. The yellow tape contrasted with the pale blue wall. The police would have removed the tape by now under normal circumstances, which meant there was nothing normal about Holden's death.

A wave of sadness hit Raina. She leaned against the opposite wall, taking loud breaths through flared nostrils. Holden just died, and the only thing marking his passing was some yellow tape and the scent of Pine-Sol. Where were the flowers and candles marking his passage? She closed her eyes and said a silent prayer.

As she straightened, the fine hairs on her arms stiffened. Someone ducked into a room at the end of the hall.
Was someone in Holden's office? Maybe she should call
Matthew. No, she didn't want to run to a man at every
shadow.

Her shoes squeaked against the floor, giving fair
warning to anyone hiding in the room. She drew out the
pepper spray from her purse and held it in front of her.
She grabbed the doorknob and flung open the door. It
rebounded and bumped into her shoulder, sending the
pepper spray flying.

Time slowed, and the pepper spray took an eternity to
land next to a pair of brown sandals. Her gaze traveled up
a pair of thick hairy legs and into the shocked eyes of Sol
Cardenas.

"What—"

"You!" Raina blurted out.

She stumbled backward, but his arm snaked out,
grabbed her wrist, and pulled her into the office. He
kicked the door shut. She opened her mouth to scream,
but her stomach lodged in her throat. The only sound
she made was a pathetic eek.

Sol folded thick arms over his paunch and leaned a
hip against the edge of the desk. "It's not what it seems."

Raina cleared her throat. The stench of days-old
vomit hit her. She clutched her purse in front of her and
breathed through her mouth. She glanced in the trash
can. There was a congealed splatter with tan lumps and
an empty coffee cup with "Lois Lane" written on the side.
When did Eden search Holden's office? "Enlighten me."

"I'm looking for my letter of recommendation.
Holden promised to write it for me," Sol said.

"Why are you searching for it behind closed doors? Why can't you ask someone for a recommendation?"

"I don't have time to wait until it's okay to look through Holden's things. That could take weeks in a murder investigation. The deadline for the grant is in two days. And I can't ask anyone else because I've only done work for Holden." Sol ran both hands through his greasy hair. "Why don't you help me look for the letter?"

"And get my fingerprints on everything? No, thanks."

"Your prints are probably on everything already. What difference do you think it's going to make now?"

Raina's pulse jumped. He was right, but a lot of other students probably left their prints behind in Holden's office. "Why would you want someone you dislike to write you a letter of recommendation?"

Sol shifted his stance by the desk, seeming to fill up the closed office with his bulk.

A tingle ran down Raina's spine, and her leg muscles tightened, ready for flight.

The phone rang and broke their staring contest. Sol jerked at the noise behind him. Keeping an eye to his back, Raina swung open the door. As the phone stopped ringing, she stumbled into the hall.

Sol whipped around. His eyes widened, and his face tightened in fear.

A flutter of courage filled Raina. If things got dicey, she could outrun him. "Why did you say murder investigation?"

"I've worked for Holden for the last three years. He treated people like crap and stole other people's work. I'm sure someone bumped him off." Sol scratched his soft stomach. "He had it coming."

Raina shivered at the malice in Sol's tone. He was probably right about this too.

9

FORK WITH HAIR ON IT

Raina stared at the two eggs in her refrigerator. Her stomach rumbled in disappointment. She had secretly hoped to come home to find the refrigerator fully stocked. Irrational? Yes. Once her grand-dad's shipping company took off three decades ago, her grandma had hired someone to shop and cook for the family. Po Po was one smart lady.

Someone knocked on the front door. Raina straightened and closed the refrigerator with a thwack. A visitor during lunch could mean free food. And a sane person didn't turn down free food. She hurried to her living room and squinted at the peephole on her door.

Matthew, clean-shaven and hair still wet from a recent shower, leaned into the peephole. His warm brown eyes had a twinkle she didn't trust. "I know you're in there, Rainy."

Raina stepped back, tugging at the collar of her shirt. The apartment suddenly felt uncomfortably warm. She wasn't ready to have a tete-a-tete with him.

"Maybe your neighbors would like to hear about our business!" he said.

She flung open the door, leaning against the door-frame. The hot air curled around her and made the back of her neck instantly sticky. "We don't have any more business. You made that crystal clear in Vegas."

"In case you've forgotten, you were the one who wanted our marriage annulled." Matthew smiled, and his brown eyes crinkled in the corners. "I saw your car when I pulled in. I can't believe you're still driving the old thing." He shifted his weight. "Had lunch yet?"

Raina crossed her arms. She hadn't forgotten, but it was much easier to blame him for the failed relationship.

"I'm not going to bite. And you always liked free food," he said.

"What can I do for you, Detective?"

"How about a quick lunch where you tell me what happened on the night Holden Merritt died?"

"I gave my statement already."

He raised an eyebrow. "I want to hear it for myself. Either we go over the statement here, or we go over it while eating lunch. And you know how cranky we both get when we're hungry."

"I had lunch already."

"I'm sorry about dinner last night." His eyes lost their humor. "I was called to a scene."

Raina swallowed the lump in her throat. That's right. The baby in the ditch. "I'll be ready in a few minutes." She closed the door and took a deep breath. No good would come from this. He would leave her again.

But she couldn't help but want to wrap her arms around his neck and offer comfort in the only way she knew how, just like she had done for most of her life. He had been the kid who hung around her family to escape his own, her best friend, and later her first lover. While he was off saving the world, death and mayhem must have been his regular bedfellows. This Matthew should be a stranger, but he wasn't. Not where it counted.

She should let him in, so he didn't have to wait in the heat. Her gaze flicked around the piles in her apartment. She'd always been a piler: mail, books, or clothes. As long as it was stackable, she made little molehills around her living space. Matthew shouldn't see this. His eyes would twitch, and his fingers would curl from his desire to straightened things out. It was more torture than mercy to let him see her one trait that drove him crazy.

Raina stripped off her clothes and hurled herself into the shower. Fifteen minutes later, she was dressed in a linen purple top and tan shorts. Her curly hair was somewhat tamed by her French braid, and she had on a smear of lipstick. The faded fingernail marks left by Gail on her forearms were covered with concealer. As long as there was no licking involved, he wouldn't know whether she rinsed cleanly or not.

She stepped out the front door to find Matthew with his cell phone wedged between his shoulder and ear and his back to her. Should she make a noise to alert him of her presence?

"What does the toxicology report say?" he asked.

Her eyes widened. Was this Holden's toxicology report? She put her finger over the latch and closed the door. The lock slid home with a soft click.

He grabbed a small notebook from his back pocket and flipped it open. "Poisoned? Are you sure?"

She gasped.

Matthew swung around and glowered at her. "Give me a call back when they're done processing his home," he said into the phone. He slipped the cell phone and notebook back into his pockets. "You shouldn't be listening to police business," he said to Raina.

"Then don't conduct it in front of a private citizen."

He sighed and mumbled something unflattering about women.

"Excuse me?" Raina said, hands on her hips.

"See what I mean about hunger crankiness?"

"How was Holden poisoned?"

"I can't tell you."

"Then I'm not going with you. Just ask your questions."

Matthew lifted a hand and rubbed the back of his neck. She leaned back against her door. She had learned patience since he had last seen her. He glared at her and took a step forward.

Raina lifted her chin. A mere four inches separated them. A curl on the side of her face moved each time Matthew exhaled. She flushed. The heady scent of his skin, a combination of sage and clean water, clogged the back of her throat.

His nostrils flared, and his eyes darkened. He took a step back and ran a shaky hand through his hair. "What-ever I tell you stays between us."

She licked her lips. "Yes." She blinked at the low husky tone. Stop it! This was not the time for a teenage infatuation.

"The initial toxicology tests came back positive. The lab has to run more tests to identify the substance. The location of the toxin in his stomach and liver strongly suggests he was poisoned."

"He looked fine when I saw him in the morning. Gail mentioned he asked her for Pepto around two o'clock. Maybe the upset stomach he complained about was the first sign of the poison." Raina froze. What if Holden had already ingested the poison when he cornered her by the vending machine?

"She didn't mention Pepto in her statement. When did she tell you this?"

"The morning after Holden died."

"What else did she tell you?"

"Are we planning to share?"

Matthew grabbed her chin and tilted her head until she could count the gold flecks in his eyes. "Don't. Get. Involved."

Raina jerked her head loose. "Why would I get involved?"

"You tell me."

About Holden? Or Sol? Like it or not, she was up to her armpits in muck. And once Matthew heard about the fake pregnancy, she could kiss any affection he might still have for her good-bye. Not that she still wanted him. She just didn't want him to think badly of her. "I'm going to stay off your radar."

"Your curiosity has gotten you in trouble before."

"I was trying to help you out."

"And I appreciated it. Just don't do it again." His eyes softened. "You know how much I hate the role of a super-hero and you as the damsel in distress."

Raina rolled her eyes. "I can save myself. So are you going to buy me lunch or what?"

The corner of his lips curled into a half smile. "Let's go."

A few minutes later, he parked in front of the Venus Café on the corner of Main Street and Second Avenue. The olive green bungalow with white trim had been converted into a commercial space more than a decade ago. The cafe featured a large front room with half a dozen small tables and a large fireplace surrounded by cracked leather reading chairs.

Unlike your typical mom-and-pop cafes, the Venus Café's interior walls had floor-to-ceiling murals of handsome men frolicking with naked nymphs with strategically placed flowing hair or bits of leaves. The town's elders hated this place, but a thrill ran through Raina each time she stepped inside the cafe. It felt good to be a little naughty, even if it was vicariously through painted women.

They placed their orders at the counter, grabbed their coffees, and found a table in a quiet corner. Sitting a foot from Matthew, Raina's knees kept bumping into his every time one of them shifted. His eyes kept straying to the painted women, and they grew wider at each encounter.

"I take it you haven't been here before," said Raina with a smirk.

"I'd been here before the murals. I wasn't impressed with the coffee then." He held up his iced coffee. "This is much better."

"New ownership. Brenda and Joe bought the place nine months ago."

Matthew tapped his fingers against his glass. No wedding ring. "I never imagined I would run into you at a crime scene." He tore his eyes from the painted walls to study her.

Raina met his eyes, and a jolt ran down her spine. A sense of déjà vu settled on her. She averted her gaze, hoping he didn't notice her reaction. The clink of forks hitting plates and the low buzz of conversation faded into a mute din. No, she couldn't let this happen again.

"How long have you been living in Gold Springs?" Raina asked. "It's a strange coincidence we both moved to this town. After shooting and exploding things for the feds, being a small town cop must be a change."

"Almost two years. I feel like I can breathe here. Your grandma visits mine quite often."

Raina slumped in her chair. And no doubt the two grandmas spoke of her, which meant he must have known she was in town and hadn't bothered looking her up. Yes, her feelings were hurt because they were old friends. Nothing more.

"I know why you moved here," Matthew said.

Raina blinked. "What?" She better save the brooding thoughts for later when she was alone.

"You moved to town because of me."

"Get over yourself. I thought you were still in Washington, D.C."

"You tracked me down by talking to my grandma. And waving a dead body in front of me?" He winked. "That's prime. You're good. Real good."

Raina burst out laughing. Uh-huh. He had it all figured out. She had forgotten he could always make her laugh. "It was the cheesecake."

Matthew leaned back and smacked his lips. "My

grandma always had a soft spot for you. It's been a while since I had your cheesecake."

"I made one for you last night."

The jovial mood vanished. The hissing espresso machine and someone's laughter filled the silence between them. Raina stared at the painted gyrating nymph on the wall closest to her. She needed to stop. They already had their chance at happiness, and it didn't work out.

Brenda Sullivan, the café owner, slid a club salad in front of Raina and a cheeseburger with fries in front of Matthew. The whiff of grease made Raina's stomach churn. For the next few minutes, she picked at her salad and watched Matthew devour his food with gusto. His appetite hadn't changed. Good thing her cooking had improved.

She fought the urge to reach across the table and wipe the ketchup off his chin. He had left her broken-hearted one too many times. Melodramatic? Yes, but she couldn't let the man in front of her charm his way back into her life again. She stabbed at a piece of spinach, twisting the fork until the leaf shredded.

He wiped his mouth and crumpled the paper napkin in his hands. "How well did you know Holden Merritt?"

"He was my advisor for my graduate studies."

"What were you doing in the building after hours?"

Raina wiped her sweaty palms on her shorts. Matthew would find out when he checked the phone records. "Holden texted me. He wanted to talk."

"About what?"

She licked her lips. Stick to the truth. "He owed me money. I had asked for it back the day before when we met to go over my coursework." Good thing no one could verify the amount.

"Why did he owe you money?"

"What do you mean?" She shifted in her seat and bumped into his knees. "Sorry. He needed cash and didn't have time to go to the ATM. And I had a twenty." Liar, liar, pants on fire.

Matthew stared at her for a long moment. His face became professionally blank. "How well do you know Gail Drakos?"

"Why would she poison Holden?"

He dipped another soggy fry into his pool of ketchup. "That's not my question."

"We're friends." She left off the "sometimes." He didn't need that information. "What was Natalie's reaction to her brother's death?"

"She answered our questions and then closed the door."

Raina rubbed her hands on her shorts again. "If he didn't stay late to meet with me, do you think he would be alive now?"

Matthew studied her expression, and his eyes softened. "Rainy, someone was out to get him. Whether he stayed late or went home wouldn't change the outcome, just the location of the crime."

She shifted, her bare knee skimming across the rough fabric of his jeans. A strand slipped from the knot in her heart. Not her fault. Her fake pregnancy and Holden's urgent desire to talk had nothing to do with his untimely death. She should tell Matthew the truth. "There's something I want to tell—"

"Let me take those for you." Brenda's hand reached

for the empty plates. "Dessert? We're starting our fall menu early this year."

Matthew glanced over Raina's shoulder.

Raina turned to look at the display cases featuring a dozen baked goods next to the coffee bar. She froze as her gaze swept past the fireplace. Eden and Officer Hopper pored over several pages on the large coffee table. How long had they been here?

"The pumpkin marble coffee cake looks good," Raina said.

Matthew pushed his chair back as if to get up.

"No, I'll get it. You two keep talking," said Brenda with a warm smile.

After the café owner was out of the earshot, Matthew asked, "What were you just saying?"

Raina shook her head. This wasn't the time to confess all her sins. "It wasn't important."

Brenda returned and slid a small plate with a generous slice of coffee cake between them. "I brought two forks." She winked at Raina and sashayed away.

Raina stared at the two forks, and heat rose from her neck. Was she wearing a dopey lovesick expression? Why did Brenda assume she wanted to share the cake?

"I can't say no to two forks," said a beaming Matthew, lopping off a large piece.

Raina rolled her eyes. Just like old times. She ordered dessert, and he finished it off. "There's been something I've been meaning to ask you. What did my grandfather say to you in high school? Before you left..." The "me" hung unspoken in the air between them.

Matthew coughed and reached for his coffee. He took a long swallow before meeting her eyes. "I—"

Officer Hopper thumped her cup on the table and sat on the vacant chair between them.

Raina wanted to scream at the look of relief on Matthew's face. She scooted her chair back at the sudden crowd around the small table. A quick glance behind her confirmed that Eden was long gone.

"Chancellor wants to meet with you in an hour." Officer Hopper grabbed a fork and popped a piece of the cake into her mouth. Her flinty blue eyes slid sideways to Raina and just as quickly dismissed her. "Wow, this is good cake, Matthew." The fork dangled off her slim hands in the space between Matthew and Raina.

Raina wanted to laugh. So that was it. "That fork fell on the floor. Is that piece of hair still on the tines? I'm waiting for Brenda to bring me a new one."

Officer Hopper's eyes widened. The fork dropped onto the table with a resounding clang.

Matthew's lips twitched, but he quickly suppressed it. His eyes were bright with amusement. "Any idea what the meeting is about?"

Officer Hopper flicked a glance at Raina, her scowl firmly back in place.

"Meet you outside in a minute," Matthew said.

Officer Hopper shoved away from the table and stalked to the entrance, banging open the door.

Right, police business. As if Raina couldn't find out what the Chancellor said. All it took was a quick phone call to Gail. "Did Officer Cake Snatcher miss a coffee run this morning or something?"

Matthew popped another piece of cake into his mouth. "You can use my fork. It doesn't have hair on it."

Raina laughed and grabbed the plate before he could

lop another piece off. He handed her the fork, their hands touching. A tingle of excitement ran up her arm. Warmth spread across her chest. The noise of the café once again faded into the background.

Matthew leaned in and tapped her nose. "It's good to spend time with you again, Rainy. See you later." He joined Officer Hopper outside.

Raina chuckled to herself and dug into the cake with Matthew's fork. She made an enemy all right. Officer Cake Snatcher wanted Matthew, but she'd no idea he was just as emotionally unavailable to her as he was to Raina.

10

SEX, MONEY, AND LIES

R aina pressed her back against the rough bark and huddled under the shade of the tree. She'd been sitting here for the last thirty minutes, but time had a surreal quality when her wet T-shirt clung to even wetter skin. Eden was late, as usual, even though her text message had said she was on her way. Waiting outside the freshman dorms in one-hundred-degree heat without a bottle of water wasn't one of her smarter moves.

While finishing off the cake at the Venus Cafe yesterday, finding Cora had seemed like a brilliant idea. Any sane person would let the police investigate Holden's murder. And Raina was normally sane, except Matthew was the police. She couldn't risk him finding out about the fake pregnancy during his investigation. He would think she was trying to trap Holden just like his mom had trapped his dad into a disastrous marriage.

Raina glanced at the names written on the notebook resting on her knee. Olivia Kline and Sol Cardenas.

Reluctantly, she added Cora Campos to the list. What reason did any of them have for killing Holden?

If Olivia was a jealous lover, why didn't she kill her rival? Raina swallowed. What if she was the rival? Not that she wanted Olivia to correct the situation.

Why would Sol search Holden's office behind closed doors if he had nothing to hide? And how did Cora fit into this? Why did the police seek her out at the bookstore? In hindsight, her reaction yesterday was suspicious.

A clinking noise dragged Raina's attention from the notebook, and she glanced at the cluster of two-story buildings. A golf cart pulled up next to the bike racks. Tony came over. "Someone called Campus Security about a woman passed out under a tree."

Raina gave him what she hoped was her cutest smile. Unbelievable. How could a man just glisten when she smelled like the underside of a moldy mushroom? "Give me another hour. I don't think I'm ready to swoon yet."

"It's dangerous to sit out in this heat." Tony tilted his head toward the golf cart. "I'll give you a ride back to your car. By the way, I'm going to have to confiscate your faculty parking pass."

Raina got into the cart. "It's too hot to walk from the student lot. I only use the parking pass for the greater good. And it's not like the faculty lots are full during the summer." She pulled out her lower lip in an exaggerated pout, blinking her eyes.

Tony laughed. "Nice try, but I'm just doing my job. And stop that blinking. You look more like a toad than a cute puppy." He weaved the cart around two bikers.

Raina handed over her parking pass when they got to her car. It wasn't as if she didn't pay for a parking pass, just that she chose to give herself an upgrade once in a while. It was one of the perks of working with computer geeks.

"Why would someone call Campus Security?" Raina asked.

Tony shrugged. "Maybe someone is concerned about you."

"Who called?"

"Cora Campos."

Raina sucked in a breath. So she was on the right trail, enough to rattle Cora into calling Campus Security to get rid of her. Now she was more convinced than ever that she needed to talk to the freshman.

The ding on Raina's cell phone distracted her from further thoughts about the matter. The text message was from Eden, asking Raina to swing by the newspaper office to pick her up for a little snooping at Olivia's house. Raina was miffed, but her friend's plan was more appealing than sitting here in this heat. As Raina pulled out of the parking lot, she waved to Tony.

A few minutes later, Eden hopped into Raina's car. "Sorry, my desk phone rang as I was heading out."

"Uh-huh. How can you be on your way when you haven't even left the building?" Raina asked.

"I was heading toward the door. Close enough." Eden pulled out a Starbucks Frappuccino from her purse. "Here's my peace offering. Ice cold from the vending machine."

Raina twisted off the cap and downed half the bottle in one gulp.

Eden smirked. "I guess I'm forgiven. Let's get on the road, Robin."

Raina pulled away from the curb. "No, I'm Batman."

"I'm almost a foot taller than you."

Raina rolled her eyes. "Fine, you can be the muscle. So why are we going to Olivia's house?"

"The Dean put her on admin leave this morning."

"Because of the missing grant money?"

Eden shrugged. "Let's find out."

Raina parked in front of the single-story ranch-style house. Eden jumped out of the car like she had been ejected from her seat. Raina followed her friend to the front door. She shifted her weight and kicked a few scattered leaves off the porch while the bell chimed inside. In the far corner, there were cobwebs, and the giant potted plant had more weeds than flowers. Olivia wasn't one of those proud homeowners who believed in curb appeal.

Olivia cracked open the door, and a rancid odor drifted out. Her body blocked the view into the house. "What do you want?"

Raina stepped back from the smell. "What's that awful stench?" She swallowed the bitter tang in her mouth. Apparently Olivia didn't believe in air fresheners either.

Olivia stiffened and started to push the door closed.

Eden stopped it with her foot. "Did you have a romantic relationship with Holden? What happened to the missing grant money? Do you think Holden's death has anything to do with the missing money?"

Olivia's eyes grew wider at each question. "What the —? Who are you?"

"Eden Small. *Gold Springs Weekly*. Are you on admin leave because of the missing money?"

"Get off my porch. You have three seconds before I call the police."

"Why did you want me on the fundraiser committee? Was it because of Holden?" Raina asked.

Olivia raised an eyebrow. "They say you need to keep your enemies close."

Raina wiped her hands on her shorts. She doubted Olivia would admit it, but it was worth a shot to see her reaction. "Did you kill Holden?"

"Wouldn't you like to know?" Olivia kicked Eden's foot out of the way and slammed the door, rattling the windows.

Eden banged on the door. "That's assault." She turned to Raina. "Well, that was a waste of time."

Raina stared at the closed door. "Actually we found out a few interesting things. Olivia is probably a secret alcoholic. You can tell by the stench in the house." Before Matthew's father left, his childhood home had the same rancid odor. She turned and walked back to her car.

Eden caught up with her. "You said a few interesting things."

"Olivia knew about my relationship with Holden. So did she want me on the committee to keep an eye on me or to rattle Holden? If it's the former, she considered me a romantic rival, and if it's the latter, she might have a vendetta against Holden."

∾

RAINA DROPPED Eden off at the newspaper office and rolled through the drive-thru on her way to campus for her closing shift. She chugged a supersize iced coffee and greasy burger while she droved one-handed. When she logged in to her computer, she sent a message to her supervisor, retracting her earlier email begging for more hours. Bills could wait. Volunteering for the fundraiser gave her the perfect excuse to ask questions. Then she printed another faculty parking pass.

When her shift ended, she trotted over to the history building, hoping to catch Gail in a chatty mood. Her stomach heaved like a twig in a storm from the acid in the coffee and the grease in the burger. She rooted in her purse for the roll of Tums. A mint, pepper spray, a notebook, and several inkless pens. It was either time to clean her purse or buy a bigger one. Her stomach churned again. Payback could be such a bit—

Raina slammed into someone. As her butt hit the floor, it knocked the air out of her lungs. Books thumped around her, and someone yelped. A flash of pain raced up Raina's back. She grimaced. She should pay more attention to her surroundings.

Andrew Rollinger extended a hand. "Sorry. We need to hang mirrors at the corners. Are you okay?"

Raina nodded and stood with Andrew's help. The contents of her purse, three hardback books, and several sheets of paper were strewn across the floor. The elusive roll of Tums rested on the heels of his brown loafers. As they gathered their stuff, he droned about the new teaching assignments for the graduate students.

"So is that extra class okay with you?" he asked.

Raina blinked, staring at his face for half a second.

His monotonous voice sounded so much like her white noise machine she'd tuned him out. "Why are you taking over Olivia's duties while she's on admin leave? Wouldn't a professor with more seniority...I mean." She flushed. "Let me swallow my foot right now."

Andrew's normally ruddy face got even redder. "I have the experience for the job. Just..." He shrugged.

Raina raised an eyebrow. How would a senior lecturer have the experience to fill in for the department head?

"That extra undergrad class is okay?" Andrew asked.

"Yes! I need the hours." This was perfect. Not only would Raina get extra hours for the semester, but it would also give her more time at the department to snoop. "So are you also dealing with the grant money fiasco, too? Is that why Olivia is on admin leave?"

Andrew shook his head. "Someone called the Dean about Olivia's inappropriate behavior." He went on for a few more minutes about blatant favoritism and bullying, none of which was news to Raina.

"What's inappropriate?" Raina interrupted when he paused for a breath.

He made a show of looking up and down the hall but didn't lower the volume of his voice. "Sex, money, and lies."

She suppressed the urge to roll her eyes. Unbelievable. The man was having a field day. He didn't seem to be the type to spread vicious rumors. "Can you be more specific? Was there any proof of misconduct?"

"Obviously you don't understand the implication." Andrew straightened, looking down his ski-sloped nose. "Rumors can make or break an academic career. Nothing was proven in my case, but..." He trailed off, his ruddy complexion growing pale. "Never mind. You're just a student."

Raina ignored his comment. "When was the last time you talked to Holden?"

Andrew froze, licking his lower lip. "During the fundraiser meeting. Why?"

Time to put her new skill to the test. "I emailed him to ask about you becoming my new advisor. I wondered if he got a chance to talk to you about it before..." Raina looked down at her shoes when her voice trailed off. Out of the corner of her eyes, she saw his shoulders relax.

"No. When did you ask him?"

"Before the fundraiser meeting." The lie slipped out as smooth as an oiled bearing. She must be getting better at lying.

"We can talk about it later, when things die down." Andrew cleared his throat. "Uh..." He glanced at his watch. "I'm meeting Lori for an early lunch."

"Can you tell Lori to give me a call when she's free? We need to work on the details for the donors list."

"Sure, but Gail is chairing the fundraiser now. It might be a good idea to wait until Monday before putting in any more work on it." Andrew glanced at his watch again. "And she's real happy about it." He drew out the word "real."

Raina's heart sank. Gail wouldn't be in a gossipy mood today, but it was still worth a try all the same.

After a rushed good-bye, Andrew scurried down the hall. Raina chewed on a Tums and resumed her search for Gail. She stopped mid-stride. If Olivia gave Holden free rein of the grant money, could she have given him personal money? Raina pulled out her notebook and wrote down the question. It might also be worth a shot to check on Andrew's employment history. Her list of questions was growing longer by the minute.

When Raina exited the hall and stepped into the vaulted lobby area, she squinted against the sunshine coming in from the skylights and large front windows. The entire space was lit up like a stage. Her nose twitched at the dust swirling in the patches of light. The potted plants were thriving in the greenhouse-like environment.

She knocked on the sliding glass partition on top of the front counter. The two small task lights under the upper cubicle shelves lit the dim interior. Gail looked up from her files and opened the office door next to the counter.

Raina stepped inside and sank into an office chair. "My skin was starting to blister out there. Need any help with the fundraiser?" If she buttered up Gail, maybe the secretary would gossip. Besides, one extra task wasn't going to take too much time.

"I can't hire you," Gail said, her thick eyebrows forming a V on her forehead.

Raina pulled out her notebook and flipped to a blank page. "That's okay. It's just more paperwork. I'll help out until the department hires someone permanent. Tell me what you need help with."

Gail gave Raina a grateful smile and proceeded to add more items to Raina's growing list. Fifteen minutes later, Raina wished she could retract her offer to help. Maybe it was time to reconsider the black tie formal dinner and pare down to something simpler.

Someone rapped on the office door. Raina dropped her notebook at the unexpected noise. Gail opened the door, and a thin-faced student rushed in, jabbering about an arrest.

"Whoa!" Raina raised her hands. "Take a deep breath. Who got arrested?"

The thin-faced student swung around. "Cora."

Gail sagged against the door, her knuckles whitening on the doorknob. "What happened?"

The student flopped down onto an office chair. He leaned forward, resting his elbows on his knees. "Cora left with the police a few minutes ago. I don't know what to do."

"Did the police arrest her or did they bring her in for questioning?" Raina asked.

The student lifted his head and frowned. "I'm...not sure." He glanced at Gail. "Should we call her parents?"

"No. We don't know what's going on yet. There's no need to alarm them if they didn't arrest her," Gail said.

The look of relief on the student's face would have been comical, if not for the situation. "You'll take care of this? I have class in a few minutes."

Gail nodded. "Don't tell anyone about Cora. We don't want rumors flying around about the poor girl."

After the student left, Gail stared into space. When she came out of her daze, she picked up the phone and made several calls in rapid succession.

Raina shifted in her seat and lowered her eyes. She had spent the night with Po Po's knee on her back. It was either share a bed with her grandma or sleep on the uncomfortable sofa. She kept her eyes closed, and let Gail's low murmur wash over her.

Gail put down the phone and said, "According to

Donna, Cora opted to leave with the police because she didn't want to be interviewed in front of her friends."

Raina started and glanced at the clock. She covered a yawn with her hand. "I'm sorry. I must have drifted off. So it's just an interview. Then they'll let her go soon. How did you get the front desk clerk to talk? I thought she couldn't share police business with civilians."

"You owe Donna a spicy cheddar cheese quiche. She wants to bring it to our church potluck," Gail said.

Good thing Po Po had offered to stock Raina's fridge. She was willing show up with a buffet if Donna gave her the inside scoop to the police station. "Not a problem. I'll deliver it warm and toasty Sunday morning."

Gail opened a drawer and grabbed her purse. "I'm taking an early lunch to go down to the police station. Cora will probably need a ride home."

Raina stood. "You were hiding something from Eden the other day. I think it has to do with Cora."

"It's not my secret to tell."

"Do you think Cora killed Holden?"

"No."

"I want to help her, too."

Gail looked at Raina, assessing her. "Cora's nephew is Holden's son. He was paying child support to her family, and they need the money."

Raina ran a shaky hand through her curly hair. Was this the shame Holden had been too embarrassed to confess? "Wouldn't killing Holden give them immediate access to his money?" She thought about his salary and made some rapid calculations. "You're talking about two hundred thousand from just his retirement and life insurance. And with his Spartan lifestyle, there's probably more."

Gail closed her eyes and shook her head. "I don't believe it. She's the first one in her family to go to college. This is her chance to escape poverty."

A few minutes later, Raina sat in her car, mulling over her morning. The cold air blasting out the vents did little to cool the interior. She pulled her shirt away from her moist body, sighing in contentment when the chilly air drifted down her chest. Her backside felt extra crispy from the hot seat. She folded the sunshade and tucked it into the space between the seat and console.

She pulled the notebook from her purse and added the information about the nephew under Cora's name with shaking hands. First Natalie and now Cora. The police were questioning all the people who were personally involved with Holden. Raina licked her dry lips. Matthew would eventually come looking for her, if she wasn't on his radar already. Did this mean Olivia would be questioned as well?

At the sudden tears in her eyes, her vision blurred. All she'd wanted was to escape the drama at home with her move to Gold Springs. Now she was up to her armpits in muck again. She straightened and swiped a finger under each eye. Time to get cracking. Sitting here wasn't going to solve her problems.

11

SECRETS DON'T DIE WITH THE DEAD

By the time Raina got home, she was beat. She trudged from her car to her unit on autopilot, only to find her living room drapes opened. Her grandma tapped on a laptop on the dining room table. The small piles of books and magazines in her apartment looked much worse from the outside.

Raina banged open the front door, grabbed the cord for her drapes, and closed them with a whoosh. By the time she spun around, Po Po had already closed her laptop. "I don't like my neighbors looking in on their way to the laundry room."

Po Po shrugged. "If you clean up your little mole hills, then you'll have no reason to hide from your neighbors."

"And why are we talking about my housekeeping?" Raina raised an eyebrow. "I didn't exactly fall far from the apple tree."

"Touché."

Raina flopped down onto the sofa, pulled out her

notebook, and studied the timeline she'd created. Po Po came over and sat next to her, tucking her short legs on the sofa.

"What are you doing?" Po Po peered at the squiggles on the page, and her face brightened. "So the rumor is true. Someone offed Holden Merritt." She rubbed her hands together. "This is exciting."

Her grandma was a Miss Marple on training wheels among her friends in San Francisco. When the mahjong ladies wanted to find a missing tile or cheat, Po Po took to the case like white on jasmine rice. The last thing Raina needed was for Eden pressuring her to pump people for information with Po Po riding shotgun, offering to pistol-whip anyone who wouldn't squeal.

Raina shoved the notebook back into her purse. She couldn't believe her grandma had rubbed her hands together. This wasn't an invitation to a tea party. "You're reading too many Sue Grafton novels. Don't you seniors have anything better to do than sit around and spread rumors?"

Po Po rolled her eyes. "And don't you young people know how to respect your elders?"

"Touché," Raina mumbled. She turned on the TV and pretended to channel surf.

The retired senior citizens were better informed than Eden when it came to the goings-on in town. Raina was dying to know the rumors surrounding Holden's death and who was saying what, but if she asked, she would only encourage Po Po to do more snooping. But with her grandma in town, she couldn't drop by the senior center to have a chat without Po Po finding out. The timing of her grandma's visit was starting to be a tad inconvenient.

"Maggie invited us to dinner. We can get groceries on the way home," Po Po said.

"And just how long are you planning to stay?" Raina asked. She didn't mind her grandma staying, but she did mind the matchmaking.

Po Po shrugged. "I'm mighty bored at home."

In other words, her grandma was planning to snoop around Holden's murder whether Raina wanted her to or not. She sighed. "What were they saying at the center?"

Po Po beamed, rattling off names and theories that swirled over Raina's head. She listened with half an ear. UFO probing and secret science experiments indeed. Holden was a history professor, not Dr. Frankenstein.

"Wait. What's this about the mob?" Raina asked. She dragged her attention from the "real" testimonials about P90X.

"Frank Small thinks Holden was killed because he stopped doing the pickups for the triad. He had been seen with a black gym bag stuffed with money."

"What pickups are you talking about? How could there be a triad in town when there are only a few dozen Chinese families?"

"Triads are known to have a long reach." Po Po shrugged. "It could be a branch from one of the bigger cities. Kinda like how banks have branches everywhere."

Raina gave her grandma a sideways glance. "And how does Frank know the bag was full of money? It's not like Holden opened it for him to have a look-see."

Po Po rolled her eyes. "Everyone knows what a gym bag full of money looks like. It's all lumpy like on TV. Honey, you need to watch more of these crime shows. It'll teach you a thing or two about life."

Raina laughed and flipped the channel. "I'll get right on it."

"Janice Tally thinks Holden was part of the witness protection program. Her granddaughter saw two large men robbing Natalie Merritt's apartment," Po Po continued. "By the time the police arrived, Natalie downplayed the whole thing. Said she was tied up because of some kinky sex games and her partners left to respond to an emergency."

Raina's eyes widened. Kinky sex game? Words like this shouldn't come out of her grandma's mouth. "Did they take anything?"

"Natalie told the cops they didn't take anything. But the granddaughter saw the men leaving with a TV and a laptop. And that night, Natalie up and left. Nobody has seen her since." Po Po nodded. "Yep, that's why Janice thinks Natalie is now on the run."

"And what do you think?"

"That's her theory, not mine. It would explain why Matthew is having a hard time tracking Natalie down for follow-up questioning. I still think Holden got probed one too many times for some kind of experiment." Po Po laughed. "That would explain why he'd seemed to have a stick up his butt the last time I spoke to him."

Raina cringed inwardly. Good thing her brief relationship with Holden had been discreet.

"We'll have to ask your friend Eden. She seems to always know about all the conspiracies on campus," Po Po said.

"There are no conspiracies on campus. Please don't encourage her. The college is the biggest employer in town. Eden shouldn't get on their bad side."

Po Po raised an eyebrow but changed the subject. "Speaking of Matthew, he came by looking for you earlier. He looked upset. Did you do something to upset him?"

Raina clicked the button on her remote, her mind racing as the stations flickered by. "What makes you think his mood has anything to do with me?" Did he find out about her relationship with Holden? She should have confessed at lunch yesterday. It wasn't her fault. She'd wanted to. If Brenda hadn't interrupted, she would have said something.

"What happened between the two of you in high school?"

Raina dragged her eyes away from the TV, hoping she didn't look as shaken as she felt. "I'm not discussing my love life with my grandmother."

"Do you want me to ask Eden to ask you?"

"We broke up. The End."

Po Po peered into Raina's face and chuckled. "You sure you don't need my help?"

"You'll be the first one I call if I need help," Raina said through gritted teeth.

Po Po patted Raina's knee. "Now are you done hiding in Gold Springs yet? It's a cute little town, but aren't you ready to come home?"

Raina froze. "I'm not hiding. I'm just on hold until I figure things out." She wasn't going to tell her grandma about the lawsuit contesting her husband's will. It would break Po Po's heart if she knew her grandchildren were squabbling over money.

She'd been on track to become a Senior Project Manager before she'd called it quits. The view hadn't been rosy during the climb to the top. A promotion with all the travel and overtime meant she would have even less time for a personal life.

The bittersweet inheritance from her granddad had shoved her down this path. Not that her freedom from a rigid work schedule this past year had done much to improve her personal life. She wasn't any happier than before. In the right lighting and after a bottle of wine, she'd even allow herself a good cry at the emptiness.

"I grieved for your granddad too, but it's been a couple of years. And life goes on. At some point, you're going to have to live again," Po Po whispered.

Raina stared at Po Po. Was this supposed to be a joke? Grief for Ah Gong?

"Oh, don't look at me like that. He was controlling and used money to bully people around, but he provided for the family. I never had to worry about money or his love."

"But Ah Gong treated you and"—Raina gestured at herself—"the entire family like he owned us." And even after his death, he was controlling her with money. Why did she still feel such loyalty toward him?

"And you had a roof over your head and food on the table after your dad died. You went to college debt free. There are two sides to every coin. Without Ah Gong, you think you could be here moping about your life?"

Raina snapped her mouth shut and nodded. The family had been shocked by the large sum Ah Gong had left her. What they failed to understand was hush money came at a price for the giver and the recipient. The lawsuit from her cousins, the vocal complaints from the aunts, and the weight of granddad's secret had forced her on this self-imposed isolation.

As Raina showered, she wondered if dinner was a set-up for a chance dinner date with Matthew under the watchful eyes of the two grandmas. Po Po rode shotgun with a frown on her face and a death grip on her red purse. Not exactly the look of someone anticipating a happy visit with her BFF. Something was up.

"Everything okay?" Raina asked, sneaking a sideways glance at her grandma.

"Everything's peachy."

Now Raina knew something was wrong. Po Po made fun of women who used that term. Said it reminded her of Southern women with scented face powder and tea doilies. "Are you going to point your pinkie finger up in the air now when you drink tea?"

Po Po harrumphed, but a smile formed at the corner of her lips. Score one to Raina for knowing her grandma like the top of her nose.

"Something is bothering me, but I'd rather talk it through with my friend," Po Po said.

Raina nodded. There were things she didn't want her grandma to know either. Fair was fair.

"Maggie would love more of your company," Po Po said. "She only has Matthew. And he's been busy lately with the murder and the fiasco with the pileup at County Road Twenty-seven."

Raina sneaked a glance at her grandma. "What fiasco?"

Po Po's eyes lit up. "Oh, you haven't heard? It happened the evening before I came. Turned out the car that started the five-car pileup had a trunk full of marijuana. And the marijuana grew legs in the evidence room."

As strange as it sounded, Raina had unconsciously thought Matthew would have as much time as she did to follow-up on leads. This only confirmed that he needed her help all right.

They entered the wallpapered lobby of the senior center with its fussy antique furniture drowning in doilies. Po Po signed them in and strolled through the lobby, past the game room, and continued to the elevators that would take them to the living quarters. Po Po chattered the entire time about the dance scheduled for the following Thursday, but Raina wasn't listening.

Po Po knocked on a door, and Mrs. Louie opened it with a beaming smile. She held out her arms for a welcoming hug. Vanilla and lemon drops enveloped her as the warm arms encircled her. For a second, the tension of the day melted from Raina's body as she returned the soft and doughy hug. No wonder Matthew adored his doting grandma. Who wouldn't want to spend time with the human embodiment of milk and cookies?

"I'm glad it's out in the open that I'm in town. I hate having to scurry off every time I see you coming," Mrs. Louie said. "Come inside."

The condo held some of the smaller pieces of rosewood furniture from the Louies' home in San Francisco. The bigger pieces were replaced by more compact items from IKEA. The beige coloring, from the fast food version of the furniture world, did little to hide the reduced circumstances for the elderly woman. Raina tried to hide her frown. She hadn't spared much thought for the woman who had been a second grandma to her.

She ran a finger over the framed photo of Matthew in his dress uniform on the side table next to the sofa. Her heart lurched at the familiar smile. She should have been at his side, snapping photos and hugging his arm.

"That's Matthew at his graduation," Mrs. Louie said.

"I wish I could have been there," Raina whispered.

"He didn't want you to follow where his job took him. Besides, the two of you would have been too young for that kind of commitment."

"We both married in our teens," Po Po said.

"That was a different generation," Mrs. Louie said. "Matthew didn't need the distraction while he was off doing dangerous work."

"It doesn't matter." Raina flushed at the catch in her voice. "I'm sure Ah Gong didn't care one way or the other as long as I didn't leave with Matthew after he gave him the money."

"Are you talking about the trust fund Mr. Louie left for Matthew in his estate?" Po Po asked. "Ah Gong was the executor."

Raina froze. A cold hand squeezed her gut. She glanced at her grandma and Mrs. Louie.

Mrs. Louie blushed and averted her gaze. "I didn't want him to take out the money, but I couldn't afford to live in San Francisco. Not after the dot com crash."

"And so he took out his college fund to pay for this condo," Raina said through numb lips. Her granddad hadn't given Matthew money so he'd stay away from her. He'd chosen to stay away. It had always been his choice.

"It's not what you think, honey," Po Po said.

"You don't understand," Raina said.

"Matthew's choice wasn't about you. He couldn't very

well let his grandma sleep in a cardboard box on the street. He was nineteen and needed money for college, so he joined the Marines." Po Po straightened. "And he'll always have my respect for not dragging you into a life you weren't ready for."

Raina blinked rapidly, willing the tears away.

"I'm so sorry," Mrs. Louie said. Tears ran down her face. "It was my fault. I should have looked over the papers I'd signed from the brokerage house, but my husband handled everything when he was alive."

A hot flash of shame sliced through Raina's pity party. Not only had she been a tad melodramatic, but she'd also made a sweet elderly woman cry. She patted Mrs. Louie's hand. "What's done is done. And we all survived to live another day. Now where are those red bean buns?"

Po Po nodded in approval behind Mrs. Louie's back.

Raina soon found herself with a plate full of red bean buns and a mug of white tea. "I should go." She bit into her third bun a while later. "These mini buns are addicting."

She didn't realize until this moment how much she missed being surrounded by her extended family. Until she figured out what she wanted to do about her grandfather's secret family, she couldn't go home. She'd been burying her head in the sand, hoping it would disappear on its own. It wouldn't be fair to ask the family to pick sides on the lawsuit challenging the large inheritance her grandfather had left her.

"Don't worry. Matthew is at home catching up on his paperwork. No time for his grandma today," Mrs. Louie said. "It must be that nice girl he's been seeing. It's about time he started thinking about settling down."

Raina choked on the bun and gulped lukewarm tea with an unladylike slurp. Was Matthew dating someone? Her hands balled into fists. That lying no good rat! Giving her smoke signals about his availability when he already was taken. She wanted to smack him.

Mrs. Louie turned to her grandma, giving Raina a chance to recover. Po Po watched Raina with a small smile on her lips.

Raina set her plate on the coffee table. Was that a test? She snorted in disgust. She didn't have time for mind games with seniors who had all the time in the world. "It's time for me to go. I have something planned for this evening." Her plan involved her BFFs Ben and Jerry and some angry journaling.

Mrs. Louie's face fell. "Oh, you're not staying to help us plan Bonnie's move?"

Raina's eyes widened in surprise. Her grandma was moving?

Po Po squirmed in her chair. "Nothing is set in stone yet."

Several thoughts ran through Raina's head. So this visit from Po Po wasn't temporary. Did this mean she would have to find a bigger place for the two of them? Her mom was going to flip. What was going to happen to the Victorian in San Francisco?

Po Po flapped her hands. "You should get on with your evening. I'm staying with Maggie tonight, so you don't have to come back for me."

Before Raina could utter another word, she found herself standing in the hallway with a door shut in her face. Clearly, Po Po didn't want Raina involved with her moving plans. She should have banged on the door and demanded to know what was going on, but she didn't. Her grandma could be as stubborn as a toddler fixated on ice cream.

12

A DONUT WITH MY NAME

Raina jerked awake to a loud pounding on her front door Saturday morning. She cracked open a crusty eyelid. Her alarm clock showed 9:30 A.M. Swinging her legs off the bed, she sat with closed eyes for another half second. The pounding came again. Reluctantly, she rubbed the sleep from her eyes and stumbled to the door.

Peeking through the crack of the closed drapes, Raina grimaced at Matthew's pinched face. With one hand braced against the doorframe, he tapped his foot and ground his teeth. She backed away from the window, wishing that she could roll back into bed. With a sigh, she opened the door. It was time to face the music.

"Rain—"

She held up her hands. "I need coffee first."

Raina headed for the kitchen to start the coffee maker without a backward glance, leaving Matthew to close the front door. While the water boiled, she fluffed her sleep-matted hair and tugged the neckline of her tank top lower. It wouldn't hurt to show some more skin.

As the rich aroma of the hazelnut coffee filled the air, Raina leaned against the white-tile countertop in the kitchen and watched Matthew pacing in the living room. Step, step, step, turn, glare.

"Do you want a cup?" she called out.

"No. Rain—"

"Not yet." She held up a finger. "Give me a minute to wake up." She sipped the coffee, wishing she could stretch this moment out.

"Ready?" Matthew asked. "Or do you need a donut to go with the coffee?" He stalked into the kitchen and stood in front of her with crossed arms.

Raina tensed. The kitchen suddenly felt like a shoe-box. Matthew was here about Holden. Did he find out about the pregnancy lie? She lifted her chin in an attempt to look relaxed. "Yes. I would love a donut. Is there a spare one down at the station with my name on it?"

The scowl on Matthew's face warred with the smile creeping in from the corners of his mouth. "How come you didn't tell me that you and Holden were dating?"

Raina shrugged, hoping she looked unconcerned. Her traitorous stomach heaved. "We broke up a month ago. You didn't ask. And I didn't think it was pertinent to the case."

Matthew ran a hand through his hair, causing the ends on the side to stand at attention. "This makes you a suspect! There's a big difference between a person-of-interest and a suspect."

She clutched the coffee mug in front of her body. Her

heart raced. What he said didn't come as a surprise, but she was suddenly filled with fear. "But... I didn't do anything. People break up all the time."

"Did you know Holden was engaged to Olivia while you dated him?"

Raina's eyes widened. Engaged? So Olivia wasn't another victim. Did Holden and Olivia have a good laugh over how quickly Raina had whipped out her checkbook? A lump formed in her throat. She was such a fool.

"I guess I know now," she said, her voice cracking. She cleared her throat. "What else did you find out about the case?"

"Stop trying to change the subject. You had no idea you were the other woman?"

"Of course I want to change the subject." Raina gestured with her hands; coffee flew out of the mug and splashed onto the floor. "How would you like it if I grilled you about one of your ex-girlfriends?"

Matthew jumped back and banged against the refrigerator door. "Watch the coffee! I'm not grilling you about who you've dated. I'm doing my job."

"That's a convenient excuse, isn't it? You could have sent an officer. There's no need for you to come all this way." Raina knew she was blabbing but couldn't seem to stop the half-baked words from escaping.

"Fine. Joanna could come by and finish up," said Matthew through clenched teeth.

Joanna? Was that how he thought of Officer Hopper? A dull ache settled on her chest. How dare he throw another woman's name in her face like they weren't... No. She slammed the lid on that line of thought. She wasn't going down that road again. Breathe. Just breathe. There was time for tears later.

"What do you want to know?" she finally asked, tipping her chin up.

His eyes sparked with anger. "Did you know you were the other woman?"

Her voice was dulled when she answered. How could he ask such a question? Given what he knew about her family history. "I would never do that. And you know better than to ask me a question like that."

"You had no clue there was someone else?"

"None. We only saw each other once or twice a week."

"Did you kill Holden in a jealous rage?"

"No."

Matthew leaned back against the refrigerator. His voice softened. "Rainy, if you're hiding things from me, I can't help you."

"Why would I need your help?" Raina tightened her grip on the mug and held her breath. How could she explain the pregnancy lie without sounding like an enraged ex-girlfriend now? "I have nothing to hide, but I'm not going to bare my soul. Not unless you care to tell me about all your ex-girlfriends in a sleepover party."

"Right, is this the part where we do each other's nails?"

Raina closed the distance between them and rested her forehead on his chest, cradling her mug between them. She breathed in his familiar scent. "I have nothing to do with Holden's death. The relationship was a mistake that I regretted shortly after it started. I'm sorry. I know I'm not making life easy for you."

Matthew stiffened. A heartbeat later he relaxed and drew his arms around her. The ice machine hummed and clicked. His familiar heartbeat thudded in her ears. She could fall in love with him all over again for his steady and comforting heartbeat.

There was a quick tap on the front door. "Hello?" called out an unwelcome, but familiar voice. Clipped footsteps came into the apartment. Raina wished she had locked the door.

Matthew pushed Raina off him. "I'll be in touch."

Raina followed him into her living room and found Officer Hopper sneering at the small piles around her apartment. The beam of sunlight coming in through the opened door highlighted a pile of orphaned socks she hadn't gotten around to matching up. Why couldn't the light be strong enough to incinerate the darn socks?

Officer Hopper smiled brightly at Matthew. "Do we need to bring her in for questioning?"

"I got everything I need for now." He marched out without a backward glance.

Officer Hopper smirked. "Don't even think about leaving town." She sashayed out, her French braid swooshing across her back like a satisfied cat.

Raina slammed her front door and clicked the lock home. Her legs buckled, and she slid to the floor in sudden exhaustion. Matthew's anger she could handle. The more agitated he got, the more explosive his temper. All it took was for Raina to soften, and she became a balm to the spike in his mood.

What she couldn't handle was the suspicion in his eyes when he asked if she was hiding anything. Her chest

tightened. Tears fell into her coffee mug. She hadn't realized until now just how much his good opinion of her
still mattered. If he even thought she lied about a pregnancy to force Holden's hand, it would finally be over
between them. That was the last thing she wanted.

BY THE TIME Po Po waltzed through the door with a
cheerful wave, Raina sat serenely on her sofa. Or at least
she hoped her dried face and clean clothes projected
some semblance of Zen she didn't feel. She grunted in
acknowledgment and returned to staring at her
notebook.

Po Po gave Raina a hug, crushing the corner of the
notebook to Raina's cheek. "What's wrong, honey?"

Raina rubbed her cheek. "A sweaty grandma almost
took my eye out."

"Did Matthew stop by?"

"How did you know?"

Po Po wiggled her fingers. "Magic."

Raina rolled her eyes, but the corners of her mouth
twitched. "I have to go to the mall. I need a new dress for
a wedding."

Po Po brightened. "Are you going with a date?"

"It's more of a reconnaissance mission." At her grandmother's raised eyebrows, Raina explained how she got
blackmailed into the date. "I need dirt on Sol Cardenas.
And a family wedding seems like a good place to find it."

"You're better off doing surveillance on him."

"I'm not up for watching Sol scratch himself for
hours."

"It'll be fun. Think of the bonding opportunity. Me, you, in a car." Po Po wiggled her eyebrows. "Granted, I'm not a hunky young man, but I can still show you a good time."

Raina chuckled and shook her head. "I love you, Grandma, but I'm afraid of your definition of a good time." Especially if it involved junk food and Po Po's digestion.

"Don't worry about Matthew. He'll come around." Po Po squeezed Raina's knee. "Ah Gong and I had our share of problems in the beginning, but we still had a good life together."

Raina smoothed the grimace on her face. Would her grandma have such a breezy attitude if she knew about her husband's secret family? Not that she would ever say anything to burst her beloved grandma's bubble. Her chest tightened at all the secrets in her life. She closed her eyes to hide her thoughts. Ignorance was bliss when it came to her granddad's shameful legacy.

In some ways, she was thankful the family was contesting Ah Gong's will. If she had access to the inheritance, she would have to send the money to China. Though she'd promised her granddad she would take care of the secret family, she hadn't factored in how hard it would be to hide it from the rest of her family.

Raina tucked a curl back into her ponytail. "I can't take you with me, whatever I decide to do. Mom will kill me if anything happens to you. I'm actually surprised I haven't heard from her by now."

"She's going to kill me anyway," muttered Po Po. "Didn't you say we're going shopping? I need a spiffy new dress myself."

"You don't usually visit without calling first. Not that I don't want you here, but something feels off." Raina raised an eyebrow. "Why are you secretly planning to move here? Owe the mahjong ladies too much money?"

Po Po laughed, but it sounded hollow. "More like the mahjong ladies owe me money. I have the best fingers in Chinatown. I can massage those tiles like no one else." She held up a finger and blew at it like it was a smoking gun. "As for the business with the family, that's between me and the family. Let's just say... there's a difference in opinion."

Raina left the rest of her questions shriveling on the vine for now. If she kept prying, her grandma might take off to some unknown destination. At least in town, she could keep an eye on Po Po.

"I think you're supposed to touch yourself and make the sizzling sound." Raina demonstrated. "That's means you're sizzling hot. Now why do you need a new dress?"

"It's for the dance at the senior center. I need to look like hot stuff."

"You have a date?"

Po Po stiffened. "Is that so hard to believe?"

"No, I'm just surprised. I didn't know you were ready for a relationship."

"It's a date. One date a relationship doesn't make."

Raina snorted. "Okay, Yoda. Let's roll."

Fifteen minutes later, they were piled in the car and on the way to Sacramento. As Raina drove, she considered Po Po's suggestion for a stakeout. Maybe it wasn't such a bad idea. How hard could it be to follow Sol for a couple of days to learn his routine?

She would do almost anything to stop Sol from

squealing to Matthew. If she had to, she would be his pretend girlfriend for the next ten weddings. Since Sol had no qualms about blackmailing her, she needed to turn the tables. After all, mutual cooperation worked both ways.

13

PAJAMAS NINJAS

When another impatient driver cut in front of Raina on the off-ramp for the Arden Fair Mall, she slammed on the brakes. Did shaving off two seconds from his travel time warrant the possibility of getting into a car accident? There was plenty of room for him to merge in safely behind her.

She sneaked a glance at her grandma. Po Po stared out the window, tapping her fingers on the door to an internal beat. Her grandma's love life sizzled, but hers was colder than the mystery meat in the back of her freezer. Raina shook her head. Something must be off with her juju. Maybe she needed to pray to the kitchen god and sacrifice her faculty parking pass to get her mojo back.

A few minutes later, Po Po towed Raina into Macy's before she had a chance to adjust to the crowds and buzzing conversations. A hop and skip later, she found herself in a large dressing stall glaring at a pile of dresses and her grandma perched on a stool in the corner.

Raina gawked at her reflection. Her underwear peeked out from the high side slits of the red sequined dress. She exhaled and looked at the ceiling, praying for patience.

Po Po beamed and clapped her hands. "Oh, Rainy, you look fabulous. I love how the dress makes your girls pop out."

"If I sneeze, I'll have a wardrobe malfunction." Raina tugged at the skintight material. "I look like an escort." The extra padding on the bodice made her chest look two sizes larger.

"Then I suggest you hold your breath." Po Po sifted through the pile and held up a slinky gold dress. "I love how girls today don't have to be covered up all the time. We had to wear potato sacks when I was your age."

Raina pressed the heel of her palms to her forehead. A potato sack was looking more appealing by the minute. She groaned when her grandma stroked the ripple openings on the back of the gaudy gold dress, which would flaunt a tramp stamp if she had one. "I don't think these dresses are my style."

Po Po wiggled her eyebrows. "Nonsense. That red dress shows off your figure. If Matthew saw you like this, he would need a bib to catch his drool."

Raina slipped back into her clothes. "Thanks, Po Po, but I got this. See you at the food court later."

Outside the store, Raina squinted at the fluorescent tubes above her while revising her game plan. The chattering crowd shifted around her. Her sister had been a pro at picking dresses to flatter Raina's boyish frame, clearly a skill which she didn't get from their grandma. A personal shopper would have to fill in for her sister today. She weaved through the crowd to another anchor store.

Forty-five minutes later, Raina trudged toward the food court dragging two fancy paper bags. The new clingy lavender dress cost half her rent, but at least she didn't have to worry about her butt falling out while burping. The other bag held a gift-wrapped pair of silver-plated doves salt and pepper shakers. Luckily, with her grandma in town and footing the grocery bill in exchange for Raina's cooking, it would work out all right. If she could gather a rumor to stop Sol from blathering to Matthew about the pregnancy lie, this shopping trip would be worth it. It didn't matter that Raina hadn't said she was pregnant. The fact that she hadn't cleared up the confusion with Holden would be suspicious.

At least she didn't have to give a red envelope to the couple, as she would have done at a Chinese wedding. The cash in the red envelopes from four hundred guests had paid for Cassie's wedding reception. So the salt and pepper shakers could be considered a bargain.

In front of the pretzel stand, three elderly women clucked and pointed at a redheaded woman bouncing a screaming baby clawing at her chest. Poor Lori! Professor Rollinger's wife seemed frazzled by the audience.

Raina darted between two middle-aged women and picked up the stroller from the floor. She knelt and dumped the spilled items back into the shopping bags and purse. Baby T-shirts, chewed pencil, pink panties, cell phone, a pink bra, socks, and a snack cup with animal crackers.

"She's fine." Raina made shooing motions with her

hands at the gathered women. "Nothing to see. Just a crying baby."

As the crowd dispersed, the baby calmed and snuggled under her mom's neck. The strawberry blonde baby stared at Raina with wide eyes and stuck her index finger into a nostril.

Lori brushed her auburn bangs off her face. "Thank you."

"My niece freaks out in a crowd, too." Raina pushed the stroller over and held the shopping bags with the other hand. "Think she's ready to get back in yet?"

Lori nodded and buckled in her daughter. She placed the snack cup with animal crackers in her daughter's eager hands. "I need caffeine. Care to join me?"

"Sure. My grandma is still shopping." When Raina handed over the bags, she noticed the brands for the first time. "You must be a good bargain shopper. My aunts are like that, but I never mastered the art." She rattled her two bags. "I just spent my entire month's income on a dress." A slight exaggeration, but there was nothing like two women bonding over spending beyond their budget.

After giving the barista their order, they waited at the other end of the counter. The hiss of the espresso machine competed with the happy gurgle of the baby examining each cracker before jamming it into her mouth.

When they got their orders, Lori pushed the stroller to a nearby table. She pulled out a baby wipe and cleaned the child's hands. "Are you going to Sol's sister's wedding?" She settled into her chair, pushing the stroller back and forth with her foot.

Raina nodded and sipped her coffee. "Are you going?"

"No, just heard it through the rumor mill."

The baby's head dipped and her eyes closed. A thumb found its way to her mouth. Lori pulled out the canopy and placed a blanket over it, dimming the interior of the stroller. Her moss green eyes widened in exaggeration and placed both hands to her heart. "I love nap time."

Raina chuckled. "My sister says the same thing."

"Are you going to the wedding with a plus one?"

"I'm Sol's plus one." Raina hid her grimace behind her coffee cup. She'd rather be Matthew's plus one, but that wasn't going to happen any time soon. Would it be too nosy to ask about the Rollingers' relationship? They had all the trappings of a happy marriage.

Lori raised an eyebrow, but thankfully kept silent.

"What's the secret to a happy marriage?" Raina asked.

Lori stared at the stroller, her knuckles whitening around her coffee cup. "The life I'm living is very different from the one I envisioned for myself." She forced a chuckle and gestured at the extra fifteen pounds on her stomach. "And now I'm your typical soccer mom, complete with the requisite mini-van. Thank God none of my exes can see me now."

Raina frowned. What did it matter what her exes thought about her marriage?

"Daddy didn't like Andrew because he didn't come from the right family, didn't go to the right school, and didn't have the right job. If only Daddy liked Andrew..." Lori's voice trailed off.

"I know what you mean. Some fathers don't think any man is good enough for their daughter." Raina shrugged. "In my case, my grandpa filled that role."

Lori looked up sharply. "So what happened?"

Raina told her how she'd initially thought Ah Gong paid Matthew off, but it turned out he was entitled to the money and used it to buy his granny a condo.

"The sad thing is, I don't think either of us ever got over it." Surprisingly, it was easier to tell an acquaintance about her feelings for Matthew than her best friend. Eden would have judged.

"Are you sure it's not wishful thinking on your part?"

Raina shook her head. "I don't know. Every time we got together in the last decade, it was like a glimpse of what we could have been. Tantalizing and seductive. When he leaves, I feel like a fool for waiting and hoping. No wonder my other relationships never worked out. They just filled the time until Matthew appears again."

"You can't change what's in front of you. Believe me, I've tried." Lori's shoulders drooped and she stared at the other shoppers in the food court. "Daddy could make things bearable for us."

Raina flicked a glance at the shopping bags hanging off the stroller. How unbearable could things be if Lori could afford those items? "At least Andrew is getting a temporary raise for taking over Olivia's duties, right?"

"Yeah, right." Lori studied Raina's face. "Andrew said you've been asking a lot of questions about Holden's death. I know you dated him briefly—"

Raina held up her hands. "Wait a minute. How did you know?"

"Rumor mill. I don't remember." Concern filled Lori's eyes. "Just be careful. Whoever killed Holden might decide you're a threat."

Before Raina could reply, Po Po sauntered over and dropped her bags on the table with a thump. The baby whimpered at the noise, and Lori gathered her things and left with a hurried good-bye.

Raina lugged Po Po's loot to the car, listening with half an ear to her grandma's prattle about the shopping deals. If her relationship with Holden wasn't a secret, did it also mean everyone knew about her fake pregnancy? As the murder investigation dragged on, how could she stop the fingers pointing at her?

LATER THAT EVENING, Raina inspected her grandma's black silk pajamas in her bedroom. When she gave the thumbs up for a stakeout, she had assumed Po Po would be wearing something similar to her own black T-shirt and black shorts. She stared at the blackened orthopedic shoes beneath the pajamas and bit her lip to keep the laughter from escaping.

"The silver stitching on the back of your top is too reflective," Raina said.

Po Po twisted in front of the full-length mirror and eyed the dragon on her back. "Got a long sleeve black shirt?"

Raina dug in her closet and handed one to her grandma. Po Po swung the shirt over her shoulders and knotted the sleeves around her neck. Great. Now her grandma had a cape over her pajamas.

Po Po tilted her shoes to show them off. "I used your black permanent marker. Not bad, huh?" She beamed at her shoes like a kindergartener showing off her artwork.

"There are still white spots on the shoes."

Po Po wrinkled her nose. "Why are you always so

quick to zoom in on the details?" She shrugged. "The marker ran out of ink."

"Are you planning to wear those to the senior center tomorrow?"

Po Po chewed her bottom lip. "What size do you wear?"

"I don't wear custom orthopedic shoes. My shoes are going to hurt your feet."

"I'm not wearing these ugly things to see my friends." Po Po glared at her shoes. "I'm giving you fair warning. Tomorrow I'm raiding your closet."

Raina sighed. Apparently vanity didn't disappear with age. "How come you didn't buy black shoes at the mall?"

"I didn't know I needed ninja clothes. You should have told me earlier. I would have picked up a baton or nun chucks."

"You're right. It's my fault." Raina shook her head. "Let's roll."

She parked the Honda under a tree across the street from Sol's two-story apartment complex. She turned off the engine, cracked the windows, and leaned the seat back. Po Po pulled out a small pair of binoculars from her purse.

"Where did you get those?" Raina whispered.

Windows glowed along the street and many were opened to the cool evening breeze. Clinks of silverware on dishes and snatches of conversation drifted toward them. Raina wished they were at a restaurant ordering their meal, but her grandma had promised to take her to a nice dinner after an hour of surveillance work.

"These are my bird watching binoculars." Po Po looked through them. "Which one is his unit?"

Raina had dropped off some research material for Sol once when they were still friendly. "Top floor. The second door from the left."

"Drat! He closed his blinds. I can't see a thing. Not even a shadow." Po Po tossed the binoculars on the dash. She grabbed her purse and pulled out a bag and a can.

Raina squinted in the dim light. Doritos and Red Bull? She cleared her throat. "Po Po, you are not supposed to eat junk food."

Her grandma opened the bag and stuffed a handful of chips into her mouth. She crunched and swallowed. "Don't you start, young lady. Your mom nags me enough as it is."

"When did you start drinking Red Bull?"

"The volunteers at the senior center drink it all the time. They tell me it's like drinking ten cups of tea. Except I won't have to go to the bathroom as often." Po Po bounced on the seat. "I thought I could use the extra caffeine in case we get into a car chase."

"We're not getting into a car chase. He'll probably spend a quiet evening at home." Raina checked the time on her cell phone. "One hour and then I want the dinner you promised me." She yawned.

Po Po shook her head. "Young people these days have no stamina." She popped the top of the can and took a big gulp. "Look!" She pointed to Sol's apartment. "He is leaving."

Raina slumped deeper into her seat, hoping he didn't see her as he got into a green beat-up Ford Taurus. She pulled away from the curb to follow the grad student. She couldn't believe she was driving twenty-five miles an hour with a granny chugging Red Bull on a Friday night. Some social life. The only thing that could make this evening worse would be for Matthew to miraculously appear in the backseat. Her eyes flicked to the rearview mirror and saw the passing street reflected on it. And no Matthew. So her world wasn't completely crazy yet.

Po Po leaned out the passenger side window, her binoculars glued to her eyes. "I told you there would be a car chase."

"He's probably just picking up something from the drugstore."

A few minutes later, Raina parked half a block from Olivia's house. She watched as Sol jumped out of the Ford in the driveway and rapped on the front door. The single bulb on the porch gave enough light to silhouette his paunch. When the door opened, he slipped inside.

Po Po bounced out of the car and bolted for the house. A sense of unease filled Raina. This was supposed to be a simple surveillance mission where she would stuff her face with Moo Shu chicken an hour later.

"Stop!" Raina whispered. Things always got derailed whenever Po Po was involved. She fumbled with the seatbelt and half fell out of the car in her rush. She winced as she clicked the door shut.

A light turned on at the side of the house. The diffused light from behind a curtain spilled into the darkened yard. Two shadows appeared on the curtains and disappeared. Probably Olivia and Sol settling into the room. Po Po tiptoed across the fresh-cut grass like Sylvester going after Tweety and crouched below the window. Her grandma was a shadow, blending with the night, except for the white reflective strips on her shoes.

Raina ground her teeth and ran after her grandma.

She held her breath, expecting the curtain to open and the occupants to catch them skulking. The chirping crickets competed with her pounding heart as the muscles on her shoulders tensed. The house next door was dark.

As she crept toward the window on the side of the house, her gaze scanned the yard for cover. There! Next to the trash and recycle bins was a small shed set back from the house. She touched her grandma's shoulder and pointed at the shed. "Hiding place," she whispered.

Po Po nodded. Raina pressed her ear next to the opened window.

From inside the house, ice clicked against a glass.

"Want one?" Olivia's question came out in a slow slur. "I hate to drink alone, but that seems to be what I've been doing a lot lately."

"Sure," Sol said.

Raina couldn't believe she morphed from an amateur detective to a peeping Tom in less than half an hour.

The voices were low inside the house. If not for the mismatched duo, it might have been considered intimate. Good thing the street was quiet. Glass clinked against glass. Someone sighed.

Raina rubbed her nose. Her allergy medication was no match for the fresh cut grass. She pulled a tissue from the pocket of her shorts and blotted her nose. Would they please get on with it?

Po Po rose to her feet and peered in the crack between the window and curtain.

"I need your help," Sol said.

Olivia laughed. A low cackle that sounded more witch-like than it should. "Why should I help you?"

The fine hair on the back of Raina's neck stiffened. She blotted her nose again and peeked into the house.

Sol leaned one hip against the kitchen island, one hand swirling the dark amber liquid in a glass tumbler. If he had been more suave, the move would appear less calculated. As it was, the liquid sloshed high up against the glass. Olivia sat opposite on a bar stool, her back to the window. The pendant lights above the kitchen island left the rest of the room in shadows.

Sol smirked. "Because by helping me, you'll help yourself."

Olivia grunted, tossed back her drink, and slammed the glass on the granite counter top. "What the hell is that supposed to mean?"

"Natalie owes me."

Olivia jerked, knocking her glass off the counter. The glass smashed against the tiled floor and shattered. Sol leapt back, surprisingly quick for a man his size.

Raina's nose twitched again, and she sneezed. The tissue shot from her hands and landed somewhere in the darkened yard. She held her breath as her mouth went dry.

"Damn raccoon! I swear this is the last time he comes into my yard," Olivia said.

"Sounds more like a person," Sol said.

A cabinet banged open and several items clattered to the floor.

"What the—" Sol's voice came out in a squeak. "Put that gun away!"

Raina grabbed Po Po's arm and pushed her toward the shed. Her heart slammed against her chest, but she kept a step behind her grandma even though she wanted to sprint ahead. The once soothing cricket chirps became a countdown to D-day. The weak moonlight became a spotlight.

Po Po tripped over a tree root and fell with a thud. Raina couldn't stop in time and crashed on top of her grandma. Her butt landed on something squishy and a flash of pain went up her spine. She gritted her teeth and stood.

The light flicked on by the back door.

Raina lifted her tiny grandma and threw her like a sack of rice over her shoulders. There were only three feet between them and the welcoming shadows behind the shed. She sprinted.

The screen door banged open.

Raina slid Po Po off her shoulders. Her grandma whimpered, but tucked herself further into the space.

Muttered curses came closer.

Raina gulped air as her heart galloped.

Po Po clutched Raina's arm with clammy hands.

The trash bin lid rattled inches from their hiding spot. A whiff of rotten trash made Raina want to gag, and she pressed her lips together in a tight line.

"Damn raccoon!" Olivia said.

Raina held her breath and squeezed her eyes shut.

Fading footsteps. A door slammed. A car roared off the driveway.

Silence.

It took several heartbeats before Raina peeked around the shed. "She's gone," she whispered, dizzy from relief.

Another half an hour passed before Raina deemed it safe to leave their hiding place. She helped her limping grandma to the car, half expecting Olivia to pop out of her house waving her gun.

Raina drove across town to the twenty-four-hour urgent care center. Po Po grunted from time to time, but didn't otherwise complain. By the time the doctor had given her some pain medication and strapped a boot on her ankle, she was back to her chipper self.

"How did you get hurt?" the medical assistant asked.

"Spy work. We were listening in on a shady deal, and we had to make a run for it." Po Po gave her a loopy smile. "Yep, we were almost in a shoot-out."

The medical assistant glanced at Raina.

So Raina did the only thing she could think of at the moment. She pointed to her head and circled her finger. "Crazy," she mouthed.

She didn't want to mock her grandma, but neither did she want to broadcast their business. It was supposed to be an hour of listening to jazz music in her car while Po Po spied on Sol with her binoculars.

Raina ran a shaking hand through her hair. There was nothing to fear. She glanced at Po Po, who continued to chat as if she had all the time in the world. Deep breaths. She needed to send her grandma packing. Things were getting out of hand.

14

SOL'S PLUS ONE

When the alarm went off the next morning, Raina wanted to throw it against the wall. Po Po's soft snore on the other side of the bed was soothing. Since her grandma usually left for her exercise class long before the alarm went off, last night must have worn her out.

Raina started the coffee maker and jumped into the shower. She tucked her curly hair into a neat chignon at the back of her neck and smoothed her hands over the clingy lavender dress. Too bad Matthew wouldn't get to see her like this.

By the time she was on the road to the wedding reception at the Indian casino's banquet hall, she'd had enough caffeine to feel human again. The forty-minute drive wound through farmland and open fields on the back roads of Yolo County. The homemade signs on the side of the road for this season's crop of peaches and nectarines clamored for her attention. If only she had time to stop.

Raina daydreamed about unveiling Holden's murderer and Matthew begging for another chance. Her skills at detection fell on the amateur side, but daydreams didn't have to make sense.

The jazz music faded, and the disc jockey made jokes about deadly burritos. As the host made disparaging remarks about pimple-faced teenagers running the Eatery without proper food handling knowledge, Raina's amusement over her daydreams disappeared. So the police hadn't announced foul play yet.

When she pulled into the crowded parking lot of the casino resort, her mood plummeted even further. She stared at the huge stone-faced building. The warm stone, the tinted glass, and dark wood trim blended in with the surrounding landscape. The manicured parking lot with blooming plantings between the rows of cars wasn't cheap to maintain. The place reminded her of a massive squatting spider in the middle of rolling green fields.

Raina trudged toward the massive entry as if she had concrete blocks tied to her feet. She clutched the wrapped gift and the silver-colored shawl in front of her like a talisman against the pulsating energy of the cheering crowd and the clanging slot machines.

Gambling was widespread in Chinese culture, where every occasion was an excuse to open the card table. Raina had grown up watching families destroyed by this acceptable recreation. She hadn't seen one of her aunts and her family for over two decades since they ran away from the loan sharks.

Raina straightened her shoulders and relaxed her grip on the gift. One fingernail had pierced the paper. She would spend her entire day inside this building. First, the wedding reception and then dinner with Eden. She was looking forward to touching base with her friend. A million questions were whirling around in her head.

Even after last night, Raina was sure Sol wasn't the murderer. Not that she would want to be alone with him. She regretted her decision to wear three-inch heels since running in these shoes was out of the question. At least she could do some damage if she aimed them at the right body parts, but that would mean the other person would be within kissing distance. Not exactly the comforting thought she needed at the moment.

Raina squeezed through openings in the crowd, following the signs to the banquet room and squinting at the smoky interior of the casino floor. A couple of men at the Blackjack table smiled in appreciation when she walked past them. One man took a step in her direction but stopped when his friend called him back. She hurried past, wishing she had packed a change of clothes for the evening.

The welcome line for the reception was a mile long. Wonderful. As she waited in the back of the line, she could take off her heels.

"Raina!" Sol called from behind her.

She turned, and her mouth fell open.

Sol strolled toward her, tugging at the collar of his white shirt. His clean black hair fell to his shoulders and reminded her of a hero in a romance novel cover. The structured black fabric and the silhouette of his black tuxedo hid his paunchy stomach and emphasized his height. When he stood next to her, she stared at his face in confusion. His vivid hazel eyes bore little of what transpired last night at Olivia's house, unlike her supersized eye bags.

"Your eyes are different. Did you put on colored contacts?" Raina asked.

Sol laughed. "I'm wearing contacts, but not colored ones." He held out an arm. "Ready?"

Raina's stomach fluttered, and she didn't know whether it was from fear of the man or anxiety for her assigned role as his girlfriend. Eden would have loved to see this transformation. It certainly was more dramatic than the losers her friend picked up at the bar. She never understood her friend's obsession with saving wounded men.

As he led her over to the newly married couple, Raina had to trot to keep up with his long legs. He waved to several people in the receiving line with a goofy grin on his face like he just got lucky but didn't stop even when people signaled for him to come over.

"Sonia!" He gave his sister a hug that lifted her off the ground. "Miguel." He shook his brother-in-law's hand and slapped his back. He beamed and brandished his hand in her direction. "And this is my Raina."

Sonia gave a loud squeal, bounced on her toes, and hugged Raina. "It was too bad you had to miss the ceremony at the church this morning."

Raina pasted on a wide smile and returned her hug, confused at the warm welcome. "Congratulations, Sonia." She gave Miguel a finger wave from over Sonia's shoulders and stepped back. "Congratulations, Miguel."

"Thank you so much for the reception." Sonia glanced from Sol to Raina, tears welling up in her eyes. She blinked rapidly, fluttering her gloved hands next to her face. Miguel handed her a tissue, and she wiped at the corner of an eye. She grabbed Sol's hand and one of Raina's, beaming at both of them.

Raina sneaked a glance at Sol. He had on a jack-o-lantern smile, and his puffed chest looked as if he were wearing one of those padded superhero Halloween costumes little boys liked to wear. As a teaching assistant, how did he have the money to pay for this reception? Of course, his verbal invite at the grocery store wasn't exactly brimming with details on what to expect.

"Honey, we have other guests," Miguel said, gesturing at the long receiving line.

Sonia nodded and let go of their hands. "Go inside and have a drink. I hope we get a chance to chat later, Raina. Sol told me so much about you."

Sol blushed and hustled Raina into the banquet room, guiding her to the table closest to the wedding table and pulling out a chair. "What do you want to drink?"

"Isn't Sonia a little too excited about meeting me? I mean, she knows this is our 'first date,' right?" Raina asked.

Sol grimaced. "I might have exaggerated our relationship."

Before Raina could ask him to clarify, Sol scurried to the bar. He moved fast for such a big man. She glanced at the dozens of formally dressed servers, fragrant flowers, festive balloons, and live band. She had expected an informal buffet lunch, where she would be able to mingle with others at the food tables and gather dirt on her blackmailer.

Sol returned and handed her a glass of chardonnay,

taking the chair next to hers. "Figured you're one of those white wine types. I told Sonia we've been dating for a while." He twirled his beer bottle in his meaty hands. "That wasn't one of my best decisions."

Raina snorted. "Thanks for the wine." Time to get cracking. The status of their fake relationship wasn't why she was here. "The detective questioned me yesterday about my relationship with Holden."

His eyes widened, and he held both hands up in the air. "It had nothing to do with me. I didn't tell anyone. I just needed a date for today." He lowered his voice and hands. "I'm sick of being the loser without a girl."

Raina raised an eyebrow. "And you think black-mailing me would solve your problem?" If he didn't squeal, then who did? Or he could be lying.

He shrugged. "I thought it might be worth a shot in case you didn't want the attention of the police."

Raina sipped from her glass. Uh-huh. Did he think she was born yesterday? Time to turn up the heat. "Did you ever get that recommendation letter?"

Sol averted his gaze. "Yes. Olivia wrote one for me."

Raina studied him. Right. "Olivia and I talked and came to an understanding." The lie slipped out of her mouth with ease. Wow, practice did make everything better. At the rate she was going, she could pass a lie detector with flying colors.

He tapped his fingers on the neck of the bottle. "Really?"

"And she told me about Natalie, but I don't know how to help."

Sol took a long swallow and belched. "There's not

much anyone can do at this point. Natalie had emails documenting the affair."

Raina straightened. Bingo! If Olivia and Holden were engaged, why would Natalie do this to her future sister-in-law? "Olivia didn't tell me about that part. The proof, I mean. Can you help her?"

Sol stiffened and his fingers tightened around the neck of the bottle. "What makes you think I can or want to help?"

Raina shrugged in pretend nonchalance. She was fishing in the dark, but sometimes it was worth the risk. "You were Holden's assistant for the last few years. I thought you might know his sister well enough to ask."

He studied her for a long moment. "I was at Olivia's last night, and I heard someone sneeze outside her kitchen window."

A bead of sweat rolled down the small of her back, but Raina forced herself to return his stare. There was no way to prove she was outside Olivia's house.

"You have a cute nose," he said. "It'll be a shame if something happens to it. Be careful."

Raina lifted her chin. "Is that a threat?"

Sol laughed. "Heck no. You're like one of those pygmy goats that'll chew my ass off for looking at you cross-eyed." He shook his head. "There's someone I care about who cares about you. I just don't want her unhappy."

Raina couldn't follow the hamster wheels in this man's head. Who was this mysterious person? "How come I'm in her place here?"

"Timing. It was off."

"What—"

"Sol!" called out a gravelly voice from across the room.

A full figured, elderly woman flapped one hand and dragged her husband to the table. She pounced on the empty chair next to Raina and stared at her with interest. "Aren't you a pretty little thing? Sol, you didn't tell me you have a girlfriend."

Sol cleared his throat. "Aunt Bee—"

"Henry, look at Sol's girlfriend. Isn't she a pretty little thing? Why, I remember when I was a young slip of a gel." Aunt Bee patted her silver frosted beehive hair. "Henry here couldn't keep his hands off me." She reached over and patted her husband's hand.

Raina glanced at Sol. He shrugged and nursed his beer. Looked like their cozy little chat was over for now.

Aunt Bee swung her head from side to side, waving at people sitting at other tables, and launched into the tale of how Henry battled her other suitors to win her heart. Henry slouched in his chair and closed his eyes. By the time Aunt Bee got to the duel in the soccer field, his soft snores became a dull chainsaw ripping through hardwood, so she spoke even louder.

Raina rubbed her temples. It was going to be a long lunch. Sol already had the glassy-eyed look men wore outside the dressing room while waiting for their girlfriends.

One of the bridesmaids had to rearrange the seating chart to accommodate Aunt Bee's refusal to leave their table. Aunt Bee's chatter dominated the entire luncheon. She pecked at her food, unlike the others eating as if this was their last meal. Another couple finally joined them, after standing at the doorway scanning the crowd. The wife gave Aunt Bee a limp hug but sat so she didn't have to make eye contact without turning her head. Raina hid her smile behind a napkin. Theirs was the only table with empty seats.

An hour later, Raina excused herself and went to the restroom. A quick glance at the mirror showed dull eyes. She applied a fresh layer of pink lip balm, pressing her lips together to distribute the color. If she pretended to have a massive diarrhea attack, could she hide here for the rest of the reception? Better to embarrass herself than to have to jab a dessert fork in her eye to stop the stream of Aunt Bee's "young slip of a gel" stories.

Sometimes it felt like her ancestors were slacking on their job. Shouldn't they send her a spiritual guide from the great beyond like the ancestors did in Disney's *Mulan* cartoon?

A toilet flushed, and Sonia emerged from the handicap stall. She washed her hands and fluffed already puffy hair. She made eye contact with Raina's reflection in the mirror. "I'm so glad you made it today. Sol said you've been too busy to come to the pre-wedding parties."

"The reception is wonderful. Sol must have saved a long time to pay for it."

Sonia gave her a puzzled look. "I thought you loaned him the money. He said he got the money from a co-worker. I thought he just wanted to downplay his relationship with you."

Raina shook her head. "Not me."

Sonia licked her lip and fluffed her hair again. "Oh."

"What's wrong?"

"Sol said that he didn't have to repay the loan. I thought maybe you guys got engaged, and he didn't have to pay you back." She blinked rapidly and averted her gaze. "I guess you guys aren't engaged after all."

Raina forced herself to smile. She wanted to kick in Sol's teeth for putting her in this awkward position. "Sol and I are enjoying each other's company for now. You know how it is when you're still at the honeymoon stage in a relationship."

Sonia brightened. "That's true. You never know with these things. And my brother is a great catch. It sounds like they are starting the karaoke." She gave Raina a mischievous wink. "Wait until you hear Aunt Bee on the mic."

15

SWIMMING WITH SHARKS

After wishing the couple a happy life together, Raina hightailed out of the reception just as Aunt Bee finished her second solo. She had another three hours to kill before meeting Eden for dinner. The casino lounge was as good a place as any for serious thinking. She pulled her wrap closer and stepped inside the dim and smoky room.

Standing in front of a booth in the far corner, two aging men with bellies that hid their rhinestone belts tried to impress four young women by flashing a lot of bling. One man slouched with bejeweled thumbs hooked in the belt loops on his jeans while the other hovered with an arm on the backrest. From the eye rolls and bored expressions on the women's faces, the men needed to work on their pickup lines. Women could tell real diamonds from cubic zirconias.

Raina slipped onto a stool at the bar opposite another three men huddled with their backs to the entrance, angling her body so she could see everyone in the room.

Three hours to people watch was an improvement over listening to Aunt Bee yowling and Henry doing the Electric Slide in the background.

A skinny man with adult acne and rimless glasses came over and asked for her drink order in a deep baritone.

"Do you have any coffee?" Raina rubbed her temples. "And Motrin?"

The bartender didn't even blink. He slipped a single dose packet of extra strength Motrin across the polished bar and pulled a mug from underneath, holding it out to a passing waitress. She came back and gave him the steaming mug, which he placed in front of Raina along with a small tray filled with an assortment of creamers and sweeteners.

The bartender glided over to the three huddled men. When the dark-haired man turned to look at the bartender, Raina's heart skipped a beat. What was Matthew doing here? Checking up on her? Or Sol?

Matthew briefly scanned the room. His gaze slid past her and jerked back. His eyes widened in surprise. He nodded with an appreciative smile at the corners of his lips.

Raina finger-waved and purposely turned her back on him to stare at the couples swaying to the smooth jazz music and the faint clang of "winning" slot machines. She hid her grin behind the coffee mug, but it didn't stop the butterflies fluttering in her stomach. She had gotten her wish after all. It appeared Matthew liked the dress as much as she did. Her wrap slid off one shoulder, and she ignored it. Tucking a curly strand back into her chignon, she peered behind her bare shoulder. Where did Matthew go?

The three men had disappeared. A blonde sat two stools over, leaning over the bar and whispering to the smiling bartender.

Raina scanned the lounge, but she didn't see Matthew. Her shoulders drooped. Why did he always seem to be in a chatty mood when she was sweaty and her hair frizzed into a rat's nest, but never when she actually looked pretty?

The murmurs next to her grew louder. Raina turned to study the bartender and the back of the blonde. He poured shots into the glasses. When he placed them on a tray, he knocked over a drink.

"Come crash at my place. You'll be safe there," the bartender said.

The blonde shook her head. "I can't let you get involved."

Raina rolled her eyes. The blonde meant "of course I want you involved, but you'll have to convince me to let you help." The bartender probably had no idea he was being played. Men usually didn't when they had that puppy dog look on their faces.

The bartender slid a drink in front of the blonde. "I'm already involved whether you like it or not."

The blonde dropped her head and whispered, "Thank you."

The bartender patted her hand and shuffled over to get orders from the waitress. The blonde turned to watch him.

When Raina saw the familiar face, she gasped. Natalie

Merritt! The blonde was several years older than the photograph on Holden's desk, but there was no mistaking the striking resemblance between the siblings now that she knew they were related. Wasn't Matthew looking for Natalie?

Natalie's blood-shot blue eyes narrowed in recognition. She sauntered over to Raina, eyeing her up and down. She tossed back her drink and slammed the glass tumbler on the bar. "I know you. You're the slut who dumped my brother because he had to drive me to rehab."

Raina stared at her with wide eyes. "Excuse me?"

Natalie leaned forward. "You're that slut who cleaned out his checking account. You look just like your picture."

Raina's nose wrinkled at the stale breath and musky body odor. "Are you sure you have the right woman? Last I heard I wasn't his only girlfriend. And don't forget, he was engaged to another woman at the time."

Natalie picked up the tumbler and held it in the air. The bartender replaced her glass with another drink. He refilled the peanut bowls, one nut at a time, in front of them.

"I know your type. Dressed to get a man hot and bothered. Was it fun making my brother beg?" Natalie asked.

Raina flushed. She flicked a glance at the deep cleavage on Natalie's red halter top and skintight black leather pants with no panty lines. Oh, she so wanted to toss in a zinger, but antagonizing Natalie wouldn't help the situation. "I don't want to fight with you. Let me buy you a drink."

Natalie glowered at her, hands on her hips.

"Please." Raina held up open palms. "I'm trying to figure out what happened to Holden."

Natalie froze, but her face registered several emotions before settling on a grimace. She slid onto the barstool next to Raina. A new drink appeared on the bar, and the bartender now pretended to polish a spot next to Natalie.

"I have no idea what Holden told you about our relationship. He dumped me by sending a text message." Raina's voice cracked. "Didn't even explain why."

"A gold digger like you doesn't need an explanation. He probably got tired of giving you money."

Raina flushed. Was that the official story from Holden? "He owed me money, not the other way around. He was always broke. I thought he had massive student loans."

Natalie shook her head. "Yeah, right."

"I have the cashed checks. I figured that was why he dumped me. I'd stopped giving him money."

Natalie rolled her eyes. "Whatever."

Raina took a deep breath. "I'm a murder suspect because we had a relationship. Just like you're a murder suspect because you're related."

The blood drained from Natalie's face.

The bartender's eyes widened. "Now, wait a minute—"

"We're having a private conversation, Kendall." Natalie waved him off. "Go. I'll holler if I need anything."

Kendall glared at Raina and drifted to the opposite end of the bar.

Natalie tossed back another drink. "What the hell is that supposed to mean?"

Raina winced. By her count, Natalie should be sliding under the table by now. Instead, the red-eyed blonde pulsed with suppressed energy.

"Who has the most to gain from Holden's death?" Raina shrugged. "It's not me. I'm never going to see my money again. That kind of leaves you and his son."

Natalie spat on the floor, and the spittle dribbled unnoticed on her chin. "If that rugrat is even his son. The whore." She grabbed her silver sequined purse and tottered out of the lounge on her four-inch stilettos.

Raina exhaled, feeling relief and regret for not handling the situation better. Natalie hadn't even blinked when Raina had mentioned murder.

The bartender returned and glared at Raina. "She would've been safer in here where I could keep an eye on her. If anything happens to her, it's on you." He slapped her tab on the bar and stomped over to other customers.

Cheeks burning, Raina propped her face on her palms, ignoring the cloying cigarette smoke and the sudden tears in her eyes. Her mind tried to make sense of everything she'd learned about Holden since his death. What did he do with all the money? As an associate professor, he made a decent living. She massaged the side of her head. Her hands shook, and she couldn't tear open the Motrin.

"Let me help you." Large, warm hands enveloped hers.

Raina glanced up to meet gold-flecked brown eyes. Matthew tucked her wrap back on her shoulder. She twisted her body toward him and slipped her arms around his waist for a hug. He wrapped both arms around her and tucked his chin on top of her head. She relaxed at his clean scent, a breath of rolling countryside in a congested city.

Matthew pulled away. "Let's go someplace quieter."

He tore open the package and dropped two pills into her palm.

Raina popped the Motrin in her mouth and chased them with cold coffee. She put five dollars under her mug and slid off the stool. "You lead, I'll follow."

Matthew stared at her for half a heartbeat, a smile tugging at his mouth. "I remember the last time you said that." He winked. "You almost got me killed."

"I can be quite dangerous."

He laughed and held her hand while leading her out of the lounge. She sneaked glances at his profile, barely noticing the passing earth-toned hallways or the plush carpeting underneath. At a quiet alcove off the now empty banquet room, he sat on the wooden bench and tugged her onto his lap, draping his arms around her.

She rested her head on his shoulders, settling her legs more comfortably on the bench. "Why does it always have to be this way between us? This push and pull. Why can't we just be happy together?"

Matthew sighed. "I'm sorry about the other day. I thought... I don't know what I was thinking."

Raina lifted her head and looked into his eyes. "You're thinking that I would be here waiting all these years."

He blushed. "No. Of course not. That would be ridiculous."

She raised an eyebrow. "Uh-huh. There's rational thought, and then there's hope. At first, I thought we might pick up where we left off."

He was quiet for a moment. "Not as long as you're a murder suspect."

Raina smiled and stroked his cheek. "I know the timing is off." She grew serious. "I wouldn't kill Holden for another woman. I cared about him, but not enough for that kind of passion ..." Her voice trailed off. It had always been Matthew.

His grip tightened around her.

She lowered her gaze and stared at her hands. Had she said too much? Did she sound too clingy? She scratched at the scabs on her hands. At least the hives were disappearing.

"Stop scratching. You're only going to make it worse."

"I just can't seem to stop." She didn't mean the scratching.

"Me neither." He kissed her forehead and sighed. "What are you doing here?"

"I could ask you the same question. I came for a wedding."

"Ah yes, the sister. Any idea how Sol got the money to pay for it?"

"Are we talking shop now? I'm not sure I can do it in this position."

Matthew unceremoniously pushed her off his lap and onto the bench. "Better?"

Raina adjusted her dress, making sure he got a glance down her chest. She was a tart all right, but only with Matthew. She gave him a saucy wink. "Yes."

He smiled and shook his head. "You're going to be the death of me."

The fine hair on her neck stiffened. Her playful mood vanished in an instant. "I hope not."

He frowned. "You okay?"

"The air conditioning is always too cold." She pulled her wrap closer. "No idea, but the sister is under the impression he got it from a love interest."

Matthew raised an eyebrow. "You're not going to stay out of this, are you?"

"Of course not. I'm your secret weapon."

Matthew stared at her and nodded reluctantly as if he came to a decision. "Swear to me you won't say anything to your reporter friend. She can't be trusted."

"Eden?"

"How do you think I found out about your relationship with Holden?"

Raina froze and an icy knot settled in her stomach. The image of Eden and Officer Hopper chatting at the Venus Café whirled into focus. No! She shoved the memory away. Eden wouldn't betray her. She glanced at Matthew. But he wouldn't lie to her either. She jerked her chin in a stiff nod and crammed thoughts of Eden into a box marked for later. "You didn't answer my question. What are you doing here?"

"I heard that Natalie practically lives at the casino and I also wanted to check out the wedding."

"You just missed her at the lounge."

He frowned. "I'll have to send Joanna here tomorrow to track her down."

"Did the lab results come back yet?"

"The victim was poisoned by black hellebore. There is no injection site."

"What's black hellebore?"

"It's a garden plant. Looks like a dark purple buttercup. You can find it at most nurseries. The toxin is most concentrated at the roots."

"What happens now?"

"We have to look at who has a grudge against Holden and knows his habits."

"You mean like his pencil chewing habit." She frowned and tilted her head considering. "You don't think …"

"Your guess is as good as mine. He picked up lunch, but he didn't appear to eat any." Matthew pulled out his notebook and made a note. "I'll have someone test his pencils. What do you know about Holden's enemies?"

Raina shrugged. "There are a lot of people who didn't like him."

"You mean like his co-workers?"

"Exactly."

"What do you know about Holden's finances?"

"He was always broke. I thought it was student loans." Raina hesitated. She winced and the words came out in a rush. "I'd given him some money."

His eyes softened. "I just can't leave you alone for a minute."

"It was longer than a minute. Try years."

"Did he get any suspicious phone calls or lose his temper?"

"No …" What about those calls that Holden never picked up? "Maybe."

"What does that mean?"

She twisted the ends of her wrap around her fingers. "I don't know. The calls came in around dinner. I thought it was credit card companies. He never answered them. Just turned off his phone."

"What gave you that impression?"

"He'd mentioned he was bad with money. I figured he was one of those types who lived beyond his means." Raina shrugged. "But you couldn't tell because of his Spartan home."

"And you're attracted to that?"

She flushed, irritated at his tone. "Well, you can't tell by looking at someone on the outside."

Matthew raised an eyebrow. "What do you know about Natalie Merritt?"

"Why would she kill her brother?"

"She has a lot to gain from his death. Holden has a quarter-million-dollar life insurance policy. And then there are the retirement funds from his IRA and his pension."

Raina gave him a disgusted look. "The same could be said about me if my mother dies. That doesn't make me want to kill her."

"You don't have the kind of debts that Natalie does. Besides, you've told me you're going to kill your mom all the time."

"So what if she has debts. She can always declare bankruptcy."

"For her legit debts. You can't declare bankruptcy for gambling debts. She practically lives at the casinos."

Raina frowned as she recalled the two men with Holden at the bank parking lot before his death. She hadn't thought much about the incident at the time. "Loan sharks?"

"Maybe. But rumor has it that someone has been steadily paying them off."

"Holden?" she asked.

"Maybe. His finances didn't add up."

An image of Olivia's face flashed through Raina's mind. Just how many women did Holden "borrow" money from?

Matthew frowned. "The college wants the case

wrapped up before school starts. So I have a week and a half to pull a *CSI* episode. I'm getting the runaround whenever I ask the school for any help."

"You would think they'd jump at any chance to help."

"I think they want everything brushed under a rug. Murder isn't exactly the best way to open a new school year."

They sat in comfortable silence for several long minutes, just like old times. Raina resisted the urge to lean her head on his shoulder and slip an arm around his waist.

Matthew cleared his throat. "I thought it would fade by now."

"Me, too."

Raina stared into his dark eyes. He had destroyed her the last time. It had always been a matter of when, but like the serviceable granny panties in the back of the lingerie drawer, he always turned up when she looked for something sexy. She wanted more than brief moments of bliss followed by long periods of waiting.

If Matthew thought he could use this murder investigation as an excuse to delay their much-needed talk about their non-relationship, then he better start counting the minutes until she solved this case. She'd grown tired of waiting.

16

POLYESTER CLAD THIGHS

By the time Raina slid into the chair across from Eden, dinner service was in full swing. A third of the restaurant spilled out to a roped off section on the main casino floor. An hour ago, Matthew had disappeared after a phone call. Not that she had expected a resolution between them, but she did hope for something more than a quick peck on the cheek.

Raina squinted against the flashing neon sign above a group of slot machines behind Eden's head. Great. She'd be dining with the casino's version of a Christmas light display guaranteed to short circuit a few of her optic nerves.

After a bit of small talk, the server left with their orders. Raina had long since lost her enthusiasm for the dinner date. She still didn't understand why Eden would tell Officer Hopper about her relationship with Holden.

Eden's eyes glowed. "Didn't Sol look great?"

"Were you spying on Sol?" Raina gave her a sidelong glance. "Or were you spying on me?"

Eden tried to hide her blush by taking a sip of soda. "I just wanted to make sure you were okay."

"And then you did what?"

"What is this about?"

"So have you found any new information since Friday?"

Eden set the edge of her glass on her fork and soda spilled onto her half of the table. She jumped off her chair. "Fu—"

The server appeared with a pile of napkins as if he'd been buzzed on the intercom. Eden made a big production of wiping and dabbing long after the server moved to another table. When her friend settled down, an awkward silence lengthened the distance between them. The murmurs of conversation, the occasional shriek of excitement, the clang of slot machines, and the clink of silverware on plates. Everyone was having a good time, except at their table.

Raina crossed her arms and leaned back on her chair. "What were you doing with Officer Hopper at the Venus Café on Thursday? Share any secrets?"

The server slid their plates in front of them. Eden squirted ketchup, laid her napkin across her lap, and sliced the steak like this was her last meal.

Raina's chicken marsala could've been made of cardboard for all the attention she gave it. The muscles in her shoulders tightened with each passing minute, and the scraping of Eden's fork grated on her already strung nerves. "Why did you tell Officer Hopper about my relationship with Holden?"

Eden choked, spraying pieces of mashed potatoes across her steak. Raina pounded on her back. When

Eden whispered that she was fine, Raina gave her an extra thump. Just to be on the safe side.

Raina settled back into her chair and watched Eden gulp soda. She blinked rapidly as the block in her stomach spread to her chest. She ran through the multiplication tables in her mind. Her best friend had betrayed her.

"It's not what you think," Eden said after an eternity.

Raina swallowed, and her voice was flat when she said, "I can't believe you'd betray me for a story."

Eden's eyes widened "No! That's not why I did it."

Raina stared at her hands on her lap. She couldn't cry. Her ex-friend didn't deserve her tears. "No wonder you don't have any other friends."

Eden pushed a napkin into her lap. "I'd be lying if I told you it has nothing to do with the story. But mostly I did it for you. You need to get Matthew out of your system. He's toxic. I thought I could push the issue forward."

Raina dabbed at her eyes. What if Matthew was the love of her life? "Things are complicated between us. You're not going to understand." Especially since her friend's relationships only lasted until she realized the frog she wanted to turn into a prince had always been a frog.

"I just want you to be happy," Eden said.

"I will be. But don't interfere with my love life. Just like I don't interfere with yours."

"Yeah, but you sure turn up your nose fast enough when I introduce you to my boyfriends."

Raina rubbed her temples. Now all of a sudden she was a bad friend? "Let's agree to disagree okay? No more talk about boyfriends. Made any progress with the murder investigation?"

"Nada. You?"

It took all of Raina's willpower to stop her eyes from rolling. She didn't believe for a millisecond Eden hadn't dug up something in the past two days.

Raina shook her head. She forced a smile and made small talk for the next half hour as she pretended to finish her meal. The subject of men didn't come up again. And even if it did, she wasn't sure whether she could trust Eden with the new information she'd gotten from Matthew.

RAINA SPENT the night tossing and turning. By the time the sky was a pale pink, she dragged herself into the kitchen to start the coffee machine. Birds chirped and cars rumbled past as she sipped and stared out her kitchen window. Her life had clipped along at a mind-numbing pace for the past year. No drama. No family. And no Matthew. It'd been perfect.

The murder investigation had not only brought to the surface her unresolved relationship with Matthew, but it revealed cracks in her best friend she'd rather not scrutinize. She closed her eyes as if this would stop her tumbling thoughts.

Closure was overrated. She should bury her head in the sand. The police didn't have any evidence to arrest her even if the fake pregnancy came to light. She didn't need to know why Holden played her like he did. Nope, she didn't need to know why men disappeared from her life without explanations. She was a wimp for letting them use her and leave her. That was all there was to it.

She opened her eyes and sighed. Burying her head could mean losing Matthew for good, and it wasn't a risk she was willing to take.

Movement at Eden's apartment caught her eye. Her tousle-haired friend leaned against the opened doorway, hugging her skimpy blue robe over her body. The raised hemline exposed too much thigh.

Raina stiffened at the familiar back in front of her. When the man turned, the sunlight caught the slope of his nose and five o'clock shadow on his jaw. What was Matthew doing at Eden's place this early in the morning? Whatever it was, they were up to no good.

Eden spoke, and Matthew shook his head. She pleaded with her hands, and he reluctantly nodded. He stalked toward the sidewalk, unaware of the extra bystander watching his progress.

The kitchen became unbearably hot. Raina almost turned away when another movement caught her eye.

Sol appeared behind Eden, snaking an arm around her waist. Her friend leaned back, and he spoke intimately into her ear.

Raina stumbled into the living room and collapsed onto the sofa. She leaned her head between her knees and took several rattled breaths. Would Eden sleep with Sol for a story? Was it that unbelievable when she was willing to sell Raina's secrets? It shouldn't matter, but it stung all the same.

But big girls didn't cry; they got even. She'd find the murderer and feed the details to Eden's biggest competitor for the Assistant EIC position. Heck, she might even submit the article under her own byline.

BY THE TIME Po Po left for her exercise class, Raina had added several pages of scribble to her notebook. When she realized she'd forgotten to check Holden's house for clues, her first instinct was to tell Eden to grab her purse. She made it to Eden's front door before realizing that she and Eden were playing on different teams.

When Raina parked in front of Holden's unremarkable single-story brick house, the sun was a blazing torch above her head. The neighborhood was pleasant with overgrown trees canopying the entire street like a green tunnel. She looked up and down the street. It was lunchtime, but most people were still at work. She glanced at the house again. It'd been a week since his death, plenty of time for the police to finish their business with the place.

During the time they'd dated, she'd visited his house once on a drunken night when Holden had lost his key. He'd made a big production of his secret hiding spot. She cringed at how she'd clapped and cheered, but it had flattered him so much he'd shared his other favorite hiding spots with her.

Time to get cracking. Raina leapt out of her car, pulling on a floppy straw hat, sunglasses, and white gloves. The hat and gloves complimented her sundress and strappy sandals. A perfect church outfit, except it was a Monday.

The house looked abandoned like it had been waiting

for its owners to return from a long trip. The drapes were drawn tight. Small twigs and brown leaves were scattered among the legs of the wooden bench on the front patio. Several bundles of newspapers were tossed into the flowerbeds.

After a glance around, she sprinted to the side yard, lifted a small moss-covered rock, and pulled out the taped spare key. Her heart hammered against her chest, but quick steps took her through the front door and into the house. When the door clicked shut, she sighed in relief. Breaking and entering was more glamorous on TV.

Raina tucked her hat under an arm and pushed her sunglasses over her head. The air was stale. It had developed the musty odor of vacant homes in need of a good airing. The three-bedroom house was shabbily furnished, giving no clue as to where Holden had spent his ill-gotten money, which supported the rumor he might have been paying off his sister's gambling debts. Her new-to-me furniture from Cassie appeared luxurious by comparison.

From where she stood, she studied the sagging sofa with its unraveling seams, the scratched coffee table loaded with books and stacks of paper held together by large clips. She rifled through the clipped piles of paper, which consisted of manuscripts at various stages mixed with pages of handwritten notes. Too bad these manuscripts would end up in the trash when Natalie cleaned out the house.

Raina peeked into the kitchen. The appliances were old but clean. The simple folding table and chairs served as a dining room set. A lonely red mug sat next to the sink on the empty tiled counter top, waiting to be washed. She blinked rapidly at the tightness in her chest and tore her gaze from the mug.

Walking to the small bedroom Holden used as an office, she stood at the doorway, her glance flicking from object to object. The police had taken his laptop. Did they find his tablet or look through his safe?

Raina made her way to the laundry room and retrieved a battered cardboard box from behind his ware-house-size tub of detergent. Holden liked to hide his important things in the most unlikely places. He was under the assumption burglars would go straight to the bedrooms for valuables. She rifled through his box of rags and touched the rubber case of his tablet. Bingo! She grinned and stuffed it into her purse.

She replaced the box and opened the door to the attached two-car garage. After flipping on the light, she went inside. Holden hid a small fireproof safe on the wall behind several boxes of Christmas decorations. She stared at his car parked in the middle of the space. He must have taken his bike to work on the day he died. What happened to his bike?

A swish came from inside the house. She spun to face the connecting door. What was that? Her muscles tensed and her ears strained to hear the small shuffle again. Nothing. Dust whirled lazily in the patch of sunlight coming in from the garage door window. Maybe the noise she heard was from outside the house. Probably a squirrel on the roof.

She cocked her head to one side and held her breath. Should she go back into the house or leave through the side door in the garage? She couldn't hear a thing over her racing heart.

There! The rustle of polyester-clad thighs rubbing together. Someone was in the house.

Raina tiptoed around the car to the side door. The rushing noise in her ears competed with her uneven breaths. Her clammy hands gripped the doorknob. She twisted and pulled. The door scraped against the concrete floor, ripping through the silence. It opened an inch. Gooseflesh peppered her arms. Darn! So much for being quiet.

She glanced over her shoulder while pulling at the door again. It protested even louder. She braced one leg on the doorframe and pulled again, grunting at the effort. The door shuddered. Twelve inches. Bright morning sun fell into the garage from the gap. A squirrel stopped in its track and stared at her.

A gloved hand snaked out and clamped over her mouth, muffling her scream. Another meaty hand wrapped around her waist, jerking her from the door. Her feet left the ground.

Raina jabbed her elbows at her attacker's soft stomach. He grunted and tightened his grip. She jerked and bucked her body, hoping her attacker would loosen his hold. Her feet kicked out and knocked things off the shelves. Cans thumped to the floor. Hand tools clanked against each other. Her attacker held tight.

She was weakening and slick with sweat. Her muscles ached with tension and trembled with fatigue. Sagging against him, she rammed her head on his chin. Her eyes watered, but she did it again. This time she hit the side of his jaw. He grunted with pain and loosened his grip. He stumbled on something. For a split second, they hung in the air. And they crashed onto the hood of the car.

Raina twisted around and slammed her purse at his face. Something crunched. She kicked his groin and lurched for the side door. Squeezed through the gap. Ran on shaking legs to her car.

It took her three tries before she was able to open her car door. The entire time, she kept glancing behind her, expecting the big man to grab her. She slid into the driver's seat and clicked the locks shut.

The jangled keys grated on her strung nerves and slipped from her slick fingers. Her fingers patted around the floorboard and made contact with the keys. She jammed the key in the ignition and roared off the curb. Her tires squealed as she tore away from Holden's house.

Raina turned right and left, and left again, hoping her random turns would make it difficult for her attacker to follow her. After several minutes, she parked in front of a stranger's house and gripped the steering wheel with both hands. The adrenaline had worn off, and she trembled like the last leaf on a barren tree. Blood stained her left hand. With a grimace of distaste, she wiped it on her torn dress. She pulled out her cell phone and dialed a number she knew by heart.

"Matthew," Raina said in a clogged voice. She cleared her throat. "Sol Cardenas just attacked me."

17

EDEN IS NO PARADISE

After a brief conversation with Matthew, Raina turned off the engine but kept the keys in the ignition. She took inventory of her injuries. More purple bruises blossomed over the fading yellow ones Gail had left on her arms last week. Her right knee ached. The heel had broken off her sandal. The scrape on her knee had a smear of dirt in it, and the darkening bruise promised more pain to come. She must have fallen in her haste to the car and not even noticed it.

Raina smoothed her hands over her dress. The unraveling seam on her side bothered her. She pulled at it and opened a bigger gap. She stared at the exposed flesh and chuckled. What would Matthew's reaction be when he showed up to find her entire left side exposed, flashing her yellow bra and panties?

A shrill laugh rose from her throat. Her eyes widened at the sound of her panic, and she slapped both hands over her mouth. Her nostrils flared when she attempted to breathe deeply to calm down. Her entire body trembled, and everything started to spin. Her vision turned foggy and sound disappeared.

Raina gripped the steering wheel and squeezed her eyes shut. "It's okay. You're okay." She repeated the mantra until her heart rate slowed. Her body relaxed. Birds tweeted. A breeze rustled leaves. A car rumbled past. Taking one final deep breath, she cracked open an eyelid. Sunshine. A leaf spun in the air and landed on her windshield. She was okay.

She frowned at the dried blood on her hand and dress. The blood wasn't hers. How come Sol didn't throw her against the wall or hit her? He was big enough to do more damage than just give her bruises on her arms. Heck, she probably broke his nose and turned him into a eunuch.

Tap. Tap. Tap.

Raina jumped at the noise. Matthew stood next to her car, frowning at her. She couldn't see his eyes behind his dark sunglasses, but his stiff posture meant he wasn't happy. She opened the door and shuffled out.

Matthew exhaled sharply at his first sight of her full appearance. He turned and headed back to his car, slamming the door.

Raina blushed and attempted to pat her hair back into place. She couldn't hear what he said in the radio, but the scowl on his face spoke volumes. She shifted her weight to the opposite foot. A flash of pain ran down her right leg. Ouch! Her darn busted knee.

A hand steadied her. "The EMT is on the way," Matthew said.

"I'm fine. I just need ice and ibuprofen." Raina gave him a weak grin. "But you should see the other guy."

Matthew stared at her, and his lips thinned. His fingers tightened around her arm.

"Ouch!" Raina jerked her arm from him. She propped herself against the side of her car. "I have enough bruises already."

"Sorry." Matthew ran a hand through his black hair. "What were you doing at Holden's house?"

Raina licked her lip. "Ah..." This was it. Time to confess everything. "I was collecting his mail." She knew she wasn't behaving rationally, but she couldn't stop poking the bear. "What were you doing at Eden's house this morning?"

"Where's the mail?"

"Are you trying to find me a babysitter?"

"What were you looking for?" he asked.

"I thought you said I couldn't trust her."

"And you shouldn't." Matthew crossed his arms. "I can arrest you for trespassing and interfering with a police investigation."

"I had a key and how was I interfering when I'm picking up his mail?"

He raised an eyebrow and held out his hand. "What were you looking for in his house?"

Raina dug around her purse and dropped the key into his palm. "His safe."

"Where is it?"

"Take me with you. Please."

"No."

Another police cruiser pulled up. Officer Hopper sauntered up to Matthew. Her eyes lit up when she glanced at Raina.

"Looks like someone got herself into a pickle," Officer Hopper said.

"Anyone at the house?" Matthew asked.

Officer Hopper shook her head. "Looks like Miss Sun was the only one doing some B&E."

"She was collecting his mail," Matthew said, through gritted teeth.

Officer Hopper gave him a sideways glance but kept silent.

An ambulance pulled up and parked in front of Raina's car.

"Please give Officer Hopper your statement after the EMT checks you out." Matthew stepped closer and whispered into her ear. "I'm going to make you squeal one way or another about the safe."

Raina whispered back, "Not unless I make you squeal first." When he stalked back to his cruiser, she caught the tail end of his sage and clean water scent. He took off without a backward glance.

Officer Hopper gave her a chilly smile and pulled out her notebook. She waved off the approaching EMT. "So tell me what happened."

FOUR HOURS LATER, Raina stood in front of her apartment and hunted for the keys in her purse. Her fingers brushed Holden's tablet. Giving her statement had taken much longer than she thought necessary.

Officer Hopper had grilled Raina the first hour before allowing the EMT to check her out. After the EMT had left, she'd asked the same questions in a handful of creative ways.

Raina limped to the kitchen and filled a glass with water. She grabbed a bottle of Motrin from a drawer and checked the expiration date on the bottle. The pills had expired a year ago. She shrugged and swallowed two pills. They couldn't make her feel any worse than she did now.

Bracing a hand against the counter, she retrieved a plastic bag from under her kitchen sink. She placed the plastic bag under the ice dispenser on her refrigerator. Ice cubes clicked against each other as they fell into the bag. The humming refrigerator was a balm to her eventful morning. She tied off the homemade ice pack.

"Your front door is open again!" called out a familiar voice.

Raina jerked, and the bag fell from her hands. It crashed onto the grungy orange linoleum. Blood rushed to her head, and she swayed until she gripped the edge of the countertop.

Eden stood with her mouth hanging open at the entrance to the kitchen. When their eyes met, she snapped her mouth shut and swooped the ice pack off the floor. She gave Raina a gentle hug and helped her to the sofa. Her face was hard as a boulder, and she pressed her lips into a thin line.

Raina placed the icepack on her knee and relaxed for the first time today. Her breathing slowed. She closed her eyes as she stretched out on the sofa.

Eden clattered in the kitchen, and someone opened the front door. The whispered conversation of the familiar voices was calming.

A cool hand brushed her forehead. She sighed and fell asleep.

Raina roused to the smell of fresh coffee and greasy takeout. Her stomach growled, but she showered and changed first. A few minutes later, she huddled over a steaming mug of coffee at the dining room table. Po Po propped her booted foot on the extra chair, while Eden twisted a strand of hair around her finger. The koi clock ticked while Raina wolfed down a cheese and spinach omelet covered in mushroom sauce from the Venus Café.

"I vote you stop looking into Holden's death," Po Po said. "Eden agrees with me."

Eden averted her gaze. "I think Raina should be more careful."

Po Po glared at Eden. "My granddaughter is not risking her life so that you can get a promotion."

"You really think this is about me?" Eden frowned. "It's Matthew. It's always been about Matthew."

Raina rubbed her temples. "This is not about Matthew."

Po Po and Eden both stared at her.

Okay, it was about Matthew, but Raina wasn't going to admit it. It bothered her. This pull and push nature of their relationship. At some point, they would have to decide where they were going. She couldn't force the issue, not while she was a murder suspect and he was the detective, but once the case was over...

Her shoulders dropped. His parents had made him afraid of tethers, but she relished the idea of growing deep roots that would weather any storm. So for the last ten years, they had clashed, clawing clothes and skin off each other at every encounter. He'd disappeared, only to turn up every time she thought she'd gotten him out of her system.

"So what happened?" Po Po finally asked.

Raina described the attack.

Eden paled and licked her lips. "Why would Sol hurt you?"

Raina glared at her. "Why not? He'd been acting suspiciously since Holden's death. Maybe he is the killer."

Eden shook her head.

Po Po cocked her head, watching the two of them. "What's going on between you two?"

"Nothing." Raina crossed her arms. "She's just not welcome here."

Eden pleaded with her eyes. "Please let me explain. I knew Matthew was the guy you've been hung up on all these years. Even a blind person could feel the chemistry—"

"I don't care about that. I told you Matthew is none of your business. What was Sol doing at your apartment this morning?"

Eden averted her gaze. "I...I don't know what you're talking about."

Raina slammed her mug on the table. "You were wearing your peacock silk robe with half your ass hanging out."

Po Po gasped.

Eden blushed. "It was a regular length robe."

"Yeah, on a normal person. The robe ended halfway up this Amazon's thigh. I guess you'll do anything for a story," Raina said.

"Raina!" admonished Po Po.

Raina ducked her head to stare at the table. What was wrong with her? She normally didn't get this angry.

"I have a confession to make." Eden took a deep breath. "I've been dating Sol."

Raina's jaw dropped as if her friend had socked her in the stomach. Eden and Sol a couple? Was her friend the special someone Sol had mentioned at the wedding?

Po Po scowled at Eden. "You're dating the guy who just attacked my granddaughter?"

"It must be a big misunderstanding. You said yourself that Sol didn't seem to want to hurt you," Eden said.

"How long has this been going on?" Raina asked.

"After he blackmailed you for a date. I confronted him about it." Eden gave her a sheepish smile. "Things just took off from there."

Raina kept her tone neutral. "Is it possible he's trying to distract you from the murder investigation?" And it'd worked since her normally terrier of a friend hadn't gotten around to asking her hard-nosed questions.

Eden's face flashed through several emotions but settled on a pinched expression. "My instinct says he's not."

Raina wanted to shout that her friend's instinct was blind when it came to men. The scruffier they were, the more Eden thought she could save them. While the men eventually turned out to be decent guys, it didn't mean Sol was part of that camp. "Then why the big secret if there's nothing wrong with the guy?"

"I didn't say there's nothing wrong with Sol. He has some anger to work through, but it has nothing to do with the murder. And you've met his sister, Sonia. I'm not ready for that kind of reception yet."

Her friend was hiding something. "Did you find anything in Holden's office?"

"How—"

"The coffee cup with 'Lois' on it. What did you find, Ms. Lane?"

Eden smacked her forehead. "Does anyone else know about that?"

"I don't think so. The janitors empty the trash in the offices every other day. The coffee cup should be thrown out by now." Raina slid a sideways glance at Eden. "Sol pulled me into the office on that particular occasion. Said he was looking for a recommendation letter."

"I honestly don't know what Sol was looking for." Eden squirmed and blushed. "We've been too busy...you know, doing other things...to talk about the murder."

"Uh-huh." Raina had a feeling Eden wasn't telling the whole story. They might have been too busy to talk, but she was sure her friend could make an educated guess. So technically, she wasn't lied to. "Where does your loyalty lie? With Sol or with me?"

"You!" Eden shook her head. "I can't believe you had to ask."

"Sorry. I need to be sure our conversations stay between us. We're either a team or we're not. It's better to clear the air."

"Okay." Eden drew out the word. "Then let me flip the mirror. Is your loyalty with me or with Matthew?"

Raina squirmed. "That's unfair. I've known him since I was a kid."

Eden shrugged. "What does that have to do with anything?"

"Matthew has never once lied to me in the twenty-one

years I've known him. Nor has he betrayed my trust. You've done both in less than forty-eight hours. What am I to think?"

Eden's face collapsed. The tears and the look of admonishment on her grandma twisted the guilt in Raina's gut. She should apologize, but it'd sound hollow when her heart ached. Instead, Raina stumbled into her bedroom with tears of her own. What did this final nail mean to their friendship?

18

DEADLY FROU-FROU DRINKS

Instead of her usual morning run, Raina drove out to Hook Park to hide until her grandma left for the senior center. Po Po's hovering last night was bad enough. She limped over to the wooden bench under an ancient oak tree in front of Mildred's Pond.

Ducks lined the pond, some with their necks tucked in their chests. The water rippled as fishes glided underneath. The tranquility of the place didn't mirror the turmoil in Raina's heart. She didn't know what to make of Eden's relationship with Sol. Or her own quasi-relationship with Matthew. And then there was her grandma.

When Raina had checked the mailbox this morning, she'd found a letter from the executor of her grandfather's estate asking for the lawyer's fees she'd paid to date. This meant someone had contacted the executor on her behalf. And the only person who would care enough to do this would be her grandma. So did Po Po come to Gold Springs to confront Raina about Ah Gong's secret family and her role in the fiasco?

A twig snapped behind her, and she turned to find Matthew juggling two coffee cups and a white pastry bag. Her moment of Zen was over for the day.

He handed her a cup as he sat. "Po Po said I'd find you here. Raised crumbs or chocolate glazed?"

"Surprise me."

He gave her the raised crumbs. How could she let go of a man who could guess her donut mood? She sighed. Love shouldn't be this complicated. They sat in silence, sipping and munching.

"Sol claimed you attacked him." Matthew leaned forward and shot the balled white bag into the trashcan next to her. "He's pressing charges."

"Of course he is. I need to talk to him."

"That's not a good idea."

"Did you find out what he was looking for in Holden's house?"

"Apparently, you're not the only one who wants to remain silent."

Raina rolled her eyes. "Sarcasm doesn't suit you, Elliot. He might talk to me."

"Matthew. You know I hate my first name. Unless you're planning to charm his pants off in a holding cell, that's not going to happen."

She sat back down, her mind racing. Matthew might not let her talk to Sol at the station, but it didn't mean she couldn't find another way.

"What does Joanna think about you not bringing me in?" She couldn't help dragging out Officer Hopper's name. It was petty, but Matthew always made her do stupid things.

He grimaced. "She trusts my judgment."

Right. Officer Hopper wanted her butt in a sling, and he was too male to notice it. "So what were you doing getting cozy with a reporter yesterday morning?"

"Are you jealous?"

Raina wanted to smack him. "No." She forced herself to smile at him. "I just don't want to be excluded from pillow talk."

Matthew snorted and looked amused.

"It's not fair for you to share insider information with…" She hesitated. A reporter? A lover?

"Relax. Eden isn't my type. She's too high maintenance, especially that hair of hers."

The knot in Raina's chest loosened.

"I like a girl who's not afraid of rolling out of bed looking like an Asian version of Carrot Top. Kind of like you."

This time she did smack him on the arm.

Matthew cleared his throat. "I asked Eden to keep you out of trouble. In exchange, I'd give her information about the case the day before it would be made public."

"Really? A babysitter?"

Matthew gave her a bemused smile. "I thought having someone to distract you might do the trick." He glanced at the Ace bandage on her knee. "But trouble always seems to find its way to you no matter what."

"This is bordering on stalker behavior."

"Good thing we understand each other. It's not like you didn't stalk me before either."

Raina chuckled as she recalled the disguises she wore in Las Vegas. "We had some good times." Too bad they always had to wake up to reality. "Were you able to open the safe?"

"Yes." Matthew's face became professionally blank. "The combination was your birthday."

Raina gasped. If Holden didn't care enough to break things off face-to-face, why would he use her birthday? Even in death, he had to play mind games with her.

A heavy silence hung between them as they sat frozen, staring at the pond and avoiding eye contact. She had no idea what was running through Matthew's head, but she didn't want him to think she'd felt any intense passion for Holden.

A bird chirped.

Raina took it as a signal that she had to make the next move. She cleared her throat. "It wasn't like that between us. At least not for me."

Matthew pulled out his cell phone, ignoring her comment. "I want you to look at this and tell me if this was the victim's handwriting."

She squinted at the barely legible print in the photos. It wasn't Holden's handwriting. An idea tickled the back of her mind, but she couldn't quite grasp it. "It's research notes for his last book, but it was written with a pen."

"So?"

"Holden only used a pen when necessary. He preferred a pencil. He liked to chew on them when he was thinking." Raina grimaced in distaste. "Whatever happened to testing his pencils for the toxin?"

"A dead end there."

"What else did you find in the safe?"

"Cash and a paternity test. The victim sent a sample to a private lab, and it came back negative."

"What does that mean?"

"He's not the father. And before you ask, it didn't say who the mother was."

Assuming the child in question was Cora's nephew, Holden had continued to pay child support for the last two years even though he didn't legally have to. If Cora's family knew he wasn't the child's biological father, then there would be no motive for her to kill him.

"How much money is there?"

"Twenty thousand dollars."

Raina's eyes widened. Did she have a shot at getting her money back? "Where did he get all that money? And what happens to it now?"

"That's for the judge to figure out."

"I think the child in question might be Cora Campos's nephew."

Matthew studied her. "There is no court order for child support on file."

"Maybe it's an informal arrangement."

He nodded. "I'll ask Joanna to have a chat with Cora."

"No. Let me do it." Raina gave him a cheeky smile. "After all, I'm your secret weapon. I think Cora would rather open up to me than an officer in a uniform."

"You mean more like my dirty little secret. All right. But if things get dicey, you call me. If anything happens to you again..." He sighed. "I don't know why I bother. You never listen to me."

She leaned her head on his shoulder. "I love you."

His arm came around and pulled her closer. "I know."

"You're not your dad. You're not going to become an abusive drunk."

"How can you be so sure? The darkness is in me. My unhappy childhood. All the time I spent in Afghanistan only made it worse. I can't risk having you around when I snap."

Raina nestled closer, breathing in his clean water and sage scent. "You're not going to snap."

"I wish I could believe you."

"Why don't we find out together?"

He shook his head. "I would rather be alone for the rest of my life than risk it."

She pulled away from him and folded her arms. "So what does that mean? We're supposed to be friends with benefits for the rest of my life?"

Matthew gave her a wounded look. "I... That's not what I mean."

Raina stood, gathering her purse and coffee. "Let me know when you figure it out. But do it soon. As my mom would say, my eggs are shriveling from the wait." She limped to her car with a straight back even as tears gathered at the corners of her eyes. Love shouldn't be this complicated.

AFTER RAINA DRIED HER EYES, she drove to the freshman dorms. It was time to see what Cora knew about the murder. Her shifty behavior inside the bookstore meant she either had something to hide or she knew something. Standing outside the three-story building, Raina pulled out her phone and pretended to talk next to the front door. When a student hurried inside, she piggybacked in, grabbing the handle before the door could swing shut.

She walked through each floor, checking the names or notes left on the small bulletin boards outside each door. Most of the bulletin boards had lots of exclamation points, smiley faces, and glitter. Some even had toothy group photos. It had been a long time since Raina was a freshman, but youthful enthusiasm for life was the same no matter what the year on the calendar said.

On the third floor, Raina found a room with the initials CC and ST on it. Bingo! She knocked. There was a slight shuffle inside, and the door opened. Cora's eyes looked huge behind her thick glasses, and she looked even more like a baby stork in her baggy T-shirt and tight shorts.

Cora licked her lips. "Hi, Raina. Did Olivia send you here for something?"

"What? Did you take something from the office?"

"No, but that doesn't mean she wouldn't accuse me of making off with a stapler or something. She's that petty."

"I can see that, but she's on admin leave." Raina studied her face. "I'm here to talk to you about Holden."

Cora took a step back, so the door shielded her body. "I don't know anything. I only started the student assistant position at the beginning of summer."

Raina raised an eyebrow. "His son is your nephew. There's a lot more you can tell me. Can I come in or do you want to have this conversation in the hall?"

"I don't have to talk to you."

"Did you kill Holden so your nephew could inherit his money?"

Cora blanched and swayed. Raina pushed her way into the room and reached out to steady her. She led the girl to one of the twin beds and closed the door. Her aggression had gotten the response she knew it would.

Weak sunlight filtered through the sheers on the single window above the side-by-side desks.

Raina perched on the chair closest to Cora. "You killed him for nothing. Holden wasn't the father."

Cora stiffened. "I've no reason to want him dead."

So she did know Holden wasn't the child's father. "Because he was worth more alive, paying child support to your family."

"This is none of your business."

"Aren't you ashamed of your sister's behavior?"

Cora glared at Raina, her eyes flashing with anger. "My sister is dead. From complications during labor. She said Holden raped her."

"Are you sure?"

Cora hung her head, trying to hide her burning cheeks. "I found out later Holden didn't rape my sister. He was in a conference in another city at the time."

Raina frowned. Did he view his child support as charity? Or was there more to the story? "So your family took child support money that they weren't entitled to?"

"My parents need the money. They're living off Social Security as it is. And Holden provided the health insurance for my nephew. The poor kid has a lot of medical problems. My sister didn't take care of herself during the pregnancy."

"But what about welfare? Isn't there some kind of state program that could help your family out?"

"I'm working on that now. Things were much easier when Holden was alive."

"So who is the real father?" Raina asked.

Cora shrugged.

Raina understood why Cora's family kept taking

Holden's money. It was easy, and the money came at regular intervals. She hoped she would have the strength to make a different choice if she was ever in a similar situation. "Do you need help? I have a friend who works for a non-profit that helps people with the paperwork for government programs."

Cora brightened. "That would be wonderful. I'm in over my head, and my parents speak limited English."

"I'll give my friend a call and get back to you." Raina bit her lip. Should she press on with her questions? "The few times I'd seen you and Holden together, he seemed nice to you."

"He was a nice man and didn't deserve to die," Cora mumbled. "I don't know why he paid for my nephew, but I knew he felt sorry for him."

"Then help me out. I'm trying to figure out how he was poisoned. He seemed fine at the fundraiser meeting. I heard he threw up when the two of you went to pick up lunch afterward."

"He looked kind of pale when we left, but he wanted to help. I was picking up lunch for the entire department so I could use an extra set of hands."

Raina cocked her head. A tingling started at the back of her neck. Cora had just confirmed that Holden had been poisoned before lunch, which meant the poison was in the coffee. He didn't look well when he'd confronted her by the vending machines, but she had thought it was nerves. "Do you regularly pick up coffee and lunch for everyone?"

Cora shook her head. "The Dean was questioning the staff about something that week. Olivia thought it would boost morale to provide coffee and lunch."

"I'm assuming Gail called in the order, and you got the food from someone at the Eatery."

Cora nodded reluctantly.

"You didn't get the food orders from someone," Raina said slowly.

"The coffee was already sitting on the counter when I showed up. I checked to make sure it had everyone's drink on the tray. I saw the barista on the way out. He was carrying several cartons of milk back to the coffee bar."

"So they didn't just order regular coffee?"

Cora snorted. "Everyone had a frou-frou drink. It seems to be a requirement if you want to work there. Same with lunch. Hold the sour cream, extra cheese, no rice. Geez, you would think I was picking up food for Hollywood divas."

Raina smiled, pretending to be amused. The murderer must have known the coffee and lunch would come from the Eatery on campus. The killer must be someone in the department. And the person only had to wait for an opportunity to add the poison to Holden's coffee. No one would even raise an eyebrow if someone grabbed the "wrong" drink by accident and then returned the doctored coffee to the tray afterward.

"Did he ever ask you to spy on Olivia?" Raina asked.

Cora picked at an unraveling seam on her bed. "No."

Raina glanced at the girl's hand working on the floral bedspread. Careful. The girl was clamming up again. "I'm sure you heard things, working so closely with Olivia. Was there something he seemed particularly interested in? Or someone?"

Cora glanced at the clock on her desk. "I'm going to be late for class. There's nothing else I can tell you."

Raina followed Cora out and made small talk about summer classes as she walked beside the girl. There were no classes the week before school starts. Cora gripped her backpack and looked as if she was deep in thought as she trudged down the stairs.

Once outside, Raina said, "I'll be in touch with my friend's contact info. I'm sure she would be able to help you with the paperwork for your nephew."

Cora twisted the hem of her shirt on a finger, staring at her shoes. "There's nothing I can say that'll... make things worse for him?"

"Not at this point."

Cora took a deep breath and looked up. "Andrew."

"Why was Holden interested in Andrew?"

Cora shook her head.

"What kind of things did you hear?"

"Just normal stuff. Like where he had last worked. Makes no sense to me." Cora shrugged. "The Dean is his wife's godfather."

Raina thanked the girl for her time and headed back to her car. Did Holden think Andrew could be a threat to his position? Or was he worried Andrew might be helping the Dean investigate the missing grant funds? It made no sense to her either.

19

SHIFTING CURRENTS

Raina peered into the Venus Café through a front window. The low hum of steady conversations was as lulling as the delectable baked goods on display. The aromatic coffee wafting outside through the cracks in the door already increased her caffeine headache. Her mouth watered at the thought of downing a creamy iced coffee.

Eden stared out the side window with a chin propped on one hand. The other hand swirled the spoon in the mug in front of her. Po Po was nowhere in sight.

Not that Raina had expected her grandma to show up for lunch when she'd received the text half an hour ago. She limped over and sat across from her friend. "Let me guess. Po Po had a last-minute appointment. And she forgot her cell phone, so you had to stay to let me know."

"That about sums it up." Eden took a sip of her coffee. "But you forgot the 'you girls have fun without me' part."

Raina grimaced. "Sounds just like the blind dates she used to set up for me."

A smile tugged at the corners of Eden's lips. "I ordered your usual."

"Thanks."

Raina pretended to study the nearest painted Venus on the wall while sneaking sideways glances at Eden. Her friend returned to gazing out the window. It wasn't until Brenda slid an iced coffee in front of Raina that she realized she'd been staring at a berry branch strategically placed at chest level across the naked nymph. These painted ladies had a sizzling love life compared to her frostbitten one. Go figure.

Brenda slid two plates on the table. "Do you want dessert later? We're starting our seasonal menu early this year. Pumpkin cheesecake cupcakes and homemade pumpkin caramel ice cream."

Eden glanced at her tuna sandwich with gooey cheese oozing out of the sides. She made a face and shook her head. "I'm on a diet."

Raina drizzled balsamic vinaigrette into her Fiji apple salad. "Sure. The cupcake sounds good."

They ate in silence for several minutes. Raina picked at her salad, pushing the spinach around. Eden ate with gusto, licking the cheese off her fingers.

Raina leaned back on her chair. "Sol is threatening to press charges against me."

"I think he's using it as a ploy to get you to talk to him," Eden said.

Brenda returned with the pumpkin cheesecake cupcake. A whiff of nutmeg hit Raina's nose, and she grinned in anticipation.

Eden eyed the gleaming drop of creamy cheesecake on top of the cake. "Maybe—"

Brenda smirked and revealed another plate with a cupcake hidden behind her back. "I got you covered."

Eden laughed. "You know me too well. And I can't have Raina feel bad about eating dessert in front of me."

"Tell yourself what lies you need, girl," Brenda said over her shoulder and sashayed to another table.

Eden bit into her cupcake and moaned. "This is good."

Raina did the same. Yep, this cupcake just made the day better.

"You need to talk to Sol," Eden said.

"He's in a holding cell. Matthew wouldn't let me see him. I could talk to him tomorrow when they have to release him. I'm sure he won't be charged with anything," Raina said.

"Let me call Joanna Hopper. She might be able to help us." Eden got up and strolled over to the fireplace with her cell phone glued to her ear.

Raina pulled out Holden's tablet. It asked for a lock code. She held her breath and tapped in her birthday. The lock screen disappeared. She jammed her iced coffee in her mouth with shaking hands. Why did Holden use her birthday for his safe and tablet? If he cared so much about her, then why did he disappear after a two-word text saying: "We're done"?

She was more confused now about their relationship than when he was alive. At least she knew where she stood a few days ago, but now the current was shifting too rapidly for her to know top from bottom.

Eden slipped into her chair. "When did you get a tablet?"

Raina stuffed the tablet back into her purse. "What did Officer Hopper have to say?"

"Joanna is on the late shift tonight. We can stop by around eleven." Eden twisted her napkin. "I don't know what to say when I see him."

Raina could think of plenty of things to say, none of which was flattering. "Maybe I should just talk to Sol one on one." While they weren't arguing anymore, she still wasn't sure she could completely trust Eden's motives.

During the short drive to campus, Raina replayed her lunch with Eden. How could her friend let Sol touch her without cringing? Story or no story. Yuck. But that was her friend's business. However, Eden crossed a line when she told Officer Hopper about her relationship with Holden. She could try to justify it all she wanted, but she still told a secret that wasn't hers to tell.

Raina's bruised knee ached, but she managed to scurry from beneath one tree canopy to the next. When she opened the door of the history building, a blast of air lifted the strands of curls around her face. Raina waved to two other graduate students talking next to the receptionist desk, but Gail was nowhere in sight.

She hastened down the hallway toward the conference room. The fundraiser meeting would start in a few minutes, and she wanted to gauge the mood of the staff. Her steps slowed when she passed Olivia's office. The open door beckoned her. Only a person with the willpower of a saint could resist. And she was no saint.

Raina whipped her head left and right, scanned the hallway, and ducked into the office. She pushed the door partially closed to block the view into the room from the hallway. Closing the door completely would have been too suspicious. A glance at the desk clock showed she had ten minutes before the meeting started. She better hurry.

The filing cabinet behind the desk was locked. The drawers on the desk didn't reveal much. A Sierra Club newsletter, a coupon for a downtown beauty parlor, and a slip of paper with "N.M. 752-2900" on it. Could this be Natalie's phone number? She pocketed the paper. In the last drawer, she found a key that might fit the locked cabinet.

Her thumping heart kept pace with the ticking clock. Four minutes had passed. Someone eventually would notice the partially closed door. The serenity of the Lake Tahoe poster on the wall mocked the tension in her body.

Raina inserted the key into the filing cabinet. Bingo! She finger-combed through the files as she read the names on the tabs. A blank tab was wedged between the thick files of "Undergrad Requirements" and "Welcome Week." She pulled out the file and rifled through the contents. Why would Olivia have a file on Andrew Rollinger? Resume, job application, and newspaper clippings. Nothing out of the ordinary, except there weren't any files of the other staff in the locked cabinet.

Heels clicked outside in the hallway, each step louder than the one before. Raina's hands turned clammy, and a bead of sweat rolled down her back. In one swift move, she shoved the file back in and locked the cabinet. She pocketed the key and rifled noisily through the files in the inbox of the desk.

"Now where did she put the list?" Raina sighed, hoping her pretense at frustration sounded natural.

Someone tapped on the door, and the door swung

open. Gail frowned, her unplucked eyebrows forming a tight V across her forehead. "Hello?"

Raina gestured at the piles of folders on the inbox tray. "Hey, Gail. Any idea where Olivia put the confirmed donors' list? I gave it to her before she went on leave. I saw her tuck it in one of these folders."

Raina sighed again. Was that too trite? She concentrated on slowing down her breathing. "I can't find anything in this mess."

Gail glared at the desk. "Hurricane Kline probably took it with her. Come on. We have to go. We're late for the meeting as it is." She turned and strolled down the hall.

Raina sagged with relief but trotted after the secretary, babying her right knee. The Ace bandage was visible below her shorts. She was surprised Gail didn't comment on it.

"How are you holding up?" Raina asked.

"The Admin staff always end up picking up all the pieces," Gail said through gritted teeth. "Olivia is setting me up to fail. She took everything home. The donors list. The vendors list. The decorations list. Everything. What sane person would take that stuff home?"

Raina's shoulders relaxed. She nodded and smiled with sympathy like a puppet on cue, tuning out Gail's list of complaints. In the past year, she'd learned the secretary's monologues didn't require any participation on her part.

At the entrance of the conference room, Gail paused and straightened her shoulders. "Thanks, Raina. I knew I could count on you."

Raina gave Gail a sideways glance. What had she just agreed to?

Gail sailed into the conference room and slid into the mesh chair opposite Andrew and Lori. The group had shrunk. It made the conference room appear even larger and colder than last week. The space between Andrew and Lori could have fit another person. Andrew's shoulders drooped more than the last time. His chin dipped close to his chest. When Raina sat down, Lori gave her a tight smile.

Raina wondered if she'd just walked in on an argument. No snacks and an hour of sitting across from a couple shooting snide remarks and dark looks at each other wasn't her idea of a good time.

Gail glanced at the clock on the wall. "Olivia took all the files for the fundraiser home with her. Raina volunteered to drop by and see if she could get them back before the end of the week."

Raina gave herself a mental head slap. So that was what she'd agreed to. At least it would give her an excuse to snoop around Olivia's house again.

"Want me to come with you?" Lori asked. "I might be able to help since she likes me."

"Tomorrow morning? Nine o'clock?" Raina asked. "I have a shift at the computer lab after this meeting." Perfect. Someone to distract Olivia while Raina snooped under the guise of a diarrhea attack. No one would dare question how much time she was taking in the bathroom.

Lori nodded. "Sure. Meet you at her house."

"Is the lodge in the arboretum available for the event?" Gail asked.

"Is it possible to turn this into something simpler? A

buffet, perhaps? It'll be less work for everyone," Raina said.

Gail grimaced. "I wish, but the Dean has already approved Olivia's plans. The Titanic has left the dock; we're just steering at this point." She looked at Lori.

Lori cleared her throat and spoke about the rental options.

Andrew watched his wife from the corner of his eyes, fiddling with the sleeve on his coffee cup. When he pulled the cup out for the fourth time, Lori shot him an angry look.

Raina wanted to snicker. Somebody was in the doghouse.

Gail looked down at her notebook and made a couple of marks. "Thanks, Raina. I'm glad you're going to take care of those details. Moving on. Andrew, did you call the campus printers for the pricing on the flyers and posters?"

The smile slid off Raina's face. What did she volunteer to do again? There was an empty feeling in the pit of her stomach. No more nodding and smiling. At the rate she agreed to things, she'd end up planning the entire fundraiser.

As late as it was, the police station had its own hum of activity from the rolling wheels of the janitor's cart somewhere down the hall to the whirling overhead fan. A bench lined one wall in the waiting area behind her. A snoring, slack-jawed man lay at one end. The lights were dimmed, as if to discourage miscreants from committing any crime until morning.

Raina shook the bag of cake pops she'd made for the visit. "I call them Chocolate Dirt."

Donna's eyes lit up at the sight of the gummy worms wrapped around the chocolate coating. "My boys would love these. Mind if I take a couple of them home?"

"Sure. Take as many as you want."

The front desk clerk grabbed a half dozen of the cake pops from the bag.

Raina suppressed the urge to grin. "Is Officer Hopper free? She's expecting me."

"Let's see." Donna spoke into her phone and hung up. "She's out back in the warehouse." She lifted the hinged counter top. "Said you can wait at her desk."

Raina followed Donna to the unoccupied office space behind the front counter. All the desks looked the same: overflowing inbox trays, battered filing cabinets, and thick folders. There wasn't much in the way of personal items.

Donna gestured toward a desk in the far corner and went back to the front desk.

Raina took a deep breath when she sat. She'd no idea what to say to Officer Hopper. At least Matthew was at home. If she was lucky, he wouldn't even find out about her visit.

Her gaze drifted to Donna's back and the bitten cake pop in one hand. The desk clerk didn't have a malicious bone in her body, but she did like talking about her food. All it would take was one mention of the cake pop at the water cooler. Well, she'd worry about Matthew later. He would understand once she explained her suspicion. She just needed Sol to confirm what she had seen in the photos of Holden's safe.

Officer Hopper strolled through an archway in the opposite corner of the room and sat behind her desk with steeple fingers in front of her. She didn't wear her usual scowl, but why should she? She knew she had the upper hand at the moment.

Raina shifted in her chair, wishing she'd taken a lesson on groveling. The steely gaze of the woman was unnerving. "I need to talk to Sol Cardenas. Can you please ask if he's willing to see me?"

Officer Hopper raised an eyebrow. "If I had my way, you'd be in the holding cell next to him. You could talk to him all you want then."

Raina's mouth went dry. "I'm sorry." She'd no idea what she was apologizing for, but it seemed like a safe comment.

Officer Hopper blinked and a slow smile spread across her face. "How about I put you in the next holding cell? Just until morning." She glanced at her watch. "It's only six more hours until the morning shift. Matthew wouldn't even know you've been here."

Raina wiped her hands on her shorts. She didn't trust the woman. "No, thanks." She stood. "I'll try to catch Matthew at his home."

The smile disappeared from Officer Hopper's face. For a fraction of a second, Raina got a glimpse of the nice woman she'd met at the crime scene behind the stiff façade in front of her. With those round cheeks and blonde curls, Joanna Hopper could have her choice in men. Instead, she had her sights on the same emotionally unavailable one that Raina did.

"You'll be listening in," Raina said. "I plan to ask him something about the murder case. And if you get something from the conversation, you can relay it to Matthew."

Officer Hopper nodded. "I'll let you have twenty minutes with Sol, but only if he wants to talk to you."

This was more generous than Raina expected. She held up the bag. "Cake pops?"

20

I'D RATHER SHOOT HIM

Raina sat on a hard chair with her hands folded on the small table in the interrogation room. The industrial lemon scent irritated her nose, but didn't hide the fear and sweat permeating the space from its previous occupants. Her scalp prickled at the bright fluorescent lights and bare walls. She glanced sideways at the large darkened window. Officer Hopper was on the other side, watching her every move and listening for an excuse to arrest her. Oh, happy thoughts.

Sol sat across from her with swollen red eyes and a badly bandaged nose. His hair looked even greasier and hung lifeless around his face. The new growth of hair on his jawline made him look like a one-eyed alley cat.

Raina cleared her throat. "I'm sorry about..." She touched her nose.

"Sonia has been hysterical since my arrest."

"Eden told me the two of you are...dating."

He sneered. "Let me guess. You don't approve."

She studied him until he looked away. "It's not up to

me who Eden dates. But if you make her cry, I'm coming after your kneecaps."

"I'm sorry. You looked so panicked at the house. I thought you were going to scream." He gave her a ghost of a smile. "I didn't want to be caught."

In hindsight, Raina's wild bucking did more damage to the garage and herself than his bear hug. And he looked far worse than she felt, but he wasn't getting off easy. "How are your boys?"

"I know who to blame if I don't have any kids in the future."

She shuddered at the thought of mini-Sols. "I heard you were going to press charges."

"I wanted to talk to you and it was the fastest way to get you here."

"What were you looking for? The three spiral notebooks?"

Sol leaned forward in his seat. "Do you have them?"

"They're in police custody."

He sank back into his chair with drooping shoulders.

"It wasn't Holden's handwriting. They looked like research material for his last book."

"That's my book. I wrote it."

"I figured as much. He gave you the money for Sonia's wedding reception."

His eyes widened. "How did you know about the money?"

"Girl talk. You know how it is in the restrooms. Sonia thought you got the money from me."

Sol half rose, the palms of his hands pressing against the table. As he strained against the handcuffs, they clinked. "What did you tell her?"

Raina held up her palms. "Nothing. She still thinks we're an item, but how are you going to explain Eden?"

He settled back into his chair. "I already told her I dumped you and found someone else."

She suppressed the urge to roll her eyes. As if his sister would believe he was a ladies' man. "About the book?"

"The money was a loan. The manuscript and research material were collateral. I was supposed to have a year to repay him."

"But he published it."

He nodded glumly.

"And you went to see Olivia a few nights ago to see if she could help you."

"So it was you! You're so damn lucky."

A chill ran down her back and Raina shivered. Yes, she'd been lucky so far. A drunken Olivia waving a gun around in the dark wasn't an experience she wanted to repeat. "I have to go. I'm sorry you're in here. You'll be out tomorrow?"

Sol eyed her. "We're even if you help me get my notebooks back."

"Sorry, no can do. It's evidence now."

"I heard you're chummy with the detective. I'm sure you wouldn't want him to know you faked a pregnancy before Holden died. It might complicate things for you."

Raina clenched her jaw. "You're dating my best friend. You're supposed to be nice to me."

He scratched his paunchy stomach. "It was worth a try, just in case the friend card didn't work."

She gave him a disgusted look. The man was incurable. Who would threaten a potential ally "just in case?"

The light clicked on behind the darkened window. A signal her time with Sol had run out. Her gaze slid sideways to the window, expecting to see Officer Hopper.

Raina's heart stopped. It was Matthew. His face was tight, the golden flecks in his eyes were dull, and his lips were pressed together. She forced herself to breathe again.

Officer Hopper stood behind Matthew. She gave Raina a cocky smile and held her hand to her ear to signal she'd called him.

Raina crossed her arms to hide her trembling hands. She should have known better than to trust a romantic rival.

A few minutes later, Officer Hopper and Matthew stood outside the opened door of the interrogation room. Officer Hopper grinned as if she'd won the lottery and glided off with Sol as if she had wings. Matthew cocked his head and marched down the hall to escort her out.

The walk to her car was the longest journey Raina had ever taken. The hall was dimmer than a few minutes ago. The air stale and quiet. She would have wrung her hands if she were that type of woman. Instead, she held her head high and stared at a spot between his shoulder blades, concentrating on keeping her tears at bay until she could be alone. His steps pounded on the floor and echoed in the hallway and tightened the knot in her shoulders.

Once outside, Matthew stalked over to the Honda and glared at Raina while she fumbled for her keys. The street lamp spotlighted her car and darkened the rest of the world around them as if they were actors on a stage. If only they were actors.

Raina swallowed several times before she found her voice. "I didn't tell him I was pregnant. He made the assumption when I meant to say my bills were late. It was the only way I could get my money back from him. I'd asked for it several times before. Please understand. You weren't even in the picture then..." Her voice trailed off when she realized he wasn't even listening.

Matthew studied her face as if memorizing her features.

She pressed her trembling lips together and held onto to her stomach as if she was going to be sick. Her heart galloped in a race she didn't want to be in. He was saying good-bye again without saying anything. She'd seen the expression before, but she'd be damned if he'd see her cry.

Matthew jerked his chin. "Good night." He stepped back into the shadow as if exiting the stage and left her exposed in the harsh light.

A tear slid out. Raina swiped at it as she turned to open her car door. Her hands shook and the keys jangled as they fell to the ground. Tears blurred her vision and it took her several seconds of patting blindly to find them. She stifled the urge to pound her fists on the car. What if he was watching from the shadows? She drove for three blocks and pulled over.

Her hands gripped the steering wheel as fresh tears warmed her numb face. Her heart squeezed tighter and tighter until her breaths came out in rapid heaves as if she were buried alive. Raina had known she'd pay the piper at some point. She just didn't know at the time the price would be so high.

The world became silent as she replayed the scene by

her car. It blended with their other good-bye scenes until she couldn't tell if she was crying because of tonight or the other times he'd walked out of her life. She leaned her forehead on the wheel and sobbed harder as her heart broke.

She'd wanted Matthew all her life, but everything she did only made him slip further away.

RAINA PATTED MORE powder on her blotchy skin. It was the best she could do given the circumstances. When she'd stumbled into the bathroom an hour ago, she almost fainted at the sight of the puffy eyes crusted over from last night's tears.

A few minutes later, she pulled out of the driveway. She'd love nothing more than to stay in bed, but life didn't stop just because her heart did. She needed to pick up Po Po and then meet Lori at Olivia's house to get the missing files for the fundraiser. As she drove to the senior center, she replayed last night's scene in her mind again.

Matthew hadn't exactly said it was over between them. There was no reason for her to think last night's good night held more meaning than just good night. It rankled that it'd always been his choice to leave her.

In the last decade, they ran into each other more times than it would have been possible under normal circumstances. Had he been toying with her affections all these years? Somehow, he always tracked her down, probably through the grandmas, like some broken record that couldn't get past the introduction.

But then, why did she always wait around like a

groupie, happy for scraps? Wasn't she worth more than the leftovers he gave her? Maybe last night was a sign to finally move on.

Po Po hopped into the car, humming off-key. She glanced at Raina's face and reached across to hug her.

Raina relaxed into the familiar arms and tears welled up in her eyes.

"What happened, Rainy?" asked Po Po.

Raina told her grandma everything that had transpired after dropping her off with Mrs. Louie. "Officer Hopper played me. I actually felt sorry for her." She pulled away from her grandma and reversed out of the parking spot.

"Of course, you wouldn't think anything of it. You're not that kind of person. If Matthew doesn't realize his time is running out, then he doesn't deserve you." Po Po patted her shoulder. "Are you still dropping me off at Starbucks?"

Raina nodded. "You really think it's time?"

"It's long overdue. Either he needs to step up or he has to get off."

Raina's shoulders relaxed. Her grandma didn't think she was the problem. It was him.

She dropped her grandma off at the coffee shop and made it to Olivia's house a couple minutes past nine. Lori was nowhere in sight. She got out and checked her cell phone. No message. She sent a quick text to Lori but decided not to wait. Might as well get this unpleasant task over with.

A shadowy movement on one side of the house caught her attention. Raina peered at the spot but couldn't make out anything from the sidewalk. After a moment of standing like a garden gnome, she gave herself a shake. It was probably a squirrel.

She limped to the front door and rang the doorbell. "Olivia! It's Raina."

No one answered.

This was a waste of time. She'd assumed Lori would call Olivia since they were so chummy. And where was Lori?

Raina turned to leave and noticed the opened side yard gate. She shuffled over, intending to close it, but strands of radio music floated toward her. She pushed the gate wider, took two steps into the side yard. No wonder Olivia didn't hear the doorbell. Geez, the woman must be going deaf.

"Olivia! It's Raina!" She cocked her head and listened. Still no response.

The mature trees shaded the narrow walkway to the rear of the house. It was silent except for the false cheer of the host on the radio show. She took slow steps into the yard and stopped every few steps. It wasn't trespassing since she'd made her presence known.

Raina rounded the house and froze. She scanned the large landscaped backyard. A lawn chair lay on its back, spilling Olivia's bulk onto the grass. Her cocked head was hidden behind large sunglasses. One hand pointed toward Raina while the other still clutched the neck of a broken Jack Daniel's bottle.

The hair on the back of Raina's neck stiffened. She whipped around and tripped over her own feet. No one. Her skin went clammy. Birds rustled in the tree, a car engine started, and the radio played "Dancing Queen." She grew dizzy and let out the breath she'd been holding.

Raina inched forward as her gaze continued to sweep the yard. Her heart raced and her muscles tensed for the slightest excuse to run. She took a deep breath and touched the still body with a shaking hand.

The air left her lungs in a rush. "Oh my God!"

The sunburned skin was warm. Olivia was alive. And she was snoring.

The tension left Raina's body. She wrinkled her nose at the stale body odor and the drying whiskey. She prodded Olivia with her foot. The drunk snorted and turned, flipping the lawn chair on top of herself.

Raina almost laughed, except the whole scene looked like a train wreck. She glanced at the open patio door and back at the sleeping woman at her feet. This would be her only chance to snoop. With another quick glance behind her, she went inside the house.

The kitchen was a mess. Junk mail competed with takeout cartons for counter space. Glass tumblers with congealing science experiments were scattered around the room. Emptied Jack Daniel's bottles were stacked inside the sink. Her initial guess that Olivia Spider Lashes was a secret alcoholic was right on the money.

Raina swallowed the bitter tang in her mouth. The smell she'd noticed from her earlier visit grew stronger in the hallway outside the main bedroom. A quick peek inside confirmed her suspicions. There were more laundry piles than there was carpet. The source of the stench came from several congealing vomit spots on the carpet. No wonder the cleaning woman left.

In one of the smaller bedrooms, Raina opened the drawers of a battered mahogany desk and rifled through the contents: several unopened collection notices and a receipt for a downtown hair salon. A three-hundred-dollar haircut and color? No wonder Olivia's hair always looked too glossy and full for a sixty-year-old.

Raina flipped through the collection notices. Tucked amid the pile were several bank receipts for five thousand dollars each. She counted out the receipts and blew out a whistle. Twenty thousand dollars. The amount of cash found in Holden's safe. Was Olivia paying for his services? She didn't know being a gigolo was this lucrative.

Something thumped on the floor from the kitchen.

Raina dropped everything on the desk and hurried over to the window. Her blood roared inside her ears. She threw a leg over the sill.

"What are you doing here?" Olivia slurred from behind her.

Raina whipped around. "I came to pick up the files for the fundraiser. Didn't Lori call to let you know I'd be coming?"

Olivia stared at her through bloodshot eyes. She swayed as she walked into the room.

Raina wrinkled her nose and held up a hand. "Stop. When was the last time you showered?"

"What are you doing here?" Olivia blinked. "Why are you climbing in from the window? I have a front door. And where's Lori?"

Raina snapped her fingers. "I need the fundraiser files. Please don't tell me they are on your desk at campus."

"Could you step away from the window?" Olivia lifted a hand to her eyes. "When did the sun come up?"

The tension melted from Raina's shoulders. "Focus,

Olivia. Where are the files for the fundraiser? When I asked you a few minutes ago, you said they're on your desk." The lie slipped easily from her mouth.

Olivia backed away and clutched her head. "Not so loud." She closed her eyes.

Raina sighed and took hold of Olivia's arm. "Let's go into the kitchen and I'll get you some Motrin for your headache."

She helped Olivia into a chair next to the cluttered kitchen table. The grateful expression Olivia gave her almost made Raina feel guilty for taking advantage of the situation. After Olivia took the Motrin, Raina applied aloe vera gel on the woman's reddened arms.

Raina couldn't believe this haggard creature was the meticulously groomed head of the history department. Her once silky chestnut hair was faded and hung in straggly strands, highlighting more roots than youth. Sans makeup and her tailored power suits, Olivia looked frumpy and every inch her sixty years in her dirty tank top and shorts. She looked like the personification of the smell in her house.

"You're going to peel. And your skin is going to hurt once the Motrin wears off. How long have you been"— Raina looked around for a napkin, but didn't find one. She wiped the gel from her fingers on her shorts —"sleeping outside?"

Olivia shrugged. "I don't remember."

Raina licked her lips. It was now or never. "I also gave money to Holden." It was a gamble. Hopefully their shared experience might nudge Olivia into telling her story. "Two thousand dollars."

A tear slid down Olivia's wrinkled face and she closed her eyes. "You got off easy."

Raina held her breath.

Olivia looked up at the ceiling and blinked rapidly to get rid of the tears in her eyes. "It's not easy to admit you're an old fool."

"And I'm a young fool. Everyone is looking for someone to love."

Olivia's shoulders drooped. "The nightmare began after his credit card got declined earlier this year. We stopped going out for dates because Holden was so embarrassed. He wouldn't let me pay." She grimaced. "Said it unmanned him."

Raina flinched as a flash of bitterness welled up in her. She was hearing her story come out of Olivia's mouth.

"Then there were the harassing calls and the strange men following us around."

Raina straightened. Were these the same men she saw with Holden at the bank's parking lot? "What did they look like?"

"I don't know. I never got a good look at them. Holden said it was a scare tactic to collect the money he owed them." Olivia buried her face in her hands. Her voice was muffled, but the pain was raw. "He was so grateful when I gave him money the first time. He called me his beautiful angel."

Raina patted her arm but cringed inwardly. He'd called her the same thing.

"Everything was fine for a while. We went to dinners, plays, and weekend hiking trips," Olivia said.

"How long did this last?"

"A few weeks. Then he started getting moody and withdrawn again."

"He wanted more money."

Olivia stared at her for a long moment. "Yes, you would know."

Raina flushed, but kept her chin up. She was a victim just like Olivia. There should be no shame attached to the victim. "Then what happened?"

"He complained his salary as an assistant professor didn't cover his living expenses and his student loans. He wanted access to the grant fund to pay himself a salary during the off months while he worked on his book."

"And you turned a blind eye because he produced a book. I heard another twenty percent went missing."

Olivia stared at her hands. "I don't know."

Should Raina tell her about the plagiarism? No, she didn't want to get sidetracked. "Was he supposed to share the funds with anyone else?"

"Two other professors, but they were busy finishing up their other projects."

"How come you gave him more of your personal money after this?"

Olivia's lower lip trembled. "He'd stopped pretending to be in love with me by then. Two weeks later, he showed up and demanded more money. I told him I'd given him everything. Then he left." She lowered her gaze. "That was the worst night of my life. That was when I realized my vanity had cost me twenty thousand dollars."

"Then what happened?"

"He came back again. This time he said if I didn't give him more money, he'd tell the Chancellor I sexually harassed him." A vein throbbed on Olivia's forehead.

"That I'd helped him steal money from the grants for sleeping with me."

Raina's eyes widened. A moocher, a cheat, and a blackmailer. Maybe it was a blessing he'd broken up with her before she found herself in love with him.

Olivia licked her cracked lips. "I'm glad he's dead."

Raina wiped her hands on her shorts. She had to ask the million-dollar question.

She glanced behind her shoulder. The sliding patio door and screen door were shut. If she had to make a run for it, Olivia would be able to knock her over the head before she had time to slide open both doors. Olivia watched her with a half-smile on her face, as if she knew what Raina was thinking. She took a deep breath. "Did you poison Holden?"

"I'd rather shoot him."

"That would have been messy."

"Then it's a good thing someone got to him first."

Raina thought about the phone number she'd found in Olivia's office along with the file on Andrew. "Have you ever met his sister, Natalie?"

"No."

Raina asked several more questions, but Olivia only grunted or stared into space. She collected the fundraiser files and left a few minutes later.

It wasn't until she was at her car that she realized she'd asked the wrong question. Olivia didn't technically lie if she hadn't met Natalie. The question should have been why she had Natalie's number.

21

FOLLOW THE MONEY

Raina pulled into the parking lot at Starbucks. She called her grandma to let her know she was outside and texted Eden to invite her to dinner. After her talk with Sol, she was convinced the man was more weasel than killer. And if he rocked her friend's boat, then so be it. There wasn't much she could do until Eden got seasick.

She leaned across the seat and opened the passenger door. Her grandma handed her a lukewarm coffee in a plastic cup. Her iced caramel macchiato held more diluted espresso than ice.

Po Po buckled in her seat belt. "What took you so long? I got myself into an incident with the man in the tan shorts and Bluetooth headset."

Raina squinted against the glare of the reflective glass on the building. A silver-haired man scowled at her car. "What do you mean?"

"He thought I wanted"—Po Po made air quotes by curling her fingers midair—"to 'hook up.'"

Raina backed out of the parking spot. She wasn't surprised men still found her grandma attractive. Her exercise routine and her ability to laugh at herself made her a favorite among the senior crowd.

"I asked if he could plug the adaptor for my tablet in the outlet strip on the other side of him," Po Po said. "How was I supposed to know the outlet strip was his?"

"I don't get it."

"Apparently that is the way you pick up women these days. Once I was plugged in, he thought he could chat me up. Kind of like when a man buys a woman a drink at the bar."

Raina smiled. "What a cheapskate. He should at least offer to buy you a coffee."

"Oh, but I showed him."

"What did you do?"

"I knocked my empty cup onto his lap. I wanted him to think I was clumsy so he'd want to keep his laptop away from me. How was I supposed to know there was still coffee in it and he'd swat it to the woman across the table from us and that the woman would knock her coffee into the man next to her?" Po Po gave Raina a sheepish grin and her eyes glowed with glee. "Things kind of dominoed after that."

Raina's eyes widened. "Geez, I can't leave you alone for a minute. Then what happened?"

"I walked around the shopping plaza and came back. By that time, only the Bluetooth Man and the staff remembered what happened. I bought a new coffee so the staff didn't care."

Raina laughed. "Po Po, I love having you around. You always make my day better."

"You need to laugh more. Stop carrying the guilt around. Ah Gong gave you the money so you can enjoy your life. You were the only grandchild who took care of him during the last years of his life. Even if you divided it among your cousins, it wouldn't make the sting of being left off the will any less."

Enjoy her life? Her granddad's money was a leash leading Raina around from the other side of the grave. If she told Po Po about the strings attached to the "gift," it would break her grandma's spirit. "I wish he had been upfront with everyone." She blinked back tears and swallowed. What was wrong with her? She was turning into a regular weeping Nelly.

Po Po patted her shoulder. "Everything will work out. And I'm always on your side." She smiled. "By the way, that red-haired friend of yours came into the coffee shop right after you left. The one with the baby from the mall."

Raina frowned. Lori? "How long did she stay?"

Po Po shrugged. "I wasn't paying attention. Too busy trying to ignore that man's lame pick-up lines. I mean 'Hello, baby?' I haven't been a baby in sev—" She coughed. "Sixty-five years."

Raina merged onto the freeway. "She was supposed to meet me at Olivia's house. I guess she forgot."

"Where are we going?" Po Po looked at the signs, bouncing in her seat. "To the casino?"

"I thought we could have lunch out there. You can't beat the price on their buffet."

"You're going to talk to Holden's sister."

"How did you know?"

Po Po wiggled her fingers. "Magic."

"Uh-huh. What does Janice from the senior center

have to say about Natalie?"

Po Po beamed. "You do listen to me."

Raina nodded. It was more like selective hearing, but she wasn't going to admit this to her grandma.

"You remember her granddaughter?" Po Po asked.

"Natalie's neighbor?"

"Yep, that's her. She said someone broke into Natalie's apartment in the dead of the night. Turns out to be one of those skinny nerdy types that'll cower if you stare at him funny. The man said he was Natalie's fiancé, but the police hauled him off to jail anyway."

Could this be the bartender from the casino? What was his name? Kenneth? Kendall? But why would he need to break into Natalie's house?

"What are we going to do about Officer Hopper?" Po Po asked.

"Nothing." Raina gave her grandma a sidelong glance. "I'm not getting involved in someone else's drama." With her luck, Officer Hopper would come looking for her sooner or later.

Po Po smacked one fist against her palm. "No one does that to my baby and gets away with it. We have to teach her a lesson."

"I don't want to borrow trouble. I have enough of my own."

"What is life without trouble? Don't worry. My posse will take care of this."

"Just don't do anything illegal. I don't want to call Uncle Anthony to explain why you need a defense lawyer."

Po Po whipped out her cell phone. "Time to get cracking." Her fingers flew across the touch screen. "I love these smarty pants phones. I'm sending out an SOS on Facebook for a secret meeting later this evening at the center. You'll have to bake me cookies since we're fighting for your cause."

Raina chuckled. Was that a new cell phone? And posse? Geez, what were they teaching the elderly at the senior center? Her smile disappeared when she pulled into the parking spot at the casino.

The massive building loomed in front of her. Holden was a liar, a cheat, and a blackmailer. There was nothing Natalie could say that would surprise her. And yet, butterflies tap danced in her stomach.

THE CASINO WAS empty in the middle of a workday. Po Po made a beeline for the slot machines by the restroom when they got through the entrance doors. Raina strolled to the lounge. She stood in the doorway, letting her eyes adjust to the dimmer lighting. Bingo! Natalie sat in a booth in the far right corner, writing in a notebook. It didn't take a brain surgeon to figure out where an unemployed gambling addict would hang out. She draped a white cardigan over her shoulders, providing some coverage to her skintight fuchsia halter top.

Raina slid into the seat. "Hi." She squinted but couldn't make out what was on the page.

Natalie looked up and grunted in greeting. She returned to the list she was making.

The waitress dragged herself from the bar stool and sauntered over. "Anything to drink?"

Raina smiled, trying to project an air of calm friendliness. "Iced coffee, please."

Natalie scowled at Raina. "Make yourself at home."

"Thank you. I think I will." Raina nodded at the notebook. "What are you working on?"

Natalie shut her notebook with a thump and shoved it into her purse. She lit a cigarette and blew out a smoke ring. "What do you want?"

Raina ignored the stinging in her eyes. "Why did Holden dump me?"

"How would I know?"

"Guess."

Natalie tapped her cigarette on the ashtray. "You have a problem. People break up all the time. They don't go around asking strangers why."

The waitress set the cold glass on the table and Raina thanked her. "You're right. I do have a problem. Fortunately, my problem is nothing compared to yours." She sipped the coffee, hoping to clear up the grit in the back of her throat from the smoke permeating the casino. "At least the police don't suspect me of murdering my brother."

"Whatever."

"The police caught someone breaking into your apartment last night. The sharks getting restless?"

Natalie's eyes widened, but she remained silent.

Raina switched tactics. "You will gain financially from Holden's death." She shrugged, pretending a nonchalance she didn't feel. "If men are leaving your apartment with your laptop and TV for collateral, you're hurting for money."

Natalie's face tightened. Her hand trembled and the ashes from the cigarette missed the ashtray. "My brother had a son. His money-grubbing aunt and grandparents are going to make sure I don't see a dime. I have nothing to gain from my brother's death."

Raina bit her lip. If Holden had meant to provide for the boy, he would have made him a beneficiary or left a will. Anything she said now wouldn't change this outcome. "Oh, I think you do. Holden showed me a paternity test he'd done. The boy is not his son."

The cigarette fell from Natalie's hand onto the table. "What?"

Raina grabbed it and smashed it against the ashtray to put it out.

"Hey."

It took Natalie three tries before she could light another cigarette. She took a long drag, spacing out, until Raina snapped her fingers.

"Every time I'd asked him for money, he'd said he had a son to support." Natalie's mouth twisted into a bitter smile. "I couldn't get a red penny out of my brother."

Should Raina tell her about Holden paying off the loan sharks behind her back? He had probably never told her because she'd run up the tab again. Would telling her do more harm than good at this point?

"Olivia has also been harassing you for the money she gave Holden." Raina pulled out the yellow sticky note from her pocket and slid it across the table. "I found this in Olivia's office. The initials." She raised an eyebrow. "Natalie Merritt."

Natalie lifted her chin. "Well, aren't you the smart one?"

A movement at the entrance caught Raina's eyes. Olivia with lobster red skin and stained sweatpants stood at the entrance, swaying as if she'd just waved good-bye to her drinking buddies at the crack of dawn.

"Have you met Olivia?" Raina asked.

"No. And I don't want to."

Raina pointed behind Natalie. "You're about to. Let me wave her over." She lifted her hand.

Natalie grabbed her hand. "No. Don't," she whispered, her voice strained. "Cover for me, and I'll tell you what you want." She slumped on the table, angling her body toward the wall. Her hands splayed across the table and her head lay awkwardly next to them. Her fake snore rattled Raina's teeth. Just another drunk sleeping it off. The cigarette fell into the vinyl booth.

Raina reached for the cigarette, but she wasn't fast enough. It left a darkened hole on the cushion. She ground it on the ashtray to put it out. While she wasn't a fan of Natalie, having a showdown at this moment would reduce the chances of her getting more information about Holden from the woman.

Olivia scowled at the few patrons from the entrance. When her gaze connected with Raina's, she tottered over and planted herself in front of the booth.

Raina wrinkled her nose at the musty body odor and raccoon piss breath. She should have dunked Olivia in a bath instead of putting aloe vera gel on her skin earlier. She moved her iced coffee closer to the wall and covered the top with her hand.

Olivia narrowed her eyes at Natalie's blonde hair. "I'm not going to spit in your drink."

Raina raised an eyebrow. "I'm more worried about your flaking skin." Apparently, Olivia had forgotten they were on friendlier terms.

Olivia snorted and put her hands on her hips. "Where is she?"

"Who? My grandmother?"

"Natalie Merritt." Her lips curled in disgust as if spitting out the name made her teeth ache.

"You told me earlier that you don't know Natalie."

"I thought you asked if I'd met her. Holden had talked about her and I'd seen her photo."

"Uh-huh." Raina stared at her for a long moment. "Why do you think she'd be here?"

Olivia tapped the side of her head. "You asked about her. It makes sense to just follow your lead."

Raina pretended to smirk to hide her unease. If a drunken Olivia could sense her interest in the murder, then the killer could come to the same conclusion. She needed to be more careful with her questions. "That's a great deduction, Sherlock, but I don't think you can ask her for the money you gave to her brother."

Olivia slapped both hands on the table and leaned in. "That slut is the reason I'm on admin leave. She called the Dean and told him I'd sexually harassed her brother. Me." She thumped her hand on her chest. "I'm the victim and I'm still victimized even though he's dead." Her face crumbled and she swallowed. "He blackmailed me into giving him money. When will this nightmare end?"

Raina sagged against the seat. She was reminded once again how both of them were victims to Holden's lying. She should help Olivia, but there was something about her that hadn't inspired trust even before their tete-a-tete. Besides, the woman was a walking time bomb with her drinking problem. Her gaze flicked to Natalie and back to

Olivia. "I'm so sorry. Do you know what Natalie looks like?"

"I grabbed the picture off of Holden's desk. She's a blonde." Olivia glanced at the mop of blonde hair spilling across the table.

Natalie continued to snore.

"She's my friend, Brenda," Raina said.

Olivia turned to scan the lounge. "Natalie needs to make things right. I want her to call the Dean and say she made a mistake." She wiggled the purse dangling from her wrist. It rattled menacingly. "I have something that'll make her see things my way."

Raina's eyes widened and she leaned further into her seat. "You didn't bring your gun, did you?"

Olivia eyed her. "Nooo," she said slowly. "If you see her, tell her I'm looking for her."

She tottered toward the bar and bumped into a dancing couple. At the bar, she showed the Goth bartender a photograph. The bartender shook her dyed black hair and continued to polish the counter.

Olivia stumbled toward the arched entryway. She turned and made the "I'm watching you" gesture with her index and middle fingers spread and pointing at her face and back at Raina.

Clicking her tongue, Raina sent a text message to Matthew that an armed drunk was speeding back into town from the casino.

"She's gone now. You're lucky the bartender didn't give you away," Raina said.

Natalie sat up and grabbed her drink. The ice cubes clinked against each other. She took a sip and stared into space.

"Didn't you just go to rehab?" Raina asked, eyeing the glass.

"Is it true? About my brother?"

"Yes."

"What did Holden do with the money?"

Raina took a deep breath. "Did Holden ever talk about me? Did he seem to care?" The last question came out in a whisper.

Natalie shook her head. "He seemed to like you well enough. Or at least he talked about you. He never mentioned Olivia."

Raina nodded and averted her gaze. Maybe she'd never know why Holden left without saying good-bye. This was an open sore for her, never knowing why the men in her life just up and leave her. It wasn't as if she was in love with him, but she'd been in love with the idea of them while they were together.

How about Matthew? Was she only in love with the idea of being a couple with him, too? No, her relationship with Matthew was a roaring bonfire compared to the candle flame of her relationship with Holden.

"Holden kept a journal in his tablet." Natalie's lower lip trembled and a tear slid down her cheek. "I'll keep an eye out for it when I go through the house."

A jolt ran through Raina. She'd forgotten about the tablet in the last three days with all the stuff happening between Matthew, Eden, and Sol. Maybe the closure she needed could be found there. Maybe she could find something to help her move on with her life.

They sat in silence for several long minutes, letting the clanging slot machines and the jazz music fill the space between them.

"According to a friend of mine, he'd been paying off your loans," Raina whispered. "I think that was why he'd been trying to get money out of everyone...including me."

Natalie's face collapsed. Her chest heaved and strained against her top. She jerked to her feet and rushed out, bumping into the same dancing couple Olivia did earlier.

Raina sighed. She did the right thing. At least now Natalie knew her brother helped her behind her back. In some strange way, it felt right to have people grieving Holden's passing.

The waitress came back in time to watch Natalie hurry out. She frowned and shook her head. "Sorry, hon, but you're stuck with her tab." She left the bill on the table and cleared off the empty tumblers.

"Oh, joy." Raina opened the bill wallet and her bank account had heart palpitations at the amount. "Good God, does she always drink this much?"

The waitress gave her a sympathetic smile. "Kendall gives her free drinks when he thinks no one is looking so her tab is much smaller when he's working."

"Was she here Tuesday morning last week?" Raina pulled cash from her purse and laid it on top of the bill.

The waitress shrugged. "Morning, noon, night. She's here all the time."

Raina pulled out another twenty and added it to the cash on top of the bill. "I'm just interested in last Tuesday morning."

The waitress glanced at the money and licked her lips. "She came in shortly after I started my shift. About eight in the morning and left around one. She was in that booth in the back corner scribbling on her notebook."

"You guys open that early?"

"The casino is open twenty-four hours a day, three hundred sixty-five days a year. They prefer their patrons drunk."

"How come you remember when she left?"

"That's when Kendall came to fill in for our other bartender." The waitress tipped her chin at the Goth woman working behind the bar. "She felt lousy all morning and after she threw up for the second time, the manager called him. She's probably pregnant again."

Raina frowned. "Any idea why Natalie left after Kendall came in? I thought they were best buds?"

"They started fighting even before he made his first drink. And no, I have no idea what they were fighting about."

While Raina didn't believe Natalie was her brother's killer, she was relieved Natalie had an alibi. She handed the bill wallet to the waitress. "Thanks."

Raina scooped up her purse and made her way to the slot machines to search for her grandma. She hoped she'd been right to reveal the Campos boy's paternity test result to Natalie.

Holden had his reasons for supporting the boy for the last two years and paying for his sister's debts without her knowledge. Though his method for obtaining money to support both endeavors was flawed, she couldn't help but feel better the man had some redeeming qualities.

It made the bitter pill of choosing to date him much easier to swallow. It wasn't lost on her that somehow her thoughts circled back to herself. Pride was on her list of things to improve, kind of like her hair. Too bad they were both on the bottom of her long list.

22

GRANNY PANTIES

After a quick lunch at the buffet, Raina dragged a reluctant Po Po to her car, promising to take her to Bingo Night the following weekend.

"I was on a roll." Po Po stuck out her bottom lip. "I need to find a new hobby, especially since you won't let me sleuth with you. Something to keep my mind sharp. Staring at the hair growing out of the mole on my big toe is not working for me."

Raina laughed as she backed out of the parking spot. "You don't have a mole on your toe."

"How would you know? When is the last time you looked at my toe?"

Raina glanced at her grandma's open-toed sandal. "I can see your toes from here."

Po Po harrumphed and crossed her arms.

Raina softened her voice. "What's going on? Why this sudden decision to move to Gold Springs without discussing it with anyone? I thought I was your favorite granddaughter."

"As if I can pick a toe to be my favorite."

"I'm the one with the toe ring."

Raina glanced at her grandma's mulish expression and decided to wait her out. The back roads to town took an extra ten minutes. If she had to get "lost" on the drive back, then so be it. She'd pushed her family concerns to the back burner long enough.

As she drove past green fields, farm animals, and scattered homes, she reviewed the murder suspects. Natalie had the most to gain financially from Holden's death, but she had an alibi.

Cora wouldn't kill Holden since he was worth more alive than dead with his child support payments and health insurance. Now the family was scrambling to make up for the loss since they'd known the boy wasn't Holden's son.

Her thoughts wandered to Sol, and she hoped for Eden's sake the man was more an opportunist than a killer. Her intuition told her he wasn't devious enough for murder, not if he could get caught so easily while he was searching for his research material.

Olivia Flaky Skin blamed her current troubles on the Merritt family. Not only was she an older woman conned out of her money, but she also had her love, or pride, thrown back into her face when Holden had threatened to charge her with sexual harassment. However, Raina believed Olivia would shoot Holden rather than poison him. Poison seemed too underhanded for the department head.

An odd noise intruded into her thoughts. A flapping sound that came from the front. Raina glanced at her rear-view mirror. A white SUV rode her bumper. With the sun's glare reflecting off the windshield, the driver was a faceless shadow.

She frowned at the road in front of her. There was no shoulder where she could pull over in this stretch of the road. The deep ditch with the overgrown weeds mocked her earlier decision to take the long route back to town. She rolled down her window and waved her hand, hoping the other driver would pass.

The flapping sound grew louder. Yep, definitely from the front. The breeze threw her curls into her eyes, and she shook them off her face. The steering wheel rumbled under her hand. Her stomach swirled with each roll of the tire.

"Sounds like a flat tire," Po Po said.

Raina eased her foot off the gas and pressed the hazard light button on her dash. The small driveway ahead of her would have to suffice. Her car drifted to her right, and she corrected, slowing even more. Just another hundred feet and she could pull off the road.

Her car ran over something with a loud thunk, probably her tire. The steering wheel shook under her hands. She had to turn her steering wheel to the left to drive straight. She must be riding on the rim of the front passenger wheel. Sweat beaded at the small of her back. Less than fifty feet. She was now crawling at thirty-five miles per hour, and the SUV was still on her tail.

"The car is making me nervous," Po Po said, her voice shrill and tight. One hand clutched the door handle.

Raina gritted her teeth. "Tell me something I don't know."

The other vehicle pulled out from behind her. She fought for control as her car continued to pull right. The other driver pulled up next to her. Did the other car drift closer to her? She tried to correct, but it was difficult to gauge because the car no longer drove straight. The driveway was less than thirty feet in front of her.

The SUV closed in on her left. What was the driver doing? Geez, there was plenty of room for him to pass.

"Watch out!" Po Po screamed.

The SUV drifted over and tapped the driver side and knocked off Raina's side mirror. Then the other vehicle roared and hightailed away.

Raina's sweaty hands slipped off the steering wheel. Before she could grab the wheel, her car hit a bump and flew head first into the ditch.

Her heart leapt to her throat.

Poof!

The airbag exploded on her face. The material enveloped her, and she couldn't breathe. Her mouth opened, but she choked. Only her ears seemed to be working. Po Po screamed.

The front end bounced as it settled into the ditch. Then there was silence.

Raina could see again. She batted the airbag away from her, coughing and choking at the dust. The strong acrid odor burned her nostrils. The passenger side lay in the ditch while the driver side stuck above it like a tipped cow. She didn't smell gasoline.

She turned off the engine and unbuckled her seat belt. Her hands shook, but she ignored them. From previous car accidents, Raina knew she had minutes before the adrenaline surge would evaporate. She needed to get her grandma out now, or she'd be useless once the shaking started.

Raina glanced at Po Po. "Are you okay? Anything broken?"

A fine white powder covered Po Po. One hand still gripped the door handle, and the other batted at the airbag. The bruised nose on her grandma's face brought tears to Raina's eyes. She'd feared there would be more damage on her tiny grandma. Thank God she'd moved the seat back from the dash to accommodate the boot.

Po Po coughed. "This stuff stinks."

"We'll have to get out from this side. I'll get out first and pull you through."

"I don't think I can get my foot out."

Raina gasped. "Any bleeding?"

"It's the boot."

Relief spread across Raina's chest. "Let me unbuckle it for you." She squeezed her head and torso into the gap between the dash and her grandma's feet. Her sweat-slicked fingers grasped the Velcro tabs and pulled them open. She leaned back on her seat, panting. "Can you wiggle your foot out?"

Po Po's voice wavered. "Yes."

Raina opened the door, but the angle of the car made the door swing shut, so she held it open against her back. A fresh breeze drifted into the car. She braced a foot against the middle console. "Let me pull you over." She dragged her grandma across the console.

Po Po blinked at the whirling white dust around them. "Rainy, I need to get you some new underwear."

Raina stared at her grandma in confusion. Did she hit her head? "Huh?"

"I can see up your baggy shorts. The ones you're

wearing would be classified as granny panties. I don't even wear underwear with that much coverage."

Raina burst out laughing. It was either that or cry. Her grandma was making an effort to regain her equilibrium, and Raina wasn't going to spoil it for her. "TMI! I have to burn my ears. I don't need to hear things like this."

Her grandma gave her a wobbly grin. A shadow fell across her face. The weight of the door eased off of Raina's shoulder blades. She glanced up and relief flooded through her. Her legs threatened to collapse at the concern on the stranger's face.

A man held the door open. The sunlight glinted off his bald head like a halo. "You folks okay?"

Raina sucked in a breath of dust. Her body coughed and didn't stop until tears streamed down her face. She waved at the concern on the stranger's face. "I'm okay."

"Grab my hand," the man said.

"Close your eyes, Po Po," Raina said.

The man pulled while Raina scrambled over the seat, stirring up white dust. He turned to help Po Po.

Raina walked around to inspect the front of her car. Where there was once a new tire on the passenger side was now a gaping hole. She shivered. New tires didn't blow off by themselves.

THE NEXT FEW hours were a blur. Officer Hopper arrived on the scene at the same time as the mechanic's tow truck. For once, Officer Hopper took Raina's statement without any passive-aggressive snide comments. Half an hour later, Raina and Po Po rode squashed together in the cab of the tow truck.

The mechanic dropped them off at the hospital on the edge of town. After they were inspected and bandaged, Raina called Eden for a ride home. She was too shaken to think after her surge of adrenaline wore off. The only thing she remembered during the short drive home was her grandma's trembling hand and wan face.

Raina fell into a deep sleep until a loud argument outside her apartment woke her. Eden's voice was angry, and Matthew's was sarcastic. She swung her legs off the bed, careful not to wake her grandma, and closed the bedroom door. Her koi clock showed nine. They'd slept through dinner.

She opened her front door, and diffused light spilled onto the pair and exaggerated the scowls on their faces. Stepping outside, she closed the door, plunging them into darkness. "Can you two be any louder? If you wake my grandma, I'm going to have to break your knees."

Eden gave her a sheepish look. "Your detective here can come back tomorrow to get your statement. You need your rest."

Matthew glared at Eden. "Your friend here needs to mind her own business."

"Raina is my best friend."

"I'm family," Matthew said.

Eden jutted her chin and rested a hand on her cocked hip. "Uh-huh. I'm more family than you. You haven't been part of her life in years."

"She's my wife."

Raina raised both hands in the air. "Stop." She pointed at him. "Our marriage got annulled. You have no claim on me." She hugged Eden, ignoring the questioning look. "Thanks for looking out for me, but I think I can take it from here. I'm sorry about dinner. We'll catch up tomorrow?"

Eden nodded and said goodnight. She threw another glare at Matthew and crossed the courtyard to go back to her apartment.

Matthew closed the distance between them and drew her close. He studied her face, sucking in a breath. His finger grazed the cut on the side of her face. "Poor Rainy. It's been a bad week for you."

The dim moonlight gave Matthew carry-on-sized eye bags. Did some of the load come from her? "I've had worse."

"Too bad I can't tie you up until I solve this case."

She cocked her head and studied him. "What are you doing here? And cut the bull about the statement."

"I want to make sure you're okay."

She tucked her head under his chin. "I can't do this anymore."

His heartbeat was slow and steady. Steady and reliable, unlike the person she held in her arms.

"I'm sorry," he whispered into her hair.

Tears sprang to her eyes and dampened his shirt. He was toxic. Raina had never given any relationship a fighting chance because she had her ears glued to the floor, waiting for his footsteps.

"As my mom loves to tell me, my eggs are shriveling into dried husks. I don't want a family right away, but I do want a man who would stick around to start one later."

Matthew stiffened. "I can't."

Raina stepped back into the shadow. "I need to get

you out of my system." For the first time, she saw the truth in her words. She'd told herself this several times over the years, but she never acted on them. There was only one way to make him stay away from her. She was too weak to stay away herself. It was the only way.

"I told Holden I was pregnant." Her voice sounded hollow to her ears. "I wanted him to marry me."

Matthew's jaw tightened. "I see."

She gulped air and stepped back. Her heart became a dead weight around her chest. "I need to sleep. Good-bye, Matthew."

"Wait. Here." He handed her a set of keys. "Use my car until you get yours fixed." He kissed her on the forehead. "Good night, Rainy. Take care of yourself."

Raina went into the house and closed the door. Her fingers tightened around the keys. She'd said good-bye. Her chest ached at the suppressed wailing she wanted to do, but she didn't dare let it out. Instead, she kept blinking renegade tears and telling herself she was having a delayed reaction to the car accident.

23

TRADING SECRETS

Raina shuffled to the shower the next morning. Warm water sluiced down her body and mixed with the warm tears sliding down her face. The fear she'd felt when the car careened into the ditch. The heartache that hung like a noose around her neck. By the time she wiped a circle on her steamed mirror, she was ready to face the day even if her grainy eyes and stuffy nose gave away her restless night. Other than a few bruises, she and her grandma survived to tell another tale.

Someone had murdered Holden and had her marked as the next target. She didn't believe for a second it was an accident that her front passenger tire blew off or the white SUV knocked off her side mirror.

Was the car accident meant to be a warning? Raina snorted. Obviously, the killer didn't know her if they assumed she would cave to scare tactics.

She stumbled to the kitchen to start the coffee machine, staring out the window as she waited. The steel gray sky matched her lousy mood. The heat wave must have broken last night while she'd tossed and turned. If only she could hide in her apartment and stream endless episodes of the *Big Bang Theory*. Of course, she didn't have this luxury, not with a million and one details to take care of after a car accident.

By the time Po Po woke, Raina had finished her breakfast and nursed her second cup of coffee. Her grandma grimaced when she lowered herself into the chair.

"Do you need another dose of Motrin?" Raina prepared tea and toast. Her grandma was not a big breakfast eater.

"I only ache like this when I dance on the tables and swing from the rafters. What I need is an elephant tranquilizer in my butt."

"I'm sorry."

"You're supposed to laugh. Stop taking me down with you."

Raina snorted. After yesterday? "I want a time machine for my birthday."

Po Po clapped her hands. "Done!"

Raina pretended to check under the table. "Come out, little time machine. I want to go back to high school." As soon as the words left her mouth, her playful mood evaporated. Her life had derailed in her teens after her father's death. She sighed. "It can't be healthy for me to hang onto this notion of happily ever after with my high school sweetheart."

Po Po's face softened. "The two of you are different people now. Even if you get a second shot with the same person, the relationship would be different."

Raina had given Matthew more chances than he deserved. "There won't be another chance. I'm done."

She waited until her grandma finished her first slice of toast. "Po Po, you should go home. I can't seem to be able to take care of you. Mom is going to flip when she finds out about the car accident."

"I'm not going home, and I never asked you to take care of me." Po Po stuck out her lower lip. "I'm tired of the city and...living with your mom."

Raina's eyebrows shot up.

"I'm sick of her coddling me like I'm a toothless baby. I may be old, but I'm not dead yet. I still have my own teeth." She pulled her lips back to show them off. "It's going to get worse when she becomes an empty nester. This is what happens when you don't establish a life away from your children. She should have gone back to work years ago, but your Ah Gong thought it was important for a single mom to compensate for the other parent. That's a man for you. Spent his entire life growing his business outside the home, but an expert in childcare."

"It'll be nice to have you close. Do you want to live in a house or an apartment?" Raina smiled. "I love you, Po Po, but you hog the covers. So we'll need a place with at least two bedrooms."

Her grandma looked at her for a long moment. "Honey, thank you, but I'm not moving in with you. I'm closing next week on the unit down the hall from Maggie."

Raina bit her lower lip at a flash of disappointment. So this was what her grandma had been doing for the last week when she disappeared. She didn't realize she'd hate returning home to an empty apartment until Po Po showed up. Having a conversation with someone at the dinner table was much nicer than staring at her nails while she shoved food into her mouth.

"Besides, what kind of action would you get with a sixty-year-old hanging around you? But you better make a point to cook for me a few times a week though. I get lost in that gap between the fridge and stove. It's like the Grand Canyon. And Maggie might get sick of feeding me the table scraps."

Raina forced herself to laugh. "Geez, are you going to be fifty-five years old next week?"

Po Po wiggled her fingers. "The time machine might take me back to my twenties."

Raina held her grandma's gaze. The air between them changed. The smile slipped off her grandma's face. Without knowing why, she knew they were both thinking of her grandfather. Po Po had met her future husband when she was twenty. Raina's heart skipped a beat at the silence. She held her breath, afraid, and yet resigned.

Po Po's face grew tight and expressionless. "Did you know about your grandfather's other family in China?"

Raina gasped in surprise at the direct question. She'd thought it'd take them a while to get straight to the point. "Uh...I..."

She'd dreamt of confessing her family's skeleton for the past year. She'd dreamt of her relief, but not like this. Her grandma's pain-filled eyes and choked voice tightened the knot on her chest.

"His son"—Po Po took a deep breath—"he called a couple of weeks ago, demanding to know why his mother hasn't been getting her monthly allowance."

Raina fumbled to say something. This was all her

fault. She should have continued with the payments even though the inherited money had been tied up in the lawsuit from her cousins. She should have called the other woman to explain.

Her throat choked on a lump. "I'm sorry," she finally whispered. Tears filled her eyes. "I'm so sorry."

Po Po nodded. "The money he left you?"

Raina studied her hands and shook at the chill in the air. For a moment, she wished she'd gotten more seriously hurt from yesterday's accident so she wouldn't be here to have this conversation.

What could she possibly say to minimize the damage of Ah Gong's infidelity? An infidelity that lasted her grandparents' entire marriage? Did she owe any loyalty to a man with two faces? For the first time, she hated her grandfather.

Raina sneaked a glance at her grandma, who sobbed into her crumpled napkin. Her heart ached. No, she didn't owe any loyalty to a man who would do this to his family. He didn't have any right to expect her to keep maintaining his other family after his death. And she shouldn't have taken on his skeleton. He should have talked to his wife while he had a chance to explain.

"I wanted to help during his fight with lung cancer. How was I to know my hurried promise was a life sentence?" Tears ran down her face. "I thought if I ignored it long enough, it would disappear."

Po Po straightened and dabbed at her tears. "He had no right to place this burden on you. I could kill him right now."

"I'd give anything for you to never find out. I would have done anything to keep you from this pain."

"What are we going to do about this other family? They won't just stop asking for money."

Raina's hand tightened around her mug. How dare the other family destroy her grandma's peace! Especially since she'd given up hers to ensure the rest of the family could sleep soundly at night. "We'll deal with it later. It's not like they're knocking on my front door right now." She'd have to contact the other family in the near future. If nothing else, she could become the buffer for her grandma.

After breakfast, Po Po left for her exercise class at the senior center, but Raina suspected it was to hold court over her narrow escape from a car ramming. Things tended to sound larger than life when they came from her grandma's mouth.

Raina lingered in the apartment in her pajamas. She'd always thought once Ah Gong's secret was out she'd feel lighter and happier. Instead, there was an overwhelming sense of sadness and...anger? Yes, anger.

Her grandfather had been a family man and well respected in the community. This secret tarnished more than her fond memories of him. It'd changed her entire perspective of happily ever after. Her grandparents had been married for fifty years. He'd said he was protecting his family, but he didn't explain what those words had meant at the time of his death.

A part of her had secretly hoped there was an explanation. This morning hope had shriveled into a hard ball that smashed her heart, reminding her yet again, how she always had too much faith in those she loved to do the right thing.

The beep of an incoming text message distracted her

from further morose thoughts. Raina trudged to the counter to get her cell phone. She did a double take at the time on the display. Did she really spend the last two hours woolgathering?

STILL NEED THOSE COOKIES FOR MY POSSE'S TOP SECRET MEETING. WILL PICK THEM UP AFTER LUNCH.

Raina smiled for the first time since the accident. Po Po was going to be all right. The resilient old bird had cried her river and was ready to take on the rest of her life. She could learn so much from grandma.

RAINA TEXTED Eden and invited her to lunch and made four dozen cookies: oatmeal cranberry and peanut butter pumpkin. While the cookies were cooling on the counter, she dug Holden's tablet from the pile of worn gym socks under her back closet. She'd forgotten why she once thought it was a good idea to save the orphan socks, but the holes and questionable dark stains served as a good deterrent from thieves.

Her heartbeat sounded loud in the quiet bedroom. She sank into the threadbare carpet and tapped in her birth date to unlock the touch screen of the tablet. It had been three days since she figured out the unlock code, but between the drama in her life and her hesitation at this breach in privacy, she hadn't given herself a quiet moment to look through the tablet. Her finger flipped through the screens, and her eyes scanned the icons of the apps installed in the machine.

On the third screen, she froze. A daily journal app. Would she get the closure she craved in here? She took a deep breath and brushed a curl off her face.

A window popped up asking for a password. She tapped in her birthday. No dice. She tried Holden's birthday. Still nothing.

Raina closed her eyes, trying to recall the birthday on the paternity report. His son's birth date had caught her eye because it was a few days earlier than Po Po's. Two days earlier? She tapped in zero eight one five. Nope. Three days earlier? Zero eight one four. Bingo.

A blank entry page popped up. Raina hit the icon in the top left corner. A calendar appeared with a star under each day, probably indicating an entry. She opened the last entry, which happened to be the day she'd told him she was pregnant. Her hand shook when she tapped on the screen.

I'm going to be a dad. This time it'll actually be my son. Maybe I'm not meant to let Rainy go.

Raina closed her eyes and escaped from the entry. She wasn't ready to read this. Not yet. She randomly selected another entry.

I need to stop enabling Natalie. I'm letting her ruin everything. Now I have thugs following me around, pulling me into dark corners for a chat about payment. This isn't the life I signed up for.

Did Holden break things off with her because his life was unraveling? Would Raina stoop to blackmailing in a similar situation for one of her siblings? She shook her head. No, she wasn't an enabler.

But hadn't she enabled Matthew by letting him dictate the terms of their relationship? If Eden knew the extent of her non-relationship with Matthew, she'd say Raina was just his booty call. Even her mother had made disparaging remarks about her eggs shriveling into oblivion while she waited for him to stop saving the world.

If her feelings had been one-sided, then she could talk herself out of the leftovers he dished out to her. But they weren't, and that was the problem. Every time they'd gotten together in the last decade, it was like the clash of Titans. All naked flesh, blood, and tears. It'd always been exhilarating, and life had seemed dull afterward.

A knock on her front door jerked Raina out of her thoughts. For the first time, she regretted making plans with Eden. Her emotions were too raw and unsteady for company. She left the tablet on her bed.

Raina swung open her front door and smiled. "Thanks for picking up the pizza." She hugged Eden's stiff body and closed the door. She hurried to the kitchen to grab utensils and drinks.

When she came back to the dining room, Raina wiggled the soda can in her hand. "Look. I stopped by the gas station for a Diet Pepsi." She'd done this on the way to the casino yesterday when her world was still a safe place. "Here's the money back for the pizza."

Eden hung back, shifting her weight from one foot to another. "Um, thanks."

Raina pulled out her good chair and held it out for her friend.

Eden strolled over and enveloped her in a bear hug, releasing her just as quickly. "You're the best."

Raina smiled. "I'm sorry. I was unfair and, as Po Po says, some cans of worms shouldn't be examined in any lighting."

"Your grandma is one wise old lady. I'm sorry, too."

The unanswered questions about Matthew hung in the air, but Raina busied herself dispersing plates and napkins until the moment passed. She wasn't ready to share her feelings about him when she was still thinking about Holden's journal entries.

Eden flipped her weave over one shoulder. "Ever get around to looking at Holden's tablet?"

The salty bite Raina swallowed stuck to the back of her throat. She gulped water from her glass. "I hate it when you do that."

"Do what?"

"Read my mind. And how come you didn't think I just bought a tablet?"

"You were searching Holden's house. Then you showed up with a tablet. It's not rocket science."

Raina licked her lips. "Holden kept a journal in his tablet. It's more like notes. I haven't gotten a chance to read through all the entries yet."

"And?"

"I think Holden might have been a decent guy who had made some very bad decisions."

Eden gestured with her pizza slice. "Come on. Really?"

Raina shrugged. "He paid child support for a child that was not his. He paid his sister's gambling debts. I'm not saying this justified the way he went about getting money, but there is something sad about the whole situation. He probably felt he couldn't make a different choice."

"We've all been in tight situations. It's how you react to it that makes you the person you are. He chose to lie and blackmail others. To me, his questionable morals made him a bad person."

"You're right," Raina said. "But murder?"

Eden chewed and pondered the question. "I'm not saying murder was right either."

For the next few minutes, Raina ate and chatted with her friend about the suspects on her list. It was like old times, except she tiptoed around the subject of Sol and her friend did the same for Matthew. The discussion didn't lead to more than what she'd considered on her drive back from the casino before the car accident.

"I know you're wondering." Eden took a deep breath. "Sol and I are still together."

Raina forced a smile on her face. "That's good. I'm glad things are going well for the two of you."

"I've been helping him search for the material he gave to Holden."

Raina nodded. This wasn't news.

"We've gotten close, and I've met his sister, Sonia," Eden said.

"That's wonderful."

"On the morning of Holden's murder, she confirmed that he was at the florist with her and then met up with her after the meeting for more wedding planning." Eden beamed. "He has an alibi."

Raina bit her lip. What if Sonia was lying?

"She wasn't lying. It came out naturally in conversation. She made the offhand comment that Sol would be a big help when we get married." Eden reddened. "I also called the florist."

Of course, her friend would call. "Now that's my girl."

They both laughed, and the mood brightened.

"Okay, the smell is killing me. What did you make? Any samples?" Eden asked.

Raina got up and grabbed the plate she'd set aside in the kitchen. "Half a dozen for you. Where were we?"

Eden's eyes lit up, and she grabbed an oatmeal cranberry cookie. "The suspects."

"After we eliminate everyone, there's only Olivia left," Raina said. For some strange reason, she hoped it wasn't her.

"And Andrew Rollinger."

"The white noise machine?" Raina didn't see how he fit into everything, but Cora had mentioned Holden's interest in him. "If the Dean asked him to investigate Holden's involvement with the missing grant funds, shouldn't he be the victim?" And yet, there was Andrew's dossier in Olivia's office.

Eden gave her a sharp look. "He filed for Chapter 13 a month ago. His credit cards are maxed out. He's desperate for money, too. Holden and Andrew could have both been siphoning money from the grant."

"But I saw Lori at the mall, buying expensive things."

"What if she doesn't know?"

"We should get our hands on that file in Olivia's office."

Bam! Bam!

"Police! Open Up! We have a warrant," called an unfamiliar male voice from the other side of the front door.

24

WORKING THE RUMOR MILL

Raina stared into Eden's wide eyes, her pulse racing. "I better answer before they kick it in." She was proud her voice didn't wobble.

She opened the front door, leaning against the doorframe to block entry to her apartment. With Eden standing behind her, the police shouldn't be able to see inside. "What's this about?"

A short, middle-aged man with loose jowls scowled at Raina. Officer Hopper slouched against the column from the overhanging roof.

"Detective Youri Sokol, Criminal Intelligence and Organized Crime." He held up some papers.

"You're the officer who confiscated my cell phone," Eden said. "When did you become a detective?"

"Promotion," Detective Sokol said.

Eden raised an eyebrow. "Permanent or temporary?"

"We're not here to go through my entire resume, Miss Small."

"Is this part of Holden Merritt's murder investigation?" asked Eden. "Where is Detective Louie?"

The detective smirked at Raina. "Someone has tipped off the Chief that he might have been too lax in his investigation."

Raina schooled her expressive face. Had someone complained about Matthew? She flicked a glance at Officer Hopper. She wouldn't. So who then? Natalie? Olivia? Or the killer?

"Have more things gone missing from the evidence room?" asked Eden, pushing herself forward until she stood in front of Raina.

The detective straightened, the top of his head skimmed her friend's shoulder. "You're interfering with police business again."

"Can I see the warrant?" Raina asked. She thumbed through the pages and stopped at the part describing the property to be seized. A gun. "When did Olivia report her missing gun?" She had it with her yesterday at the casino.

"Did Olivia Kline accuse Raina of stealing her gun?" Eden asked.

Officer Hopper leaned forward. "How did you know it was Olivia's gun?"

The only person Raina knew who had a gun was Olivia. It didn't take a rocket scientist to figure this out, but a snarky comment might make the situation worse.

The detective held up a hand. "You should leave, Miss Small. This has nothing to do with you."

Eden locked eyes with the detective. "You're out in public. I have every right to be here."

Officer Hopper smirked and fingered the handcuffs clipped to her belt. "Should I cuff Miss Sun?"

The detective flicked a glance at his partner. "I don't think it's necessary. Why don't you just wait here?"

Raina handed the warrant back to him. "Have fun. I'll be counting my underwear after you leave."

Detective Sokol chuckled and ducked inside her apartment.

Raina was worried about the tablet she'd left on her bed, but there wasn't a sign that screamed it'd belonged to Holden. The police didn't have the right to flip through the apps to confirm ownership, and the screen was locked. Her apartment wasn't spanking clean, but she was sure they'd seen worse.

Eden continued her rapid-fire questions at Officer Hopper. Raina smiled at the mumbled "no comment" replies. She had a feeling the officer was thrown off balance by her friend's presence. By the time the detective came back out, Officer Hopper was no longer smiling. Her lips were pressed in a thin line, and her posture stiffened into a rod.

"Find anything?" Officer Hopper asked.

Detective Sokol shook his head. "Where's your car?"

Raina raised an eyebrow. "You'll have to get another warrant if you want to search my car."

The detective studied her. "What are you trying to hide?"

"The warrant specifies my apartment. My car is not within its scope."

"Are you trying to bully a private citizen into forfeiting her rights?" Eden asked.

The detective grunted, thanked everyone for their cooperation, and left with Officer Hopper.

Eden bounced on her toes. "That went well. I can't believe Olivia accused you of stealing her gun."

"Let's not jump to conclusions," Raina said. "It could be anyone."

"Someone seems to be out to make trouble for you." Eden regarded her. "I think we're closing in on the killer. You should give Matthew a call, to ask how he's doing."

Raina gave her a bemused smile. "And to charm more information from him?"

"Hey, why not kill two birds with one stone?"

Raina rolled her eyes. "I say we get to campus. We need a better look at that file on Andrew."

Until she had more control over her reactions toward Matthew, she didn't want to risk another encounter. A part of her wished she'd cried instead so he would have an excuse to hold her. It wasn't lost on her how lame it was to have this damsel-in-distress thought, especially since she was done waiting for him.

ONCE THEY GOT to the history building, Eden took off for Olivia's office with the key for the filing cabinet while Raina made her way to the front counter to collect department gossip.

Gail glanced up from the stack of papers in front of her and waved to Raina. She slid open the glass partition. "You okay? Your face looks... puffy."

Raina planted her elbows on the wood counter. "Minor car accident yesterday."

"Oh, you poor girl. But everything is okay?"

Raina nodded. "I don't want to talk about it. Here are

the fundraiser files from Olivia." She handed the folders to Gail.

"Thanks for picking up these folders. How is Olivia doing?"

"She looks like Hollywood's version of trailer trash. Bad sunburn, flaky skin, and her roots were showing. I feel sorry for her."

"What's the big deal? It's a few paid days off." Gail lowered her voice. "She's coming back next week."

"I thought the admin leave was indefinite earlier this week. What changed?"

"The Dean got a phone call this morning from Natalie Merritt."

So Natalie decided to play nice with Olivia after all. "How is Andrew taking the news? He was in hog heaven the last time I spoke with him. He was convinced he could just slide into her role."

"I don't think he knows yet. Actually nobody knows yet." Gail scratched her head. "I forgot to disconnect when I transferred the call."

Raina glanced at her shoes to hide her smile. So this was how Gail found out about everything in the department. Should Raina stir the pot? Oh, why not? A hidden spider was doing the same with her life.

She looked over her shoulder to make sure they were alone. "Gail, I need to ask for a favor. I want to tell Andrew that Sol would be substituting for Holden. I want you to say you heard the same rumor."

Gail raised an eyebrow. "What are you up to?"

"Can't tell you right now. But if it turns into something big, I'll tell you all about it before the newspaper gets wind of it." Raina shrugged. "And if it turns out to be nothing, well, no harm done, right?"

Gail tapped her pen on top of the counter. "Before the newspaper?"

"Of course."

"I don't know. I'm not the gossiping type."

Raina bit the inside of her cheek to stop a laugh from escaping. Gail not gossip? When did pigs start swinging from the trees? "Do you still need help with your daughter's bake sale? It's in two weeks, right?"

Gail chewed her lower lip. "Yes, we still need more donations. I was going to pick something up at the grocery store."

"Cupcakes or cake pops?"

"How about both?"

This time Raina did laugh. She'd asked for it. "Not a problem."

Gail studied her for a moment longer. "You sure this is harmless?"

"Yes. I want to see how he'll react to the news." Raina shrugged. "It's just a rumor. What harm could come from this?"

Gail glanced over Raina's shoulder and nodded. "Here he comes." She resumed her filing, looking busy.

Raina spun around and waved. "Hi, Andrew, how are things going?"

Andrew faltered as if he wasn't sure whether he wanted to stop and chat. Raina took a step toward him. If he wasn't willing to come to her, then she'd go to him.

"Busy. I finally finished shifting the teaching assignments for the grad students." His voice droned in her ear, rhythmic like a swirling overhead fan. He continued for another five minutes about how he brilliantly shifted everything around like pieces of a puzzle until it all sorted out.

Raina blinked. This man couldn't be the killer. Not only did he not sound like someone with the passion or the imagination to kill someone, why would he need to use poison when he could put them to sleep with his voice?

All the same, she was committed to shaking the tree. She wasn't going to let a mysterious person throw coconuts at her without making trouble for someone else. Misery loved company and all. Besides, Po Po would say the least likely suspect usually ended up being the killer.

"Then it's a good thing the department hired Sol on a limited term basis for the rest of the semester. He should be able to take some of the load off your back," Raina studied his face. "And part of his duties includes checking up on the missing funds."

Andrew frowned. "Hired him? But there are no open positions other than..."

Raina's chest tightened with guilt. "Are you okay?"

"Is this confirmed?"

"Rumor mill." Raina shrugged, hoping she appeared nonchalant. "Gail heard the same rumor."

Andrew glanced at the front counter and licked his lips. "I don't get it. Why would the Dean want to give him the position? The police detained the man for the murder."

"How do you know he is a suspect?"

"What else could it be?"

"A witness. Maybe he saw something. He always pops

up like a pimple before prom around here. I'll bet the police are trying to protect him until they make an arrest."

Andrew paled, and beads of sweat formed on his upper lip. "A witness." He repeated the words like a toddler learning to form his words.

"They can do amazing things with forensics these days. If half the stuff on TV is true, they would have collected enough evidence to determine the killer. They are probably waiting for the right opportunity to make an arrest."

"I'm sure you're right." Andrew looked at Gail over the front counter. "I need to pick up medicine for the baby, so I'll be gone for the rest of the day." He rushed out the main doors without waiting for a response.

Raina tingled all over. This was it. As she followed Andrew out of the building, She dialed Eden's number. "Meet me at the car. Andrew is making a run for it."

RAINA PARKED under the tree across from the Rollingers' house. Andrew had hurried inside a few minutes ago without any side trip to a drugstore. Medicine for the baby? Right.

The two-story house was a cookie cutout of all the other homes in the subdivision. If not for the vividly colored flowerbeds and the thriving potted plants on the porch, she wouldn't be able to pick the house out among the others on the street. Either someone in the family had a green thumb, or they had a good gardener.

Eden sat in the passenger seat, flipping through the

folder she'd gotten from Olivia's office. "The newspaper clippings are from a few years ago. There was a scandal where several large gift accounts disappeared after a professor's plagiarism was exposed. He resigned even though nothing was proven. No names were given, but I'll make a phone call to the school later. Bet it's safe to assume the professor in question was Andrew."

Raina bit her lower lip. "What are the chances that Holden might have been planning to blackmail them next? This isn't something you want your co-workers and friends to find out."

Eden shrugged. "How do we know he hadn't black-mailed them already?"

"What if Andrew knew Holden was planning to set him up as the scapegoat for the missing grant fund?"

"Or Holden and Andrew were in cahoots over the missing grant fund."

It was a lot of maybes, but it was still more than what they knew a few hours ago. It would be too bad if the Rollingers got caught up in Holden's web. Lori had ingratiated herself to Olivia by volunteering on the fundraiser with the hopes of advancing Andrew's career. And if Andrew turned out to be the killer, then where did that leave the stay-at-home mom and her baby?

"Look!" Eden pointed at the house. "They're leaving." She pulled out a DSLR camera with a zoom lens from her backpack and snapped a photo.

The garage door rolled open, squealing on its track. Andrew loaded the baby into the backseat and climbed into the white minivan. Inside was another white vehicle. Lori followed, holding a large duffel bag.

Raina made a U-turn and followed them, leaving half a block in between. "When did you get a fancy camera?"

Eden braced her hands against the dash as if urging Raina to go faster. "It's Sol's."

Raina gave her friend a sideways glance. She didn't know much about cameras, but the zoom lens looked like it could take close-up shots from half a block away. Good thing she kept her living room drapes closed.

The minivan weaved through the neighborhood streets until it hit the main thoroughfare and picked up speed.

"They're heading for the freeway. Shouldn't we call the police?" Raina asked.

"We have no proof anything is going on right now. What if they're going to the other end of town?"

Raina glanced at the gas gauge on the Jeep. "I don't think there's enough gas to go any farther than that."

"Geez, who tails someone with a quarter of a tank?" Eden's tone was waspish.

"This isn't even my car."

The minivan took the hospital exit. Raina's heart sank as she followed the car off the ramp and down the road to the parking lot. The Rollingers parked and rushed into the ER.

"The baby was sick after all," Eden said.

25

ANOTHER VICTIM

W hen Raina got home, she called her insurance company. The lady on the other line insisted the cash settlement to total Raina's car was the best they could do.

"It'll cost more to fix your car than it's worth," the lady said. "You'll need to replace the hood, the passenger side panel, and driver side mirror. There might be even more damage in the undercarriage. And then the paint job to blend it with the rest of the body. Too expensive."

Raina asked a few more questions and hung up. Her hands were shaking. Totaled her dad's car? No way. People didn't get rid of their pets when they were too old and expensive to fix up.

When she called her mechanic, he was more than happy to store her car out back until she decided what to do in exchange for a homemade meal later in the week. Taking those culinary classes in her early twenties had gotten her further in life than her looks ever did.

"All your tires have dangerously low pressure. Around

twenty-six psi. You're lucky you weren't driving on the freeway," the mechanic said over the phone.

"I haven't touched the tires since you installed them last week. Are they defective?" Raina couldn't remember whether or not the ride felt strange during the drive back from the casino. But then she had other things on her mind at the time.

"I tested them. There didn't appear to be any leaks. Strangest thing."

Someone had let the air out of her tires while she talked to Natalie and ate lunch. Olivia had plenty of time to do it, but she didn't drive a white car. The Rollingers owned two white vehicles. Could one of them be a SUV?

She wasn't sure if that person meant to scare her or hoped she would get into a serious car accident on the freeway. For the first time, she was thankful she'd chosen to take the back roads. Things could have turned out less rosy otherwise.

"I don't want to total my car," Raina said. "But new parts are going to be more than I can afford."

"It's going to take me a while to find used parts."

"Can I just make you more meals?"

He chuckled. "All right, but if I can't fit under a car anymore, then I'm blaming you."

"Don't worry. You're still eye candy even if you look like Humpty Dumpty."

For his time and her storage fee, she agreed to deliver three meals a week until he could locate the replacement parts. The insurance check wouldn't cover his labor when he got around to fixing her car. It was time to look for another part-time gig.

Later that evening, Raina curled up on her sofa

streaming *Murder She Wrote* to her TV. Her grandma squinted at the TV, dropping several stitches on her afghan. It was the first quiet evening Raina had in a while.

Po Po yanked out a knitting needle and pointed it at the TV. "I told you it was the best friend. Those closest to you often have the best motive for murder."

Raina gave the knitting needle a pointed look. "Want me to put that back into the loops for you?"

"What?" Po Po looked at her afghan and grinned. "That would be a great help. I don't have my reading glasses on."

"When was the last time you had your eyes checked? You're squinting like you're some kind of peeping Tom."

Po Po rolled her eyes and ignored Raina's question. "Your cookies were a big hit. We need more cookies tomorrow. We're rolling out Phase One of Operation Code Red."

Raina pulled the stitches back on the needle. "What is Code Red?"

Po Po shrugged. "Don't know, but it sounds cool. Frank said we need to have a name for the operation."

Raina shook her head in confusion. "Who's having an operation? Eden's grandfather?"

"No, silly. The plan to get even with Officer Hopper."

"Whoa." Raina held up her hands to indicate time-out. "What plan?"

Po Po straightened like a proud kindergartener about to give her parent the rundown on a surprise. "Phase One: Identify the mark's routine. We have four teams of two set up to follow Officer Hopper around the clock for the next two days." Her hands balled into fists, and she shook them excitedly. "We even got walkie-talkies."

Raina covered her smile by rubbing her nose with her opened palm. Phase One seemed harmless enough. "But isn't there a curfew for your friends in the nursing home?"

"They have the day shift." Po Po waved away her concern. "Phase Two: Disrupt the routine. That kind of depends on what we find out in the next two days. Frank thinks he can intercept the radio and we can pretend to be dispatch."

"What kind of disruption are we talking about here?"

Po Po leaned forward. "We can radio in an emergency every time she has to use the can." She wiggled her eyebrows. "Imagine how disruptive that would be."

Raina coughed and got up to hide her bubbling laughter. When the urge to laugh disappeared, she returned from the kitchen with a glass of water. "Just don't put a stink bomb in her patrol car."

Po Po cocked her head. "That sounds like a good idea. I bet we can improvise something from Janice's great granddaughter's diapers."

"Stop—"

Rat-a-tat!

Raina dragged herself to the front door as her heart rate sped up. A knock like that meant trouble.

Eden stood in the doorway, hastily stuffing her precious hair into a baseball cap. "Let's go. A source just texted me. Andrew Rollinger got admitted in the ER for food poisoning."

The hair on the back of Raina's neck stiffened. Like Holden? "Did the source tell you anything else?"

"No. She could lose her job for giving me details."

"What about the text message?"

"We have a secret code. No one else knows what it means." Eden glanced at the koi clock above the TV. "Will you hurry up? I don't have gas in my car."

Raina glanced at her grandma, but Po Po dismissed her with a wave. "Go. I need to call my posse about the diaper idea."

Eden alternated between tapping her fingers on her phone and the passenger door while Raina drove to the hospital. Maybe Po Po was the smart one for opting to stay home. She wasn't sure what to expect, but since neither of them was family, the best she hoped for was news that Andrew was stable.

The dim interior of Matthew's jeep mirrored her dark thoughts. If Andrew was another victim, then he couldn't be a suspect unless he poisoned himself to throw them off his track.

Raina took several rattled breaths. Could Lori poison her husband? But why? They were such a loving couple. And then there was the baby. Raina's faith in marriages was already badly shaken enough with her grandparents' example that she didn't need to follow this train of thought.

She got them to the hospital in record time. Eden shot out of the car and raced around the side of the building. Raina limped after her and rounded the corner in time to see her friend slap a key card against the reader. She held the door and gestured wildly for Raina to hurry.

"Is that an employee key card?" Raina asked when she caught up.

Eden let the door slam behind her. "I'm going ahead.

He's in room 2117." She left without waiting for a response, taking the stairs two steps at a time.

Geez, what was the rush? Andrew must be stable if they moved him into a room.

Raina strolled along the corridor, glancing at the room numbers. When she got to the nurse station at the intersection of the two wings, Eden was already conversing with a pleasant heavyset woman with mousy brown hair in purple scrubs. Her friend was scribbling on her notepad.

The elevator dinged and the doors slid open. Matthew got out and scanned the corridor. He held Raina's gaze for several heartbeats.

Time stood still as tightness spread across her chest. His eyes spoke of regrets and apologies. She gave her head one slow shake and closed her eyes. It was too late for regrets.

She opened them to see Matthew yanking the notebook from Eden's hands. He tore off the top page and stuffed it into his jeans pocket. "You shouldn't be here."

Eden snatched her notebook from his hands. "Is that your only comment? Are there any similarities between this poisoning and the poisoning of Holden Merritt?"

If her friend had been a cat, her fur would have poofed to twice her size. Her eyes widened until Raina could see more white than brown. Yep, Po Po was the smart one.

The nurse shrank back into her seat and flipped open a chart. Her eyes flickered between the folder and the two people facing off in front of her desk. Raina ducked her head and turned away. She hunched her shoulders and tried to fade into the background as she tiptoed to the elevator.

He wore one of those exasperated expressions like he was dealing with a belligerent drunk pissing in a fountain. "Raina, get your friend out of here."

Raina pasted on a weak smile and turned to see both Eden and Matthew looking at her expectantly. Like she was going to get in the middle of this. The elevator dinged.

"Duke it out. I'll be waiting in the car." She threw herself through the opened doors and slapped the button for the lobby.

A few minutes later, Eden jerked open the passenger door. "Your boyfriend is impossible! Let's go. I want to swing by the Rollingers' house."

"He's not my boyfriend." Raina started the car and pulled out of the parking spot. "I feel like an ambulance chaser."

"You have to follow the lead while it's hot."

"Great. We'll see Matthew again later when the neighbors call the cops."

Eden winked. "Just doing my part to make sure you lovebirds spend more time together. I'm going to win the bet."

"What are you talking about?"

"Po Po thinks you're finally done with him." Eden smirked. "But I don't think that's going to happen."

Raina gripped the steering wheel. "I'm done."

"But I don't think he's done with you."

"That's his problem."

"Have you created a spreadsheet yet?"

"I can make decisions without listing all the pros and cons."

Eden sat back. "Uh-huh."

"You're being offensive. How many times do I have to tell you? It's a flow chart."

Her friend rolled her eyes. "He's going to try to win you back."

Raina shrugged. She pulled into the small side street. Diffused light spilled out from the curtained windows onto the front lawns of the neighboring homes. The Rollingers' house looked empty, blending into the night sky. Even the raised solar lights lining the walkway from the sidewalk to the front door looked ashamed to be on when the family was experiencing a crisis.

"Lori drove Andrew to the hospital and then left saying she had to get the baby from her neighbor. Isn't it strange she would leave him alone at a time like this?" Eden asked.

"Someone has to take care of the baby. Maybe she didn't think it was serious."

"If it were Matthew in there, wouldn't you have stayed?"

"Feral dogs wouldn't be able to drag me away. The baby would be fine with the neighbor."

"My point exactly."

26

DAMSEL IN DISTRESS

Raina parked in the shadow of the tree across from the house like she did earlier in the afternoon. The scent of the overpowering flowers did little to improve her mood. Her eyes became grainy and itchy before she even got out of the car. By the time she stood in front of the door, her nose ran.

A block of concrete settled in her stomach. Lori couldn't have anything to do with the murder or Andrew's poisoning. She'd seemed happy at the mall, talking about how she met her husband. But people didn't survive on love alone.

She'd sounded bitter when she spoke of being cut off from her parents' money. Was the bitterness from her parents' lack of acceptance in her choice of husband or was it from their lack of financial support? Did everything circle back to money?

Eden pressed the doorbell, and the musical peal of bells filled the air.

Raina shifted her weight from one foot to another

and wiped her hands on her shorts. "What are we going to say when she answers the door?"

Eden shrugged. "I'll think of something." She waited several seconds and pressed the doorbell again.

No answer.

Eden tilted her head, indicating she wanted to go around the side of the house. She tiptoed to the side windows, crabwalking below each sill and popping up for a quick peek.

Raina's pulse raced as she followed her friend around the corner. She prayed the neighbors were busy watching TV. There was nothing unusual inside any of the windows.

She glanced back at the sidewalk in time to see a police cruiser pull up. A neighbor must have seen them skulking around the house. Matthew and Officer Hopper walked up the driveway.

As blood rushed into her head, Raina grew dizzy. Her hand trembled when she tugged on Eden's shirt and pointed behind them.

Faint peals of bells floated out from inside the house. A loud knock followed and, "Police!" Hurried footsteps from inside and the front door clicked open. Lori was home after all.

Eden disappeared behind the house. The dark lumps littering the ground were an effective booby trap. Raina's ability to trip over her own feet made dashing after her friend impossible. She would make more noise than a Mariachi band. What she needed was a hiding spot.

Raina squeezed herself into the space between two bushes, hugging her knees to her chest, and closed her eyes. Maybe Matthew wouldn't recognize his Jeep. Her nose leaked, but she didn't have a tissue. She swiped at her nose and smeared the moisture on her shorts. He would need night vision goggles to see the make and model of the car under the shadows. As long as he didn't catch her skulking in the yard, he wouldn't even know she was here.

She couldn't make out what was being said, but as long as they were talking, nobody was looking for her. Her fingers itched to slap at the mosquitoes drawn to her moist flesh. She took long breaths like she was in a Lamaze class. They sounded loud in her ears, but if she stopped, she'd start hyperventilating. Her muscles trembled with tension, but she couldn't risk moving even an inch.

The front door clicked shut, and an engine started. She sagged against the bush in relief. A slow smile spread across her face. Matthew had no idea she had been hiding here the entire time. She must be a better sleuth than she gave herself credit.

When a hand touched her knee, she jumped and bit back a yelp.

"Shush!" Eden whispered.

Raina blew out a rattled sigh. She tiptoed back to the sidewalk and peered out into the night. The street was cleared, and there weren't faces pressed against the neighboring window. The Jeep was hidden from this angle.

Once on the sidewalk, Raina scanned the quiet street and hustled to the Jeep. The hair on the back of her neck stiffened as if someone was watching her progress. She threw a glance behind her, but didn't see anyone.

Eden gasped.

Raina's nose detected the familiar scent of sage and clean water before her mind processed what it meant. A hand snaked out of the darkness and clasped her on the arm and tugged her into the shadow under the over-hanging tree branches.

"Why am I not surprised to find you here?" Matthew whispered into her ear. His warm breath tickled her, sending tingles of delight down her back. "You can never stay away from me, can you?"

Eden turned her back and pretended to watch the house. By the way she held her head, her friend was listening in on their conversation.

Raina shook him off, irritated at her body's response to his nearness. "I'm surprised your swollen head hasn't floated off."

"I want you to go home right now, Rainy. This is no time to pretend you're helping me," Matthew said.

She sucked in a breath and crossed her arms. "Pretend? I'm—"

He pushed her further into the shadow until her back was pressed against the tree trunk.

"What—" Raina whispered.

The Rollingers' garage door squealed open. A white SUV nosed out of the driveway. The dim streetlight spot-lighted the damage on the passenger side of the car. Raina gasped and her hand flew to her mouth. It was the same car that knocked off her side mirror. It took off before the garage door finished rolling shut.

Eden shoved her. "Come on."

Matthew held out his hands as if expecting Raina to toss him the keys. She unlocked the doors for the Jeep and hopped in. Her hands trembled as she pretended not to notice both Matthew and Eden reaching for the passenger door. Not only was she trailing Holden's murderer, but also two of the most important people in her life were having a pissing contest on who should ride shotgun. She started the engine and turned on the headlights.

"It's my car," Matthew said.

Eden stuck out her bottom lip but climbed into the rear.

The light traffic allowed one or two cars to get between them and the SUV. The single-family homes gave way to medium-size apartment complexes typically rented by students.

"Rainy, whatever happens, I want you to stay in the car," Matthew said. "I don't want to find you bleeding and cut up again. Promise me."

"I can take care of myself," Raina said.

His voice softened. "I'm sure you can. Just not tonight, okay?"

"All right. I'll just be the designated driver."

Lori pulled into the driveway of Sol's apartment complex. The vehicle's headlights disappeared around the back of the building where the residents parked.

A bolt of energy ran through Raina's body. Were Lori and Sol co-conspirators to Holden's murder? She glanced at the rearview mirror. Eden's face was tight, and her eyes looked worried. Raina hoped there was an explanation for Lori's late-night visit.

Raina slowed the car and parked where the streetlight ended. She turned off the headlights but kept the car running. "Now what?"

"Stay in the car." Matthew took off for the back of the apartment with Eden hot on his trail.

"Wait!" Raina called out, but the two disappeared into the darkness. She dialed Eden's phone number, and after a second of delay, music played in the backseat. Eden had left her purse behind.

Raina drummed her fingers on the steering wheel. Crickets chirped, and someone opened a window curtain. What if someone sneaked up to the Jeep? She glanced at the rearview mirror and locked the doors.

Movement on the far driveway caught her eye. The glow of headlights became brighter as a vehicle rounded the opposite side of the apartment complex. The white SUV turned back onto the street. She couldn't even tell if there was more than one occupant in the car.

Raina dialed Matthew's cell phone and got his voice mail. "Where are you? Lori just left the complex. I'm following her and heading north." She kept an eye on the sidewalk for her friends, but after two blocks, she realized she was on her own.

When the SUV hit the main thoroughfare, it zipped through the light traffic and pulled into the hospital parking lot. Lori jogged to the side door and disappeared inside.

Raina parked behind a large van and jumped out. She speed dialed Matthew again while she sprinted after the woman. "I'm at the hospital."

She hoped she wouldn't be too late. It didn't take a rocket scientist to know Lori was heading to her husband's room. Andrew had become a liability. Either he was a co-conspirator, or he'd found out about Lori's extracurricular activity. Whichever the case, things would get worse for him before the night was over.

The side door opened easily in her hands. Someone had taped the latch on the doorknob. Lori made a left through a set of doors before the empty nurse's station.

Raina ducked through and lost sight of her. The corridor had floor-to-ceiling windows on one side and a row of doors on the opposite wall leading to patient rooms. She glanced at the ceiling, but there didn't appear to be any video cameras — some security. Anyone could walk off with a patient.

Her nose burned from the lemon-scented antiseptic cleansers. The dimmed lights and the whirls and clicks of medical machinery made her skin crawl. Even amid these miracle makers, how many people checked into hospitals and never checked out?

Raina removed her pepper spray from her purse and slipped it into her shorts pocket. Tiptoeing down the hall, she placed her ear against door after door. What was Andrew's room number?

Someone snored in door number one.

The TV chattered in door number two.

Silence in door number three.

At the fourth door, she made out Lori's faint voice.

"You sure you don't want any water, honey?"

"Where's the baby?" Andrew asked between coughs.

"With my mom. Here, take a sip."

Something dropped on the floor.

"Andrew! Why did you have to knock over my purse?" Something rustled and clattered. "Here's another cup."

He coughed. "I don't want anything from you."

"You know, things didn't work out between us as I envisioned it."

He laughed, harsh and desperate.

"You were supposed to take care of me. Instead, the bank will foreclose on our tiny shoebox of a house. I slept with my godfather to get you a job. I even got rid of the blackmailing jerk. But you still manage to screw things up. How are we supposed to come up with the money to replace the missing grant funds? I just can't do this anymore."

Raina's heart sank. Why did love flip into hate like this?

"Fine. Divorce me," Andrew said.

"Call the nurse, and I'll make sure you'll never see the baby again. Now drink the damn water."

Raina jumped at the ringing and vibrating sound coming from her side. Sweat beaded on the small of her back as she clawed at her purse, her clammy hands squirting the phone onto the floor. It slammed against the tiled floor and echoed in the empty hall. Scrambling on her knees, she lunged at it, hitting the ignore button just as it rang again. The call was from Matthew.

A cloying gardenia scent made her head swim and her eyes water. The fine hair stiffened on the back of her neck and gooseflesh peppered her forearms.

She pasted on a weak smile and turned to stare into the dark barrel of a gun.

27

BROKEN

Raina lifted her gaze and met Lori's eyes. Her mouth went dry. She swallowed, but there was no moisture. She was a dead duck.

Lori gestured for her to get inside the room. Raina glanced at a pasty Andrew ineffectively reaching for the call button on the raised hospital bed. If she stalled, he might come through or a nurse might make her rounds. Rancid fear filled the small space, rolling off Andrew in waves.

Raina gripped her purse. "Detective Louie knows I'm at the hospital with Holden's killer." Her voice wobbled. She wasn't fooling anyone.

Lori narrowed her eyes, and her lips tightened into a thin line. She grabbed Raina's arm and jerked her inside the room.

When the latch clicked home, Raina broke out into a cold sweat. Why didn't she stay in the car? She wiped her clammy hands on her shorts.

Lori held out a hand. "Give it to me!"

"What—"

"Your cell phone."

Lori snatched the phone from her hands and clicked on the screen to check the last call. "Crap!" She threw it on the floor next to the lip gloss, pencil, keys, and snack cup from her knocked over purse. The display screen cracked, and the battery and back cover flew in different directions. "No more fun and games." She shoved Raina toward the hospital bed.

Andrew's shaking hands broke her fall, but in the split second that their eyes met, Raina knew she was on her own. He was in no condition to help her. Even hoping he could get to the nurse button was a stretch.

"Drink the water, Andrew," Lori said through gritted teeth. "Or I'll make sure the baby does."

Raina gasped. She had to be bluffing.

Lori swung her gaze to Raina. "Daddy was right. Andrew wasn't man enough for me." The corners of her lips curled. "Lucky your granddad took care of your problem, huh?"

Raina jerked her head in the semblance of a nod. *Agree to everything and stay calm. Stall until Matthew gets here.* "Where did you get the black hellebore?"

"My garden. It's my only joy in this marriage," Lori said. "It was featured on the Garden Club's newsletter."

Andrew swatted at the plastic cup on the tray. Liquid ran down the sides and dripped onto the scratchy fleece blanket. He flopped back onto the bed, drained from the effort.

Lori made a guttural sound that was more animal than human. Her eyes widened as her pupils dilated. Her flushed face matched her red hair. She lunged for Andrew.

Raina leapt back until she was sitting on his feet on the bed. The cloying gardenia scent floated like an A-bomb cloud next to her head.

Lori grabbed his mouth, forced it open, and tipped the remaining liquid in. He coughed and batted at her hands. She slammed his head on the tray.

Raina jerked the pepper spray from her pocket and swept her arm like she was holding a fire extinguisher. She held the other arm over her face. Her eyes stung and watered, but she kept her finger on the button. The spray ricocheted off Lori's back and hunched shoulders.

Lori spun and smashed the cold barrel of the gun on Raina's hand.

The pepper spray slipped from her numb fingers and clacked onto the floor. Another blow caught Raina on the side of the face, and she fell onto the floor. Her arm landed on a sharpened pencil and pain shot up her arm.

Lori shot out a foot and kicked Raina in the stomach. She grunted, clutching her stomach, and curled into a fetal position under the bed. Her vision blurred and tangy bile rose in her throat. She swallowed and focused on her breathing.

When Lori's foot shot out a second time, Raina grabbed the ankle with slick hands, twisted, and rolled further underneath the bed. Lori crashed onto the floor.

Raina clamped the foot between her thighs and pulled the pencil from her arm. She stabbed Lori on the side, jamming the pointed tip into the soft flesh. The gun clattered to the floor.

Lori screamed and bucked. Her foot jerked roughly against Raina's thighs.

Raina kicked the gun across the room. She yanked the pencil out. Warm blood ran down her hands.

The door banged open. Several pairs of feet came into view. A pair of hands helped Lori off the floor.

Raina clutched the pencil to her chest. Her breaths came out quick and unnatural. Her tight muscles shook with fatigue. Friend or foe? Should she crawl out or stay hidden?

Matthew's face came into view. He moved his mouth and held out his hand

She couldn't understand what he was saying. The room spun alarmingly. This was not the time to pass out. Deep breaths. She blinked, but he was still holding out his hands.

"Give me the pencil, Rainy." His voice was soft and gentle. The tone an adult would use on a frightened child.

Raina glanced down at her hands. Blood covered her arms and her shirt. She held out the pencil.

He handed it to someone and held out his hands again. "Come here, honey. It's okay."

The touch of his warm hands drained the tension from her body. She was safe. His fingers curled protectively against her clammy hands. She held onto his hand as she crawled out from underneath the bed.

Raina blinked at the too bright scene in front of her. Officer Hopper held onto a handcuffed Lori in the far corner. She held a bloody towel against her side. Another officer bagged the gun. Eden yelled and pushed against an officer blocking the doorway.

A beeping noise from the machinery cut through the din.

Matthew moved her away from the bed. Raina swayed, and he tightened his grip. He led her outside as a team of medical staff rushed in. Their white coats and colorful scrubs looked like macaws among the dark police uniforms.

He wrapped his arms around her. "I hate finding you covered in blood." His voice trembled, but his hold was steady.

She laid her head on his chest and cried.

RAINA WOKE to the aroma of fresh coffee and bacon the next morning. She winced as she sat up in bed. Bracing her hand against the side table, she slowly straightened and hobbled to the bathroom. Her body felt old, and her mood wasn't any better. What she needed was Po Po's elephant tranquilizer.

The long shower helped, and she almost felt her age again. She wiped the steam from the mirror and jerked in surprise at the sparkle in her wide brown eyes. The bruises on her body were superficial and would disappear with time.

Matthew's reappearances had always heralded the next phase in her life. This time was no different. The past two weeks had brought purpose and excitement to her dormant year of hiding in Gold Springs. She should have known better than to stick her head in the mud.

Her dysfunctional family finally caught up with her when Po Po arrived on her doorstep with her red suitcase.

She could have dealt with the demands of the other family in China and her cousins. It was the fear of losing her grandma's love that had weighed down her heart. Now that Ah Gong's secret was out, having Po Po at her side was like a jolt from a Red Bull.

Raina opened the bedroom door to find Po Po looking expectantly across the dining room table at her. Eden popped her head out from the kitchen, disappeared, and returned with a plate of food and a mug of coffee.

"Thanks for making breakfast, Eden," Raina said, cradling the mug her friend handed her.

"Hey, how did you know I didn't make breakfast?" Po Po asked.

Raina raised an eyebrow. "You call the gap between the fridge and stove The Grand Canyon."

Po Po harrumphed. "A woman's place is not in the kitchen."

Raina shoved a piece of scrambled egg in her mouth. It was too early to argue that cooking was a survival skill.

"Andrew is alive but still in critical condition." Eden glanced at the koi clock. "Lori is in a holding cell. I need to leave in a few minutes to see if the judge will let her post bail."

Raina flinched. "I feel responsible for Andrew being in the hospital. I thought the white lie about Sol investigating the grant fund would light a fire to get him to do something stupid."

"I don't think the outcome would've changed, just the timing. Lori was a walking time bomb," Po Po said. "She already thought her husband has failed to live up to his promises."

Raina gave her a sideways glance. Her grandma

would know about failing husbands. "The gun was Olivia's?"

Eden nodded. "Lori even tried to frame Sol by leaving traces of the poison on his car and throwing the rest in the trash bins. She was planning on calling in an anonymous tip later."

A weight lifted from Raina's shoulders. She wasn't a fan of Sol, but she didn't want him to have anything to do with the murder. Her friend was dating the guy after all.

"How's this for poetic justice? The pencil you used to stab Lori? It belonged to Holden," Eden said. "Of course, I can't publish this detail. It'll get my source in trouble."

Eden left shortly after. Po Po hung around the apartment, clucking at Raina and fluffing imaginary flat pillows. After lunch, her grandma left, and Raina finally felt like she could breathe again. She was watching her sixth episode of *Big Bang Theory* when someone knocked on the front door.

Raina opened the door to find Matthew holding out a blackened orthopedic white shoe. She sighed and invited him in.

"Where's Po Po?" he asked.

Raina settled into her sofa. She glanced at the koi clock. Her grandma had left three hours ago. Plenty of time to get into trouble. "What happened?"

"Someone called in that a bunch of senior citizens locked a police officer in a portable potty."

The beginning of a smile tugged on her lips. "Please don't tell me there was a stink bomb involved?"

His eyes sparkled. "There were multiple stink bombs. I'm assuming they meant to throw it inside the portable potty. But the peanut gallery ended up setting it off among themselves. One of the men screamed, 'Abort Operation Code Red' into a walkie-talkie."

"Was the caller able to identify anyone?"

Matthew shook his head. "No, but he gave a good description of the little old Chinese woman who lost this shoe."

They both laughed.

"Po Po is planning to move into the unit across from your grandma," Raina said.

"Things are going to get mighty interesting in this town." He tugged his collar. "I found a hood in Sacramento. It'll take a little while, but your car can be fixed."

Raina blinked at the tears welling up in her eyes. She reached over and squeezed his hand. "Thank you," she whispered.

The fact he knew how much her dad's car meant to her said more about his feelings toward her than what was not said. But it wouldn't change her decision to let him go.

Not one bit.

THE END

PLEASE REVIEW my books at your *ebook retailer*. As an indie author, reviews help other readers find my books. I appreciate all reviews, whether positive or negative.

Continue Raina's story now.
Gusty Lovers and Cadavers (Raina Sun #2)

ALSO BY ANNE R. TAN

Thanks for reading *Raining Men and Corpses.* I hope you enjoyed it!

Did you like this book?

Please review my books at your *ebook retailer*. As an indie author, reviews help other readers find my books. I appreciate all reviews, whether positive or negative.

Want to know about new releases, sale pricing, and exclusive content?

Sign up for Anne R. Tan's Readers Club newsletter at http://annertan.com/newsletter

Your information would not be sold or transferred. Thank you for trusting me with your email.

Want More Raina Sun?

Gusty Lovers and Cadavers (Raina Sun #2)

Breezy Friends and Bodies (Raina Sun #3)

Balmy Darlings and Death (Raina Sun #4)

Sunny Mates and Murders (Raina Sun #5)

Murky Passions and Scandals (Raina Sun #6)

Smoldering Flames and Secrets (Raina Sun #7)

Hazy Grooms and Homicides (Raina Sun #8)

Chilly Comforts and Disasters (Raina Sun #9)

Fair Cronies and Felonies (Raina Sun Mystery #10)

How about another series by Anne R. Tan?

Just Shoot Me Dead (Lucy Fong #1)

Just Lost and Found (Lucy Fong #1.5)

Just a Lucy Break-In (Lucy Fong #2)

ABOUT THE AUTHOR

Anne R. Tan fell in love with storytelling in elementary school, but decided to study engineering so she could get a "real job." Her day job is her vacation from home and she moonlights as a writer to keep the voices inside her head under control.

Her cozy mysteries feature Raina Sun, a Chinese American amateur sleuth, on the cusp of change in her life. Not only is she dealing with finding love and overcoming family betrayals, she is also solving murders.

If you are interested in learning more about Tan and her writing process, sign up for Anne R. Tan's email newsletter at http://annertan.com/newsletter for exclusive content, new release announcements, and sales.

CPSIA information can be obtained
at www.ICGtesting.com
Printed in the USA
BVHW080259280421
605945BV00004B/268

9 781087 852140